Flame of the Desert

Cindy Chubboy

PublishAmerica
Baltimore

First printing

ISBN: 1-4137-6362-6
PUBLISHED BY PUBLISHAMERICA, LLLP
www.publishamerica.com
Baltimore

Printed in the United States of America

Cover illustration by Matthew Chubboy
Cover model: Lindsey Chubboy

Author's Note

King Tutankhamun's tomb was discovered February 1923. In order to disperse historical facts involving his tomb, I have set its discovery during an earlier time period. In the book only brief references are made of the tomb's discovery and the mystery surrounding Lord Carnavon's death.

Reference Materials

Non-Fiction

The Curse of the Pharaohs

Written by: Philipp Vandenberg (1973; p. 186). On board the Titanic were 2,200 passengers; 40 tons of potatoes; 12,000 bottles of mineral water; 7,000 sacks of coffee; 35,000 eggs—and an Egyptian mummy that Lord Canterville wanted to take from England to New York...

Egypt: The World of the Pharaohs
Contributing authors
Edited by: Regine Schulz and Matthias Seidel

King Tutankhamun
Written by: T.G.H. James

Chapter 1

Egypt, 1911

I shall never forget the first time I heard about the curse of the pharaohs. I was sitting on the edge of the swimming pool of Cairo's Omar Khayyam Hotel, sipping tea with mint, and listening to Uncle Harry and Dr. Nathan Mehreiz talk of the pharaohs.

Dr. Nathan Mehreiz was the director-general of the antiquities department of the Egyptian Museum of Cairo. He was the director of a very large building housing over one hundred thousand objects, all precious treasures from the time of the Egyptians.

I was mesmerized by all those things housed in the museum: tiny scarabs; bulging, powerful stone statues of the great and mighty pharaohs; and on the upper floor, in Room 52, twenty mummies arranged according to age and sex, first the men and then the women, all in glass caskets for public viewing. It was not an uncommon sight to see people dash out of the room pale faced and nearly petrified. But I found the remains of smiling mummies with their bared teeth fascinating.

Archeology was new to me and I was extremely obsessed with learning all that I could. There was one thing in life that at the age of twenty-one I had already discovered, and that was to grasp at whatever opportunities came my way. I realized, had it not been for Uncle Harry, I would not be sipping tea in Cairo. Instead, I would be off somewhere probably fulfilling the role as a governess. This fate I had no desire to fill.

After the death of my parents I wondered what I would do for a living. Teaching seemed to be the only logical solution. For a young woman there were not many career choices available. However, after I completed my needed education, Uncle Harry came to my rescue: "You will come with me," he had said. "I need an assistant, and since I have no son, you will be of great help. There is much tedious paperwork involved in all that I do and I haven't the time to do it. You shall do it for me. Who knows, maybe even one day you will become an archeologist yourself."

He laughed about that and I joined him, for it was not conventional for English women to take up such a profession. But there was one thing about my uncle that gave me a certain amount of hope: he was not a man given to conventionalism.

So, the thought of being an assistant to a renowned archeologist was very thrilling. It did not matter that I was a woman and unlearned about many things concerning his work. I believed he loved teaching as much as he loved archeology, and for that reason he overlooked my faults and kept me on.

It was through Dr. Mehreiz that the curse of the pharaohs was made known to me. I was certain my uncle already knew of it.

As I had mentioned, I was sitting by the pool, drinking tea with mint, and listening to my uncle and Dr. Mehreiz converse about the pharaohs. I was wearing a white hat with a four-inch brim that shaded my hazel-green eyes and gave my olive complexion the needed protection from the sun. My hair, the color of honey wheat, I had tucked up inside the hat. My bare feet were dangling in the pool, and the hem of my white linen skirt was now wet from the water. I had been listening to their conversation concerning a strange occurrence that had happened to one of the Egyptian workers.

Dr. Mehreiz had commented that there are strange and unexplainable coincidences in life. Uncle Harry then asked, "So you really aren't sure there is a curse?"

A curse? This captured my full attention. I looked from my uncle and then back to Dr. Mehreiz. Their expressions revealed that they were quite serious concerning a certain curse.

Dr. Mehreiz hesitated before answering. He was not unlearned. He was an Egyptologist, and a man not weakened by folklore, but his next comment surprised me: "There have been several mysterious deaths linked to the pharaohs' tombs. It does make one speculate."

Harry laughed. "If the curse is indeed genuine...well, look at us. We have both been involved with tombs and mummies of the pharaohs for a very long time. We're living proof it is all coincidence."

I could no longer contain my curiosity. "What curse? And what mysterious deaths?" I asked.

Dr. Mehreiz was a powerful, thickset man with bushy eyebrows. He looked at me with an expression of kindness and concern. "My dear Elizabeth, what are you doing here?" he asked me, as if my presence had just occurred to him. "You should be in England courting fine young gentlemen. You're a cruel man, Harry," he then said to my uncle. "To bring your beautiful niece into a land of curses and mummies. What kind of life is that for a young woman?"

Uncle Harry gave me an apologetic smile. "He's right, Beth, you should go home."

I laughed. "What nonsense! I'll have you know, Dr. Mehreiz, my uncle saved me from a fate far worse than mummies and folklore. Besides, I love my job, it is all so—rewarding." I looked directly at Uncle Harry. "Have you forgotten that Cairo is now my home?"

Uncle rubbed his bearded chin, probably remembering the day he had me shipped and delivered to his doorstep. "That's right, Egypt is your residence, but England will always be home."

"Dear Uncle Harry," I laughed, as I arose from the pool's edge. He was lounging comfortably on a rattan with a large frond umbrella shading him from the sun. At the age of fifty-four, Uncle Harry was well fit and distinguished looking. His deep blue eyes reminded me of the clear tropical seas. His aquiline nose could have suggested arrogance, but he was not at all egotistical. Many women still found him handsome, but he had no desire to remarry after my aunt passed away, he was too involved with his work to even give marriage a passing thought. We were two misfits: he without my aunt, and I without my parents.

I stood behind my uncle and wrapped my arms about his neck; his salt and pepper beard tickled the skin of my arms. "I bet if I were a mummified princess, I would not be so easily sent away."

Dr. Mehreiz's eyes gleamed with humor. "She's right, Harry. You know more about what goes on with the dead than the living."

I laughed along with Dr. Mehreiz as Uncle scowled, then mumbled at us for making jokes about his dedication and commitment to the cause of archeology. I then sat in a vacant rattan next to Dr. Mehreiz. "Please tell me about this curse? It sounds intriguing."

"Intriguing," Dr. Mehreiz repeated with articulation. "Some things are best not known—less to feed one's imagination. Wouldn't you agree, Harry?"

"That definitely seems to be the case with our workers," said Uncle Harry. "Their vivid imaginations will certainly put a damper on the progress of my new excavation."

I crossed my legs, and then leaned back into the cushioned rattan. "I assure you, I am not one given to hokum and nonsense, Dr. Mehreiz."

He looked uncertain. I suppose he was weighing out whether or not to tell me of the curse.

Uncle Harry spoke up. "You may as well tell her, Mehreiz, she'll learn of it one way or another. Best that she hear the more intelligent side of things rather than from one of the workers."

"Yes—yes! You're right, of course. Would you like to explain, Harry, after all, she is your niece."

Uncle waved a hand in the air, as if shooing away the suggestion. "You'll do a fine job."

"I thought you would say that," said Dr. Mehreiz.

It seemed that neither of them wanted to be the one to tell me of the curse. I suppose they still looked upon me as a child: one easily afraid of the dark, or the boogeyman lurking in the closet. Even as a child I was more curious of the unknown than afraid, which often got me into trouble.

Dr. Mehreiz looked at me rather sternly. "You must understand one thing," he began. "Some things happen as just mere coincidences, other phenomena are so unusual that they don't seem to fit into any scientific explanation."

Although I had not experienced the latter, I agreed that some things probably happen in life that are not explainable. I believed God to be sovereign, and the Old Testament was full of phenomena that occurred by means of the supernatural—such as the children of Israel escaping Pharaoh by crossing the Red Sea on dry ground. I would like to hear the professors explain that one.

Dr. Mehreiz cleared his throat and then continued, "The Egyptians believed in gods and magic, curses and such. We have discovered several papyruses that talk of secret powers. The demotic Book of the Dead, the Pamont, talks about 'divine forces of the city of Bubasis that comes up from the crypts.' But what we have learned is that these powers are never called upon to protect the living, but the dead. Oh sure, they had their magic incantations for the living. Magicians were needed to conjure up wind and rain, or protection from lions in the desert and the crocodiles of the Nile. A magic spell was said every morning to protect the pharaoh against his enemies."

Uncle Harry spoke up, "Not everything that we have discovered turns to the supernatural and crude magic. There is really nothing magical about the food we find in tombs and painting on the walls of the grave chambers. Some things were done as a matter of religion or tradition, or even a way to make a little money."

I said, "But evil is a force. And if good can exist for thousands of years— is it not possible that an evil curse may also?"

Dr. Mehreiz and Uncle Harry exchanged a quick look at one another.

Uncle Harry said, "Evil will always exist, but just remember, Beth, good will always triumph."

"There was an ordinary clay tablet found in a pharaoh's tomb several years ago," Dr. Mehreiz then informed me. "It made many of the workers nervous. It was found in the antechamber. The inscription read: 'Death will slay with his wings whoever disturbs the peace of the pharaoh.'" Dr. Mehreiz shrugged his shoulders as he went on to tell the story. "The scholars, with their scientific minds, did not fear the curse then, nor did they take it seriously, but they were worried that the Egyptian laborers would. So the tablet was removed and never spoken of again. Not until just recently, one Egyptian worker found a curse in a somewhat changed manner—on the back of a statue. It read: 'It is I who will drive back the robbers of the tomb, I am the protector of the grave.' Not far from that statue lay another clay tablet with the same inscription as the first. The worker spread the word and soon fear was planted in the hearts of his fellow laborers."

I grimaced. "It seems that curses were a very popular thing to do."

"Very," said Dr. Mehreiz. "The Egyptians believed in a life after death, and curses were used to ward off anyone that wished to take what belonged to the dead king. As you know, they believed those treasured possessions would be needed in the afterlife."

"Yes, Uncle has explained all that," I told him.

Dr. Mehreiz then continued, "All was well until an archeological student on that particular site mysteriously died. The workers blame the curse, and now some are refusing to work."

"That could be a problem," I commented, knowing that without the workers, excavations on many sites would come to a halt.

Uncle let out a sigh. "I have had to almost double the pay to get some to work."

"What will you do?" I asked.

Dr. Mehreiz said, "Time always has a way of healing and forgetting."

"Yes," said Uncle. "But with time my funds will dwindle."

"I agree with Dr. Mehreiz," I said to Uncle Harry. "With time the workers will forget about the statue's curse, and the mysterious death. Why not take vacation time away from your work?"

Dr. Mehreiz agreed. "Listen to your niece, Harry—it's good advice."

Uncle squinted his eyes my direction. "Yes, I suppose it is. I imagine there is a certain young lady who wouldn't mind taking a little time off. I have worked her hard in the last month or two."

"And I have loved every minute of it," I said. "I am so eager to know more. There is so much yet to learn and understand."

Uncle said, "That is what is so fascinating about archeology—you never stop learning. A new discovery is just waiting to be uncovered, and we are going to be the ones to do it!"

"It'll be hard to tie him down for even a day," Dr. Mehreiz said concerning Uncle Harry. "It's in his blood. He can't live a minute without it. Time away from his work will be his undoing."

"You're probably right," I agreed.

"I'll take some time off and do some reading," Uncle told us.

Which he did: *The Tombs of Harmha, The Prospect of Egyptian Immortality, A History of Egypt, The Lost Pharaohs.*

One afternoon he was sitting in his favorite chair reading *Thebes City of the Dead.* He was so deeply engrossed in the book, he did not even hear me enter the room. When I told him that *Thebes City of the Dead* was not vacation reading material, and suggested he should read something entertaining to take his mind off of his work, he said to me, gruffly: "That would be a waste of time, and to waste time would be a sin."

I laughed. "You're impossible! That would not be a sin! You are only trying to justify the fact that you really cannot get away from your work."

Now I had asked for it! He slammed the book shut, looked at me pointedly, pushed his spectacles up his nose, then said, as calmly as he was able, "Look here, young lady! I find this material extremely entertaining."

It was humorous to see him so passionate. I was not trying to be disrespectful by any means. But Dr. Mehreiz was right: Uncle Harry could not take his mind off of his work. He was so enamored with Egyptian artifacts and the pharaohs that if he could not physically be on site, then he would do so with his mind. So every afternoon, there he would sit, reading about the pharaohs, his body present, but his mind with the ancient Egyptians. I thought, *In order for one to be exceptional with his or her work, then one must be totally dedicated.* Uncle certainly was.

I spent my leisure time by the pool. Often I would lounge under a frond umbrella and read. I was not as religious as Uncle Harry. My reading choices were *Jane Eyre* and *Portrait of a Lady*. Indeed I was the sinner, for neither book enlightened me on the lives of the great and mighty pharaohs.

One afternoon as I was on the final chapter of *Jane Eyre*, two young men sat behind me drinking lemonade. The frond umbrella hid me, but their conversation was easily heard. One said: "Do you think the curse may have been the cause?"

I stopped reading and then committed yet another sin—eavesdropping. The other replied: "I think there is really something to it. It was too odd. No one can explain it."

Their talk was somewhat cryptic. What was odd? And what could not be explained? I wanted to hear more, so I leaned over the arm of the rattan with my ear toward them. Their conversation continued: "It's the way the poor chap died that makes one wonder."

The other said: "I know what you mean. If it would have happened anywhere but in the tomb where—"

Several children in the pool had been playing and the remainder of conversation was drowned out by their frolic. I sat back into the cushions of the rattan greatly disappointed. What happened next took me by surprise. As I leaned over to retrieve my book, which had slid off my lap onto the pebbled concrete, my chair tilted slightly to one side, sending the frond umbrella forward and on top of me. I let out a startled cry, and was quickly assisted by the two young men, who immediately jumped to my aid.

"Say, are you all right?" the shorter of the two asked, as he managed to remove the hateful umbrella from off me, for I was certain I was being punished for eavesdropping.

"Yes," I said, embarrassed. "Only startled."

They set the umbrella upright, making sure it was secure.

"I don't believe we've met. Are you staying here?" the same asked.

"I'm living here with my uncle," I told him. "Presently, we are residing here at the hotel until our home is complete. We are adding a new addition. And you?"

"I will be here for some time. I am here assisting my father, Colonel James Whittley."

"Colonel Whittley!" I exclaimed. "Uncle has mentioned him on occasion. He's known for his discovery of the tombs of the queens?"

"The very same. I should make proper introductions. I am Philip Whittley, at your service."

I laughed. "Indeed you are. Thank you so much for coming to my rescue, Mr. Whittley."

He gave a curt bow, his light brown hair falling onto his forehead as he did so. "Philip, please," he said. "And this is my friend, David Carter."

Philip was shorter than David by about a foot. David was tall and lean.

"Mr. Carter," I said, acknowledging him with a nod of my head. "I am Elizabeth Woodruff, and it is a pleasure to meet you both. Please call me Beth."

"Beth," said David. "It is a great honor to meet you. And I insist that you call me David. When I am addressed as Mr. Carter, I feel that my father must be present."

We laughed.

The light in Philip's brown eyes began to dance. "Do you know Harry Woodruff, then?"

"Yes, he is my uncle."

"Say—that's splendid!" Philip said. "We met your uncle when he gave a lecture at the college a year ago. It was quite fascinating. Do you mind if we join you?"

"Not at all," I replied.

After they were seated across from me, David opened the conversation. "Philip and I were just discussing the curse of the pharaohs. Do you know of it?"

I was elated. I had hoped the curse would be the crux of our conversation. "It has become something of intrigue," I remarked. "This is only the second time I have heard it mentioned. Once from my uncle and Dr. Mehreiz, and now from you."

"Do you help your uncle?" Philip asked me.

"I'm his assistant," I told him, feeling a little proud of that fact.

"Then you are aware of the dangers?" David put in.

"Some. I do most of my work at the museum. I help date and catalogue the finds. As of yet I'm sort of an apprentice."

"Probably that is best," Philip then added. "The sites can be dangerous."

"The sites or the curse?" I wanted to know.

Philip's eyes took on a challenging look. "You get right to the point, I see."

I smiled. "You could say I prefer to be straightforward."

"Then we shall come right out with it. David and I believe there is something behind the curse of the pharaohs. What do you think?"

"I'm afraid I don't know all the facts," I told them. "Perhaps if you shared with me what you know, then I will be better able to give an opinion."

"That seems logical," David said. "We'll tell you what we have learned. How does your uncle feel about it?"

"He doesn't take it seriously—that I know. When Dr. Mehreiz mentioned something about mysterious deaths, and how it does make one speculate about the curse, my uncle thought it rather foolish. You have to admit, Colonel Whittley and my uncle have been meddling with the tombs for some time and they are both alive today."

"Yes, I've thought of that," Philip said. "But there is still so much that remains a mystery."

"So—then, you must tell me all that is mysterious," I said.

It was Philip who began to explain. "It was several years ago that, for the first time, scholars and newspapermen began to talk seriously about the curse of the pharaohs. An archeologist, Lord Carnarvon, who was involved with Tutankhamun's excavation, came down with a strange illness—an illness that took him suddenly. His son said that his father, Lord Carnarvon, complained of weakness, and that he ran a high fever of one hundred and four, and shook with chills. His end was respiratory failure."

"That is not so strange," I commented. "Others have died with such symptoms."

David was quick to add, "But that is not all."

Philip leaned closer. "What was so mysterious," he almost whispered, "is the fact that when his father died shortly before two o'clock in the morning, there was a power failure all over Cairo. The family asked the Cairo utility company about it the next day. They could not explain why the lights went out and then on again."

They had my full attention. "That is mystic."

David continued, "And what makes it even more sinister is yet another curious incident. Carnarvon's son said that the family learned later that something very strange happened in Highclere at about the same time as his father's death."

He paused. I was now gaping with curiosity, so I leaned closer and found myself whispering, "And what was that?"

"Lord Carnarvon's pet fox terrier, whom he was very attached to, began to howl, sat up on her hind legs, and then fell over dead," Philip finished.

"At about the same exact hour as Lord Carnarvon's death?" I inquired, incredulously.

"Yes! The very same hour," said David.

"We've talked to the family," Philip then told me. "And what we have just told you the family has confirmed to be true."

I felt goose bumps travel up my arms. No doubt about it, Lord Carnarvon's death was surrounded by strange and unexplainable happenings. Yet it was not enough to convince me that a curse was the cause. "Oddities do happen," I commented. "Why not others? I would think if the curse slays one, would it not take the lives of all those involved?"

"Maybe it depends on the curse," said David.

"There have been other incidents," Philip clarified. "Several months ago a good friend of ours had a freak accident and was killed in one of the tombs. His death frightened the workers. He was standing near the sarcophagus of a prince. He called out to us and said that he had found a cursed tablet. As he removed the tablet a rock fell, hitting him on the head. Instantly he was killed."

Again, I felt goose bumps. "I am so sorry about your friend. But you have told me yourself that the sites can be dangerous."

Philip said, "We are usually very cautious. Walls and ceilings of the chambers are always checked for weakness before we proceed into the tombs."

"I am not entirely convinced that these deaths were the result of an ancient curse," I admitted. "Curses have always been more suited for fairy tales and such."

"I have a splendid idea," said Philip. "Let's put our heads together and do some research. We'll do what we can to learn more about the curse. On Saturday we'll get together, right here—say, around five o'clock."

We agreed. I sensed excitement in the three of us. Together we would investigate the facts behind the mystery of the curse of the pharaohs.

Chapter 2

Although Uncle Harry was very devoted to his work, his dedication to God took precedence over any professional ambitions. If he had to make a choice between the two, God would always come first. Every evening we would spend time together reading from the Bible and afterwards we would discuss the scriptures. When I had difficulty understanding certain verses he would do his best to clarify its meaning. We had already completed the New Testament, and the first book of the Old, Genesis. I think Uncle enjoyed the Old Testament, simply because often there was mention of a pharaoh, or a king of some sort.

We were reading from the first chapter of the second book of Moses, called Exodus, when I became intrigued about a certain verse. After he read the verse, I interrupted by repeating the same: "And it came to pass, because the midwives feared God, that he made them houses?"

Uncle stopped his reading and eyed me over his spectacles. "Yes," he said, "the fear of the Lord is the beginning of wisdom."

"I understand all that," I told him. "But Uncle—God built them houses!? Pray tell, how can a God, who at that time had no form, build a house of brick and mortar?"

He ran a hand across his bearded chin still eyeing me with some amusement. "Yes, that would be something to see—would it not? A house built by God."

"I can tell by the gleam in your eyes that you find something a bit humorous."

He began to flip the pages of his Bible. "Turn to Psalms, one hundred twenty seven, verse one."

I did, then read: "Except the Lord build the house, they labor in vain that build it: except the Lord keep the city, the watchman waketh but in vain."

Uncle followed by reading: "But he that heareth, and doeth not, is like a man that without a foundation built an house upon the earth; against which the stream did beat vehemently, and immediately it fell; and the ruin of that house was great."

Uncle glanced up at me and said, "Now if you will go to I Peter, chapter two, verse five, you will have a better understanding.

I quickly located first I Peter, then he told me to read it aloud: "Ye also, as lively stones, are built up a spiritual house, an holy priesthood, to offer up spiritual sacrifices, acceptable to God by Jesus Christ."

"It is a spiritual house," I stated.

"The midwives will always be remembered for their reverence and obedience to God." He pointed to verse fifteen with his finger. "See here, their names are remembered and their children God thus blessed even down through their lineage. It is important," he said, "that God come first, and that you obey all of his word; then, and only then, will God establish you into his kingdom. Let God build your house, Beth, so that you will be prepared for eternity."

After our time of devotion, I gave Uncle a kiss on the cheek and then went to a room that adjoined with his. We enjoyed the comforts of the hotel, however, we were both anxious to move back into Uncle's home. A room was being added, and a bath for my convenience. He would do whatever necessary to see to my comforts, even if it meant himself doing without. I remembered as a child Uncle doting over me. Since my aunt was unable to have children, I became their object of devotion. I spent almost as much time with my aunt and uncle as I did with my parents.

I changed into my silk pajamas and then flopped down onto the bed. My Bible lay beside me, so I flipped the pages open to where we had earlier read. Again, I read the names of the midwives. I was amazed at how their reverence to God had brought about his blessings. Suddenly the thought came to me: What of curses? Does the Bible make any reference to curses? I was to meet with Philip and David tomorrow, and I had not yet found anything to share with them concerning the curse of the pharaohs.

I began to thumb through the pages. Exodus was full of interesting facts tied to the pharaohs. I began to jot down information onto my notepad. I was now excited and had difficulty sleeping. I could not wait to share with them what I had discovered.

The next day I was anxious to meet with Philip and David. I dressed early for the occasion, wearing a favorite white featherweight blouse and camisole in organdy, and a linen skirt with front pleats. I French-braided my hair, leaving the braid to fall against my back. I grabbed my straw hat and made my way down to the pool area.

Philip was already waiting, dressed casually in a white shirt with the sleeves rolled to just below his elbows and a pair of khaki pants. He greeted me with a welcoming smile, and stood when I approached. "You're early," he said, as he glanced down at his wristwatch.

"You're early, too," I repeated the same with a smile.

"It appears that we share common interest: we are both anxious to discover what the other has learned about the curse. Is this spot okay with you?" he asked, and then assisted me into one of the cushioned chairs next to a round table. His notebook lay on the tabletop ready for our discussion. I imagined that his findings would best both David and me.

"Yes, this is fine—thank you. I admit, I am anxious to share what I have discovered. What of you?"

"I couldn't sleep last night thinking of it."

I laughed. "Nor I."

"Would you like something to drink while we wait for David?" he offered.

"That would be wonderful."

Our tea was brought out to us by one of the hotel waiters, who managed to balance a silver tray laden with various items, by the use of only one hand. Many of the hotel patrons were gathered around the pool having their drinks. It was a pleasant afternoon, a refreshing breeze made sitting out of doors very enjoyable.

"It's a lovely afternoon," I said.

"Indeed it is. And what luck that we've met."

"I feel the same," I told him.

"I have a feeling we shall become very good friends."

His comment pleased me. "I hope so, since I haven't any here."

"None!?"

"Not a soul. I know Dr. Mehreiz and several others, but that is only because they are acquaintances of my uncle. Of course, I have not been here long."

"Well, I shall remedy that," he said. "What are you doing tomorrow night?"

I blinked—a bit surprised. "Well—nothing."

"Good! Then you will have dinner with me."

"How nice."

"Would six o'clock work for you?"

"Yes, six is fine."

It was then that David plopped down in the vacant chair next to mine. "You've not started without me, I hope."

His eyes were on me as he rested an elbow on the table, his chin in hand; he was giving me a charming smile. I felt myself slightly blush to his appreciative stare.

Philip cleared his throat. "You're late."

Ignoring Philip, David asked me, "What are you doing tomorrow night?"

"She's having dinner with me," Philip told him.

"Well, she should cancel it and have dinner with me."

I knew David was not being serious, so I said, "Thank you, David, for the invitation, perhaps some other time." I glanced over at Philip and smiled. I could see that he was somewhat annoyed with David. I had a feeling the two had already conversed about Philip asking me to dinner—and what a tease David was being.

"Shall we get started?" said Philip, as he opened the cover of his black leather notebook.

"Ladies first," David pointed out.

"No, please. I would rather go last if you don't mind."

"You start then, David," Philip suggested. "What have you discovered?"

"Very little," David said honestly. "I have learned something I think you might find interesting."

"Let's have it then," said Philip.

"There was a priest named Imhotep, who was an adviser to a pharaoh. This Imhotep had the kind of scientific knowledge that made people believe he was some sort of a god of healing. So, this priest could convince people that he had favor with the gods. In other words, if his administrations worked on the sick then they were blessed, if they died from his medicines then it was due to a curse from some god. Convenient, don't you think?"

"Very," I said. "Then you believe that the priests were actually very scientific, and the people, being ignorant, labeled it magic."

David said, "Precisely. It seems that the Egyptian priests knew something of modern science, and they did not share their knowledge with but a select few. For most science was as shrouded in secrecy as were the priests who practiced it. The masses saw it as gods, miracles or magic, when in fact it was a simple understanding of medicines and the constellations. Unlike other offices, priesthood was not passed down, but had to be earned. The priests had real authority and formed a kind of mysterious cult or class and were very powerful men."

"What does that have to do with the curse?" Philip asked.

"Well, it had to be through these 'magicians' that the burial rituals were performed. It was the priest who had the authority to chant a curse over their dead king? I guess what I'm trying to say is: maybe the curse is something more tangible, not just words written on the dead king's papyrus."

Philip said, "That's possible, but that would not explain the present mysterious deaths: the lights going out in Cairo, and the fox terrier falling over dead when Lord Carnarvon died."

I said, "Maybe it was a combination of both magic and science."

"I think you might have something there," said Philip. "David, learn what you can about their medicines or potions…whatever you want to call the stuff."

"Sure."

"I've been looking into the life stories of past archeologists to find out if their deaths had anything in common, and there were a number of remarkable coincidences," Philip informed us. He looked down at his notes and read the facts aloud: "Johannes Dumichen, born in 1833, Egyptian archeologist. He would spend weeks underground or in a ruin. It is recorded that his personality underwent radical change. Heinrich Brugsch, born 1827, could read demotic script by the age of sixteen. His personality also underwent change. Francois Champollion, born 1790, succeeded in decoding hieroglyphics, and at the age of five, he could repeat word for word the passages from the Bible that his mother read to him. It is recorded that Champollion was given copies of several pharaonic inscriptions, he was able to decode two of them: Ramesses and Thutmose. After decoding them he collapsed and remained unconscious for five days; when he recovered he spoke of strange visions and repeated over and over the names of the pharaohs whose characters he had decoded. Obviously the curse of the pharaohs has some magic force on its victims, when outstanding scholars were returning from Egypt somewhat mad. Strange, don't you think?"

"Almost as if he had been in some sort of trance," came David's comment.

"It appears," said Philip, "that these men all underwent personality changes. So the million-dollar question is—why? What caused these men to act almost schizophrenic at times?"

"What about deaths?" I asked. "Did any of these men die mysteriously like Lord Carnarvon?"

The golden flecks in Phillips brown eyes sparkled. "As a matter of fact, a few of them did. A James Henry Breasted, a veteran of Egyptian expeditions, before his death also had feverish malaise, and grew increasingly weak, similar to Lord Carnarvon. A Swabian doctor and scientist, Theodore Bilharz, who is known for his work in anthropology and pathology, his interest was in autopsies of mummies, also suffered violent feverish cramps before his death."

I was fascinated. "Where did you get all this information?"

Philip smiled. "The libraries and archives contain detailed descriptions of archeological discoveries and theories."

"I would love to look through them," I told him excitedly.

"Then we shall all go together," said Philip. "We'll make a day of it."

"You can count me out," David said quickly. "I'm not much for going through old papers. I'll find some old digger whose got a story to tell. That's how I like to gather my information."

Philip eyed him with brotherly impatience. "Not always the most accurate way. People like to stretch the truth."

David shrugged his shoulders. "Maybe, but it's more interesting than reading archives."

It was my turn to share what I had discovered. When I informed them that I had gleaned my information from the Bible, they stared at me as if I had lost all reason.

David was the first to speak: "The Bible?"

I was hesitant. "Y-e-s," I said slowly. "Have you gentlemen never attended Sunday school?"

Philip seemed skittish. "Oh—sure, a few times." I think he was embarrassed that his spiritual attentiveness was being held in question.

I told them, "As Uncle Harry always says: 'If there is anything that you need to know, you will find it in the Bible.' I believe he's right."

They listened keenly to my dissertation. I began with the story of Moses. I explained that when the Lord commanded Aaron to cast down his rod before Pharaoh, that Aaron's rod became a serpent. When Pharaoh called his wise men and sorcerers to perform their enchantments, they also did in like manner, for they cast down every man his rod, and they became serpents. When Aaron stretched out his hand over the waters of Egypt and the frogs came up, the magicians did so with their enchantments and also brought forth frogs.

I said with some conviction, "These magicians had real power—their enchantments worked. There were, of course, certain things that they could not perform, such as the plagues of the lice, or the death of the firstborn. However, their magic was real. And concerning curses, the Bible does speak of it. In Deuteronomy, the twenty-eighth chapter, the Lord tells the children of Israel that if they will not hearken to his commandments that certain curses would come upon them and overtake them. It appears, gentlemen, that curses were a very real thing. At least during the time of the pharaohs."

Philip looked genuinely impressed. "I do believe we have a Bible scholar in our midst."

"Say—that's some remarkable information," said David.

"I'm not a Bible scholar," I said honestly. "In fact, far from it. During Bible studies, Uncle Harry is continually explaining the scriptures to me."

"Do you think he would mind if we joined in on your Bible studies?" Philip asked. "Say, one day out of the week?"

Excitement rose up within me, for sharing the word of God with others is an important part of Christianity. "He would be thrilled, I'm sure."

We agreed that curses were real phenomena. After all, the Bible does speak of them, and the Word of God holds all truth; but we were yet in a quandary over whether or not a three-thousand-year-old curse would still be effective in our day. I was not entirely convinced that a curse from a dead pharaoh would presently affect our lives. I was reminded once more that Uncle Harry had had enough hands-on experience with mummy tombs, and if the pharaohs' curse existed, then, surely, he too would have fallen victim. The thought then occurred to me: *Maybe not all tombs had curses.* Was it possible that Uncle Harry had not yet encountered a tomb with a curse, and that was why he had not yet been a victim? If that were the case, then the possibility of Uncle finding a cursed tablet was probable.... Then what would befall Uncle Harry?

The thought alarmed me.

The next evening, Philip and I met inside the hotel's fine dining area. A waiter led us to a corner table for two where several candles were already lit, giving off a romantic glow. I had dressed carefully, choosing an elegant but simple satin evening dress of midnight blue, and my hair was twisted in a chignon with a few curls left dangling alongside my face and neck.

Once seated, I looked across at Philip. He looked quite debonair dressed in a simple black tuxedo. "This is enchanting," I told him.

Philip said sweetly, "You look lovely, Beth."

"Thank you, kind sir." I was not sure whether or not it would be proper for a lady to return the compliment, so I said nothing.

"I am the envy of every man tonight. Here I am in Cairo, Egypt, the place only some men can dream of, with the loveliest lady in the world to accompany me to dinner. What more could a man ask for?"

"The tomb of Smenkhkara," I teased, for Smenkhkara's tomb was the talk of many archeologists. It was said that whoever found his tomb would indeed find a splendid one.

Philip laughed. "Well, that would be the icing on the cake. Maybe we will discover it together."

I scowled. "That's not likely, seeing as how Uncle will only let me safari as far as the Cairo museum."

"A man will cherish his prized possessions and see that no harm come to them. Harry is looking out for your welfare."

"Yes, I know—but I would still like to go to the sites. It would be an unforgettable experience."

He looked thoughtful, then said, "Maybe I can help in that area."

"What do you mean?"

"Father has discovered a tomb that he believes may belong to an important princess. Once the chambers are secure, I will speak with your uncle. Perhaps I can convince him to come out one day and bring you with him."

"Oh, Philip! That would be wonderful!"

Our dinner was brought to us on silver trays. Philip changed the conversation by asking personal questions: What did I enjoy doing? What was my childhood like? He asked about my parents. I, in turn, asked him the same. He enjoyed being out of doors. Hunting, fishing, horseback riding, and of course, archeology. He had been taught by Cambridge scholars, and lived an exciting life helping his father at the digs.

By Uncle's request, I was to be delivered safely back to my room by nine o'clock that evening. At the door, Philip took my hand and held it gently within his own. "I had a wonderful time, Beth."

"Yes, it was a lovely evening. Thank you, Philip."

"No, I should thank you. You have made Egypt all the more fascinating."

It was a romantic statement that I would always remember. He had a way of saying the sweetest things without making them seem profuse or inappropriate.

Once a week, David and Philip would join Uncle Harry and me for Bible study. We were becoming quite a group, the four of us. We applied ourselves to the Word of God, dissecting the scriptures. It was after one of our group meetings that Philip found the opportunity to mention the expedition.

"We have come across a very interesting tomb," he told Uncle Harry.

We were sitting at a round table in the parlor area of Uncle Harry's room, and for the present; it was the only place available for our sessions. Uncle Harry had just closed his Bible; his hand was still resting on the cover. "A tomb, you say?"

"It is something to see," Philip said. "Father is certain she is Princess Ihi, of the Middle Kingdom. He found her in Thebes' City of the Dead on the eastern slope of El Cocha."

"Have you entered the burial room?" Uncle asked.

"We are now at the entrance of the actual burial chamber."

"A thrilling moment," Uncle commented.

Philip ventured on, "Father thought it would be good for you to be at the site when the seal is broken."

The seals, Uncle had informed me, were placed upon the bolted doors of the pharaoh's shrine. If you found a shrine with the seal broken, then most likely the tomb had already been plundered. It was a common occurrence among the Egyptian archeologists, that when the seal of a pharaoh's shrine was broken it became something of a celebration. When Lord Carnarvon was ready to open the main chamber of Tutankhamun's grave, there were twenty men present for the event. His partner Howard Carter even put on a dark suit in honor of the occasion. So, it was not at all unusual that Philip ask Uncle Harry to attend, and it was not the first time that Uncle had been invited, but what would be a first is that I be present.

I was growing anxious. I knew in what direction Philip was leading the conversation. I wanted to go desperately; I wanted to see for myself what I heard others talk of. I said a silent prayer.

Uncle Harry looked delighted. "I wouldn't want to miss it!"

Philip plunged ahead. "We have also invited your niece to come along."

Here, I held my breath.

Uncle Harry did not bat an eye, but did appear thoughtful. "Well," he said thoughtfully. "I suppose that would be a good experience. What of it, Beth? Would you like to go along?"

Unbelievingly, I sat gaping. He was going to let me go! I had prepared myself to plead with him—to beg him if necessary, to let me go. I would have been like Moses, who constantly became a nuisance to Pharaoh, insisting that he let the children of Israel go: Let me go that I may participate in the breaking of the seal. Let me go lest I bring the plagues of constant badgering. Day and night, I would have been a pestilence to his soul until he consented to let me go. But I did not have to go through such verbal calisthenics—he was simply going to let me go! Pharaoh's army would have done better had they been more like Uncle Harry. Realizing this, I jumped to my feet and threw my arms round him. "Oh—Uncle Harry! Thank you!"

"Well, gentlemen," Uncle Harry said, a bit embarrassed at my show of affection. "I believe her answer is yes."

So it was planned. I would go with the party, for the breaking of the seal of Princess Ihi's shrine, in Thebes' City of the Dead.

Chapter 3

I find it difficult to describe how I felt when I entered Princess Ihi's inner chamber. In all my life, I had never dreamt that I should see, upon this earth, such marvelous sights. Gold—the glint of gold was everywhere! In the sepulchral chamber, and towering above us, was a magnificent gilt shrine in which the princess's sarcophagus was kept. For over three thousand years, not a living soul had entered into the sealed tomb. I was the intruder, along with nine others, who, like myself, were awestruck at the wondrous treasures before us.

Upon our arrival to the site—an approximate six-mile safari from Luxor, I was introduced to the party. Colonel Whittley, of course, was beside himself with expectancy. He was a stalwart gentleman, sporting a thick mustache and wire-rimmed eyeglasses. Then, of course, there were Philip and David, who had traveled with Uncle Harry and I from Luxor. Also along were the archeologist Professor William Hubert and his wife. Professor Hubert had just recently retired and was spending vacation time in Luxor; he knew something of hieroglyphics. He was a heavyset man with a white walrus mustache, his hair the same color. Mrs. Hubert, who insisted that I call her "Grace," was a petite woman, with a genteel disposition. Also with our party was an American toxicologist, Dr. Maxwell Clairborne, who did not look at all like a doctor, but more like a safari hunter in his dust-covered white shirt and khaki pants; a leather coiled whip hung neatly at his side. I wondered about the whip—were there wild animals about? When I told Philip of my concerns, he assured me that whips were handy for a number of things if you know how to use one. My imagination could not venture any further than that of wild animals. However, I could not show any such fears, lest Uncle Harry forbid me to travel out again.

There were two other men present: James Wright, a journalist who would take account of the event, and Marvin Adams, the photographer. Both, according to Colonel Whittley, were extremely important to the field of archeology. "One must record all of what happens," he had said. "And the camera is indeed a marvelous piece of modern equipment. Time is saved by its use. You see, my dear," he had addressed me, "before the camera, artists sketched every artifact in its original location, and this took weeks, even months to achieve. A responsible archeologist must record everything before it is removed from its original location in the tombs. This is an extremely important thing to do. If we go about dismantling the tombs in a reckless way, vital information could easily be destroyed."

I liked Colonel Whittley, he and Uncle Harry were already on familiar terms. He seemed to take an interest in me, explaining why things had to be done the way that they were. I found him most engaging and very hospitable. For our human comforts he supervised the erecting of tents. I was certain he and Philip were to be thanked for Grace's and mine. Grace and I shared a private tent with cushioned mats and large pillows to soften the hard, canvas-covered floor; a water basin for washing; a spirit lamp with a teakettle and two china cups. And something I had not even thought of for myself—a mirror hung on the center tent pole.

It was the morning of the second day. I was up early. Grace and I took tea together before dressing. I found her very pleasant to be with.

"Isn't this exciting?" she said. She was sitting on a large cushion holding a cup of tea. She had not yet combed her grayish-blond hair, which she had plaited the night before; the braid now lay across her shoulder. Her oval face was almost youthful in appearance; only the fine lines gave away her age. The prints on her lightweight cotton robe were tiny pink rosettes. She was youthful to say the least. Perhaps the old cliché was true: "You are as young as you feel."

"Yes, this is most exciting," I told her, as I sat with my legs crossed on a nearby cushion, dressed in a sleeveless white cotton nightdress, with my own cup of hot tea.

"How fortunate we are. We will experience today what others will only read about."

"I have never seen anything like this," I told her. "This is my very first time out on location." I knew that she had probably been to other sites, since she was the wife of a retired archeologist.

"Oh, my!" came her exclamation. "Then this is a new experience for you. I have been with William to many sites, and I can truthfully say, the thrill never diminishes."

She leaned forward, the cup of tea held out with her pinkie finger raised. "Was the princess's shrine not marvelous? You can expect the coffins to be even grander—they usually are."

Today, the seal on the shrine would be broken, and the sarcophagus exposed. Philip had informed me that King Tutankhamun's tomb contained four coffins, each placed inside the other, and the third made of solid gold. They did not expect the princess's shrine to hold anything so grand, but they did believe it would be a rare find.

I said, "Philip is ecstatic."

She laughed. "He is a fine young man and very much like his father." She took a sip of her tea and then asked, "Have you known him long?"

"Actually, just recently. We met five months ago in Cairo."

She smiled knowingly. "He seems smitten with you."

"We have become good friends."

"That's good, dear. Before William and I fell in love, we mostly quarreled."

"You quarreled?"

She laughed. "Oh, yes, I was always into some sort of mischief. William, being a bit older than I, took it upon himself to correct my ways. Of course, I was rather independent and often proved to be most difficult."

I laughed. "How interesting. I would never have guessed you giving the distinguished Mr. Hubert a difficult time of it."

"Oh, indeed I did! And he claims that at times I still do. But that makes our relationship all the more interesting." She waved a hand in the air. "The making up has always been great fun."

I laughed at her candor. I could see that she was full of life, enjoying all that she could of it. But unlike Mrs. Hubert, I would not care to live with a quarrelsome spouse. Perhaps Mrs. Hubert was the instigator behind their marital disputes; she truly sounded like she enjoyed the verbal battles they shared. I had a feeling that I should be sympathizing with poor Professor Hubert.

After our tea, I dressed, wearing a khaki split skirt and a white blouse, then I went in search of Philip. Along with Dr. Clairborne and David, he was seated under a canvas awning that had been erected for the sole purpose of giving shade from the desert's hot sun.

When I approached they stood. Their etiquette was still intact, even in the middle of a remote desert where only the dead existed.

Philip greeted me with a cordial smile. "Good morning, Beth."

I said good morning to the three. They quickly offered me a chair—which I took, and a cup of coffee that I declined.

Dr. Clairborne did not appear the eccentric individual that he had upon our arrival. He was dressed as the others, donning a cool white shirt and khaki trousers. The leather whip no longer hung at his side, and he had shaved, which gave him a more civil appearance.

Philip said, "Well, this is the day, Beth. Are you excited?"

"How could I not be."

"It will be a painstaking process, you know? Things can be most fragile. Think of it. Three thousand years!"

"A very long time," I agreed.

"Dr. Clairborne was telling us something of amulets," Philip then told me.

Not knowing what they were I repeated, "Amulets?"

Dr. Clairborne then explained, "When the princess's mummy is exposed, we will probably find several amulets on her, some even wrapped within the linen shroud. The Egyptians had great faith in amulets. They come in different shapes and sizes, similar to jewelry."

David quickly added, "Tutankhamun wore twenty-one amulets just around his neck." No doubt, Philip had given him that piece of information—the great connoisseur of King Tutankhamun.

"What did they believe its purpose?" I asked.

"To protect the pharaoh on his journey to the empire of the dead. Amulets possess magic power," said Dr. Clairborne.

"Magic, Dr. Clairborne?" I asked skeptically. For one, he did not appear to be a man that would believe in any form of magic.

He smiled benignly. "No, of course not."

His response was what I had expected.

"Max, or I should say, Dr. Clairborne," Philip said, "believes that the priest used scientific discoveries to reinforce the amulets' power."

"I don't understand," I unashamedly admitted.

"Much like the sand bags sold in Bohemia's Joachim Valley as a cure for headache and rheumatism," Dr. Clairborne went on to explain. "It was labeled as 'occult nonsense,' but the patients claimed they actually worked. It was soon discovered that the bags contained earth with radium, and thus were slightly radioactive. It is possible, but has not yet been determined, that the amulets may work in the same manner. I hope to take part in discovering what magic—or I should say, what natural resources were used to produce these healing powers."

I found what he had to say interesting. I remembered what David had shared with Philip and me concerning the Egyptian priests. What in fact was science at work was magic to the people simply because of their lack of knowledge and understanding of such things.

I said to Dr. Clairborne, "I am almost convinced that it is a combination of both magic and science. David, Philip and I have spent some time studying into these matters."

Dr. Clairborne eyed me with some amusement. "Yes, so they have told me. I was intrigued with your biblical viewpoint."

He wanted to laugh—I could tell. "You think I'm foolish?"

He quickly corrected me. "No—not at all! On the contrary, I thought it a very logical explanation."

"And yet you don't believe the Egyptians possessed magic powers?"

"Well, I can't argue with the Bible. Indeed, it does appear that Pharaoh's magicians had powers. However, I don't believe their powers still exist. And yes, I am referring to the curse."

"Then you can explain the mystery surrounding Lord Carnarvon's death?"

"Not entirely. However, I will point out that curses were used to simply ward off robbers. Like glorified threats—that sort of thing. Of course, in our day and time, the media prefers to embellish whatever mishap may take place upon the opening of a pharaoh's tomb. And for certain, every time an individual who attends the 'opening' of some pharaoh's tomb, takes ill and dies, he is suddenly 'a victim of the mummy's curse.' It makes a great story."

Now I wanted to laugh! To him it was nothing more than folklore and hokum. I had decided then not to converse with the knowledgeable Dr. Clairborne about such topics.

At precisely nine that morning, we entered the tomb for the second time since our arrival. Uncle Harry had already informed me that the earlier we were able to descend into the tomb, the better, for the afternoon's heat would make the chambers below unbearable, with temperatures rising to one hundred and twenty degrees and even hotter in the direct sunlight.

Months prior, objects in the chambers had been removed by Colonel Whittley's team of workers. Philip had explained that the large sealed door to the princess's shrine could not have been dismantled until all the objects had been cleared away. Evidently, the treasures had been packed in so tightly that it was difficult to move one without other objects threatening to come crashing down.

We descended the stairs down into the inky blackness of the grave. I followed behind Philip, my hand held securely within his own. Colonel Whittley led us down the sloping passageway and into the antechamber, his torch lighting the way. Painted on the walls of the antechamber were hieroglyphs and magnificent figures of the princess and her attendants. I marveled that the colors were still so vivid, as if the artist had just recently applied the pigment.

It was amazingly quiet as we marveled once again at the grandeur before us. The golden canopic shrine; beside it, on the floor, was an alabaster jewelry box, which Philip told me was full of precious stones. Alabaster vases and wooden furnishings trimmed in gold were also within the burial chamber, for these items had not yet been removed. Colonel Whittley wanted us to view the chamber in its originality.

I am not ashamed to say that emotion caught in my throat as I gazed upon the shrine's etchings of golden goddesses, with their winged arms outstretched, as if protecting the sarcophagus. Their sweet faces stared back at us, as if pleading with us not to come closer, not to take what belongs to their beloved princess. If they had ears to hear, I would have told them that they had nothing to fear. We were not intruders come to steal, but to preserve.

The silence was soon disturbed by the sound of Mr. Wright's pencil upon his stenographer's tablet, recording every detail of this event. Mr. Adams was also quick to coax out of the semidarkness what later proved to be the most marvelous pictures suited to archeological affairs, capturing the unmistakable beauty of it all.

What we had waited days for now was upon us. The seal was photographed and then broken by Colonel Whittley. He opened the doors of the shrine, after thousands of years of being shut; the hinges gave an ominous sound. Immediately, a golden sarcophagus was revealed. Hieroglyphics were carved upon the limestone sarcophagus. Professor Hubert took a very thin piece of paper and laid it over the stone and then rubbed dark chalk over the entire surface. Amazingly enough, the hieroglyphics were now perfectly duplicated on the paper—he would later decode them. The coffins and the mummy would not be exposed for some time. Philip informed me that it would be a complex job dismantling the shrine and then lifting out the coffins and mummy.

"What will you do with her?" I asked him.

He leaned closer to my ear and then whispered, "Father hopes to send this one to the London museum."

"Really! With all of her things?"

"Some of the treasures will have to remain here."

"It seems a shame to separate the princess from her belongings."

"Yes, but that is the way things are done. It is always customary that the spoils be divided. Some treasures will remain here in the Cairo Museum."

"If only the entire burial chamber could be transported exactly as it is." I turned to him. "Wouldn't that be wonderful? If everyone could see it exactly as we are seeing it now. It makes it all the more impressive."

"I agree. It is like walking into something very sacred."

One hour later, we ascended from the tomb; the sunlight and fresh air were welcoming. It was an overwhelming experience, the party seemed to be in at state of exhaustion—I assumed it was the magnitude of it all. We gathered under the large open tent. The cook that Colonel Whittley had hired for the safari brought us water and lemon squash. Conversation centered on the magnificent things we had seen. Indeed, it was something to behold.

Later, when the sun lowered behind the Theban hills, the temperature dropped considerably. We sat close to the campfire that Philip had constructed. Uncle Harry and Colonel Whittley were in discourse over something or other, in a tent where maps and books were scattered on a tabletop. I could see Uncle from where I sat. He was leaning over a table studying what Colonel Whittley had laid out before him.

I could hear James Wright fervently tapping away on his typing machine. In a matter of days he would send out his typed manuscripts to the New York and London *Times*. "The world will soon know about Princess Ihi and her marvelous things," he had said. "And I will be the one to tell them all about it. It makes it very exciting."

David then appeared, buoyant and eager to share some sort of news. "Did Philip tell you?"

I glanced at Philip. "Tell me what?" Philip did not seem pleased that David had asked. His jaw stiffened, and his eyes sparked a warning in David's direction.

Regardless, David went on to say, "Professor Hubert has decoded the hieroglyphs that were on the sarcophagus."

"Really!" I said, and then looked from one to the other. "What's going on?"

A bit perturbed, Philip said, "Nothing is going on, Beth. I just thought it might be best to wait and let Professor Hubert explain the hieroglyphs—that's all."

I was not satisfied. He was keeping something from me and I wanted to know what. "Philip?"

David said, "Professor Hubert has retired for the night."

"You won't be so cruel as to make me wait until morning?" I asked Philip. "I can go and awaken Grace. She will tell me."

"That won't be necessary," said Philip. "I can tell you. The hieroglyphs that Professor Hubert decoded talk about Princess Ihi's beauty and her power," Philip explained. "She was loved by the people and was a prophetess; it was said that she was the 'Eyes of the Temple.' Another set of hieroglyphs were decoded as: 'Awake from the swoon in which you sleep and a glance of your eyes will triumph over everything that is done against you.'"

"A curse!" I exclaimed, my pulse quickening.

A voice from behind said, "We have disturbed a sleeping princess, who finds her tomb invaded by the curiosity of archeologists."

I turned quickly, and there stood Dr. Clairborne gazing down upon us. To be honest, I was not in the mood to listen to Dr. Clairborne, but Philip was kind enough to say, "Won't you please join us, Dr. Clairborne." Which he did, and to my discomfort, he sat directly in front of me.

There was something about Dr. Clairborne that I found at times intriguing. Perhaps, it was because he carried an air of confidence. He was an attractive gentleman. His hair was very dark—almost black; he wore it short on the sides, but combed back the longer strands on top. His eyes were a smoke-gray, and presently they were assessing me. I was determined not to let him unnerve me, so I did the same—this produced a raised brow.

"Have no fear, Miss Woodruff," he said. "You will be well protected." He patted the gun holster that lay against his chest where a revolver was conveniently carried.

"I am not afraid, Dr. Clairborne."

He said, "After our conversation earlier, I thought you a firm believer in the curse of the pharaohs."

"I am a believer. But that is no reason to fear it."

"I'm afraid," said David openly with a laugh.

Philip, his voice laced with mild irritation, said, "So glad that you're here to comfort the women, David. I wouldn't want Beth to sense that she is in any sort of danger."

David threw his hands up in the air. "I wasn't trying to frighten Beth. I was just stating the facts. We all know about Lord Carnarvon, and she's well aware of the curse before now. What did I say that..."

I interrupted with a short laugh, "David, it's quite all right." I gently laid my hand upon Philip's arm. "It's okay," I told him. "You don't have to worry about me being frightened. I assure you that I am not afraid."

Dr. Clairborne surprised me by saying, "Fear is not such a bad thing, it makes one cautious, and in these deserts watchfulness keeps one alive longer."

I wondered then, *Is it possible that Dr. Clairborne was not as severe as he appeared. Fear to many men was a show of weakness. Perhaps I had judged him too harshly.*

However, it was well after midnight when I began to question Dr. Clairborne's character.

We had all retired around eleven, and I had just put on my nightdress, when I heard voices coming from somewhere behind our tent. I could distinctly make out Dr. Clairborne's voice.

Curiosity about the man took precedence over any good common sense that I may have acquired during my lifetime. Crazy though it may seem, I donned my robe and slipped out into the night. If I were caught, what excuse would I give? I felt the need for a walk? No one would believe that story—not in the middle of a desert where creatures prowled about. The outhouse was in the opposite direction—so that was not a good alibi either. I could say that I needed a drink of water, but then I remembered a pitcher full of the precious liquid was given to us before we retired to our tent. Would I sound convincing enough if I said that I tend to walk about in my sleep, and thus here I am to prove that to be so? After considering these plausible stories, my conscience was quick to remind me that all those explanations were lies. So I capitulated: I would simply tell them the truth: I heard voices. I did not have to confess to anyone that I was wondering why Dr. Clairborne felt the need to have a clandestine meeting, with whomever, on the outer skirts of camp; nor that I was suspicious of him.

Bravely, I went ahead, staying close to the sides of the tent. What luck that the color of my silk robe was midnight blue and perfect for such a time as this. I walked cautiously to the backside of the tent, well concealed by its shadow, and then I peered out. I could see Dr. Clairborne's tall silhouette, the other man I did not recognize. I waited, listening; my heart beating faster than normal.

The other man said, "It will be tonight."

"You are sure, then?" came Dr. Clairborne's voice.

"Yes," came the reply. "Most definitely."

Dr. Clairborne's next sentence was muffled, but I did hear the words: "Let him get away." What it meant, I did not know, but it all seemed rather suspicious.

It was then that Dr. Clairborne handed the man what I assumed was money. He was paying him—for what, I was not certain. They split apart, Dr. Clairborne to his tent, and the man out into the desert, away from camp.

As I sat on my pallet, I could not help but wonder what Dr. Clairborne was up to. Questions came to mind, such as: *Who was the other man? Why the clandestine meeting?* I had no answers. However, the next day I was soon to learn about the black market. Where there are treasures, there are thieves, and thieves come in all shapes and sizes, and professions. Was Dr. Clairborne involved in the black market? Was he sinister enough to steal and sell rare finds from the archeological digs—precious things belonging in museums? Could he be the ringleader of such goings on? Eventually, I fell asleep and dreamed of a man, dark and tall, following me through the tunnels of Princess Ihi's tomb. As I was running, trying desperately to get away from the man in my dream, I was suddenly awakened by a blast.

It was very early in the morning when we heard the sound of a gunshot. The sun had not yet risen and the moon was still full. The piercing sound jolted Grace and me from our sleep.

"Dear God!" she said, as she groped for her robe. "That sounded like a gunshot!"

After I found my robe, I followed behind her, out the flaps of the tent door. The men had already gathered around Dr. Clairborne, who was holding the whip that Philip praised to be useful for a number of things. At that moment, Dr. Clairborne claimed that he had snatched the gun from a thief with the use of his whip. "But unfortunately," Dr. Clairborne said, "he got away, and he had a large canvas bag with him." He then said to Colonel Whittley, "I'm afraid he may have made off with several things from the princess's chamber."

Colonel Whittley sighed heavily. "There is nothing that we can do about it now. We'll see in the morning what great loss was done, but we best assign watches to avoid any further surprises."

Marvin Adams was the first to volunteer. "I'll watch till morning," he said.

"How terrible!" I whispered to Grace.

She shook her head sadly. "It is indeed."

After the men dispersed to go back to their tents, Dr. Clairborne looked our way. He quickly came to us, Philip following not far behind him.

Dr. Clairborne looked genuinely concerned. "Are you ladies okay?"

Grace said, "We heard the gunshot. You are not hurt then?"

"As you can see," he said, holding out his arms, "I am unharmed. The gun went off as the whip knocked it out of his hand."

Philip said, as he was still working on the buttons of his shirt, "Everyone okay?"

"Yes, we are fine," Grace told him.

I remembered then the clandestine meeting that Dr. Clairborne had taken part in, and the words that he had spoken came to mind: "...let him get away." Had he not told Colonel Whittley that the man "got away"? Was this what the clandestine meeting had been all about—tonight's robbery? I suddenly felt faint. How silly of me, but the thought of knowing that Dr. Clairborne could be a part of something so corrupt was extremely repulsive.

Involuntarily, I swayed, feeling ill. Grace noticed and quickly took me by the arm. Dr. Clairborne was quick to respond, for he immediately caught me up into his arms and carried me inside the tent.

Grace said, "Philip! Quickly warm some water for tea. She'll need a strong brew. I have just the thing." She waved her arm. "Over here!" Grace told Dr. Clairborne as he carried me to where Grace indicated, then gently placed me upon the cushions.

"That wasn't necessary," I told him. "I could have walked."

His gray eyes studied me for a moment. "I doubt it."

Grace took my hand.

Dr. Clairborne was still leaning over me, assessing my condition. He told Grace, "Make it strong, Mrs. Hubert."

"I'll fix it up. I brought along my own medicinal brew," she told us, then left me in the care of Dr. Clairborne.

Dr. Clairborne said to me, rather sympathetically, "The incident was a bit unnerving, but a hot cup of Mrs. Hubert's medicinal tea will set you right."

As I gazed into his smoke-gray eyes, I felt a surge of indignation. I wanted him to know exactly how I felt about such diabolical acts. "It was not so much the incident as the evil behind it that sickens me. That men would take, and oftentimes even kill for money is very revolting. Things that they have no right to! Things that belong in a museum! Things that are not meant to be sold!"

His dark eyebrow shot up—I think more out of being amused with my comment than considering its worth.

"The color is coming back into your cheeks, Miss Woodruff, but I would venture to say that it is due to voicing your convictions rather than your physical state. But you needn't let this incident upset you, we will find the grubby thief and hopefully bring back what may have been stolen."

The ordeal was becoming embarrassing. What was wrong with me? I tried to sit up, but was still feeling dizzy.

"I wouldn't try that," Dr. Clairborne advised.

"I feel very strange. I don't normally faint just because I'm upset."

His eyes narrowed as they gazed into mine. It was then that he began to take note of my condition. What he was looking for I was not entirely certain, until he asked, "Did you feel any stings or pricks on your skin this evening—something like an insect bite?"

"I don't think so."

"You don't think so? What about an itch?"

"An itch?"

"Like a mosquito bite."

"I'm feeling very hot, Dr. Clairborne, and it is becoming difficult for me to breathe."

He then became alarmed, for his voice held a certain amount of urgency. "Mrs. Hubert! Come here—quickly, please! Philip, go to my tent and bring me the black leather bag that is sitting next to the water basin. Please be quick!"

"What is it?" Grace asked, concerned.

Dr. Clairborne quickly gave her instructions. "Check her legs for any marks that may look like an insect bite."

"Oh, dear!" Grace gasped. "Do you really think that—?"

"We must remain calm, Mrs. Hubert," Dr. Clairborne interrupted her as he took my pulse and then checked the pupils of my eyes. "We'll not jump to any conclusions, but it is best to rule out such possibilities."

I felt Grace's hands upon my feet and ankles. In less than a minute she said, "Dr. Clairborne, you best take a look at this."

He did. Directly above my right ankle was a red puffy mark, now about the size of a quarter.

"Miss Woodruff, I do believe we have discovered what is causing you to feel ill," Dr. Clairborne said.

It was then that Philip returned with Dr. Clairborne's black bag. Uncle

Harry was right behind him.

"What's going on?" Uncle Harry asked, somewhat disconcerted.

Dr. Clairborne told him, "I believe your niece has been poisoned."

"Poisoned!" Uncle Harry repeated, as he came to stand next to Dr. Clairborne, his face twisted with concern.

"An insect bite," Dr. Clairborne clarified. "May I have permission to administer treatment to your niece?"

"Why—yes! Of course you have my permission. Will my niece be all right?"

Dr. Clairborne smiled down at me. "Oh, I think so. She will probably be ill for the next several days, but she'll live."

I gave a moan when Dr. Clairborne pulled out of his bag a hypodermic needle. I was not so certain I trusted him enough to administer anything to me—especially a needle.

"Is that necessary?" I asked.

"You don't trust me?"

"You don't look like a doctor."

He smiled. "Then you should be thankful that my credentials are not based upon my looks, otherwise you would be a very, very sick young lady. This will sting a bit," he warned.

I shut my eyes during the ordeal. After he was finished with that, he numbed my ankle with a local anesthetic, did something to the bite and then placed a bandage over it. He was extremely gentle.

I did not ask any questions.

"I'm going to put something into your tea that will help you sleep."

Grace handed me the cup of tea. Philip placed an arm across my back to give me the needed support as I sat up to drink.

"This is ghastly, Beth," Philip said.

Uncle Harry and Dr. Clairborne stepped outside the tent door. After I was finished with the tea, Philip went back to his own tent. Grace helped me out of my robe, and straightened the covers on my pallet. Being motherly, she tucked me in. "Thank God, Dr. Clairborne was here to take care of that bite," she told me. "And what luck that he specializes in poisons."

The medicine was already beginning its work on me. I was feeling extremely relaxed. "Yes," I mumbled. "It is a good thing." Approximately ten minutes later, I heard Dr. Clairborne ask Grace, "I saw that your light was still on. May I come in?"

"Why, certainly," Grace told him. "May I fix you a cup of tea while the water is still hot?"

"Thank you. That is very hospitable considering the hour."

He took his tea, and then I heard him say, "I would like for you to keep a close eye on my patient if you would. Let me know if there are any changes."

"I will definitely do that. Will she be all right, Doctor?"

"Hopefully, in a couple of days she will be feeling better."

They talked for a little while and I fell asleep—or so I thought. Medicine can cause people to do and to say strange things, and obviously I had talked with Dr. Clairborne after his tea with Grace. It was about eight o'clock when Grace went for my breakfast, and that was when Dr. Clairborne came in to check on me.

"How are you feeling?" he asked me, as he checked my pulse and looked at the bite.

I felt a bit uncomfortable being alone with him. Grace had not yet returned. "I still feel fuzzy headed," I told him. "But maybe that's due to the medication you gave me to drink."

"Best stay in bed today. And no more prowling around at night, especially in these." He held up the house slippers that I had placed beside my cot. "Always wear your boots."

I was totally taken by surprise. Not a soul, besides myself, knew that I had gone out to spy. "What do you mean?"

"You don't remember?"

"I remember you had tea with Grace."

By the way that he was smiling down at me, I could tell that he found my discomfort amusing. "You apologized for the inconvenience that you had caused me. Then you mumbled something about hearing voices outside your tent. Did you go spying, Miss Woodruff? Is that how you acquired that bite?"

I was alarmed. If he was truly as involved with all the tomb robberies as I thought, then what would he do if he suspected that I knew of his dealings?

I tried to sound indifferent. "Medicine can cause people to say such foolish things. Surely, you would not expect me to converse coherently after being sedated? Really, Dr. Clairborne, that would not be very gentlemanly of you."

His keen eyes narrowed a little, and a dark brow rose. "I give you my word, I was not trying to coax out of you any hidden secrets. But take some advice: never meddle—it will only lead you to trouble."

Never meddle! Was that advice—or a subtle threat?

I was growing angry at his audacity. "You are accusing me of meddling? Meddling into what, Dr. Clairborne?"

At that moment Uncle Harry came in. "So how's my niece this morning?" he asked. The tension in the air was thick enough to slice, but Uncle Harry was oblivious to it. He leaned down and gave me a kiss on the cheek.

"I'm fine, Uncle Harry."

"She'll be able to travel home tomorrow," Dr. Clairborne told Uncle Harry.

"Tomorrow!?" I blurted out.

"Dr. Clairborne thinks that you should continue your rest at home, where it will be cooler and more comfortable."

Why was Dr. Clairborne so concerned? Maybe he just wanted me out of the way.

"But you said that we would stay here until the end of the week! Think of all that we will miss!"

"Not so much, really," Uncle Harry assured me. "Most of what will take place will be very tedious work and the progress will be slow going."

"But I'm fine, really. And if I rest today, then tomorrow I will be quite fit."

"I will have to agree with Dr. Clairborne," Uncle said. "We will leave first thing in the morning. Now, I have some work to do. You stay in bed and get plenty of rest. I'm afraid the safari home will be a bit taxing for you."

Uncle went his way. I knew then that the expedition was now over for me. I had only one last thing to say to Dr. Clairborne, "You should not have meddled!" I told him angrily, repeating the advice he had earlier given to me.

Chapter 4

I had to swallow my pride to admit that Dr. Clairborne was right, but the following weeks proved to be very uncomfortable for me. I was certainly glad to be back at the hotel, where ceiling fans circulated cooler air. In the desert, relief from the heat was unattainable and most luxuries were nonexistent.

I had not seen Philip since our departure from Princess Ihi's tomb. I imagined he was extremely occupied with the princess and her belongings. I could almost say that I felt a twinge of jealousy, for she was certainly taking up most of his time—which meant that I was seeing less of him.

One morning, after we had made our move into Uncle's house, we were sitting out on the back patio having our morning tea. As usual, Uncle Harry was hidden behind the morning paper, leaving me to admire the scenery. Occasionally, he would make a comment about something or other that he had read.

I had just poured myself a fresh cup of English tea when Philip paid us a visit. "Hello," he said gaily, surprising both Uncle Harry and me as he stepped up onto the patio.

I was overjoyed to see him. He looked wonderful. Daily exposure to the sun had changed his light brown hair to almost blond and deepened his tan.

Uncle offered him a seat. He asked how I was feeling.

"If you are referring to that ghastly bite," I told him, as I placed a cup of hot tea before him, "then, yes, I have finally recovered. Who would have thought that a tiny insect bite could make one so ill."

Philip then brought out from under his arm a rolled newspaper. "I thought you might like to read this."

It was the *London Times* and the headlines read: "Archeologist's Niece Bitten by the Curse." Below the caption was a young woman standing by the tomb of Princess Ihi. It was me!

I was astounded. "How did they get this picture?"

"Our friend Marvin Adams."

"The photographer!?"

"The very one."

Uncle looked down at the paper and then chuckled. "Photographers and journalists, they'll sell anything for a dollar."

"Who wrote the article?" I asked.

"Take a guess."

"James Wright."

"Bingo!"

"I don't believe this!"

Philip laughed. "You made the headlines, Beth. How does it feel to be a celebrity?"

"A celebrity! Indeed! And bitten by the curse. What utter nonsense."

I read the article while Philip drank his tea and conversed with Uncle Harry. I was amazed that being bitten by an insect had suddenly made me victim of the curse. The article was very convincing. And I, who believed that the curse was a very real thing, had not given it credit for the unpleasant experience. I remembered what Dr. Clairborne had said about the media embellishing whatever mishap may take place upon the opening of a pharaoh's tomb, and that every time an individual who attends the opening of some pharaoh's tomb takes ill and dies, he is suddenly "a victim of the mummy's curse."

Again, I hated to admit it, but Dr. Clairborne was right. "Well, it makes a great story," I said, quoting Dr. Clairborne's exact wordage.

Uncle and Philip both laughed.

"What do you think of our pharaoh's curse now?" Philip then asked me.

"I still believe in it."

"What nonsense," Uncle Harry blurted out.

"Uncle Harry, I'm surprised," I said. "You being a man of the Bible, and of science, should know that it is something supernatural."

"We live in different times now, Beth," said Uncle Harry. "Things are not as they were. We don't call on God as the men of old, by way of a priest, and the Ark of the Covenant. This is a new dispensation. Remember the verse: 'Greater is he that is in me, than he that is in the world.'"

Still, I was not convinced.

Philip changed the subject. "I came for another reason besides getting your autograph, Beth."

"That's very humorous, Philip."

He slid the *London Times* over to me and then pointed. "If you'll sign right there."

Uncle Harry laughed.

I picked up the paper and slapped Philip with it. "Stop being a tease."

"Don't crumble the paper, I intend to have it framed—after you sign it of course."

He laughed. I rolled my eyes.

"What other business do you have with us, Mr. Whittley?" I asked with sarcasm.

"I'm escorting Princess Ihi from Southampton to New York for a special exhibition."

Uncle Harry was thrilled. "That's marvelous!"

I wasn't as pleased. Again, the princess was taking him away from me. "How long will you be gone?"

"Maybe a couple of months. That's what I have come to talk to you about. Would you like to go along?"

I was surprised. "Me!?"

Uncle Harry scowled. "You young people forget too often the need for propriety. What is this world coming to?"

Philip quickly eased Uncle's mind. "Of course we will be properly chaperoned. Professor Hubert and his wife Grace have already consented to the task."

"Have they now?" Uncle commented dryly.

"Grace and Professor Hubert!" I said delightedly. "Oh, what fun! When do you leave?"

"Three weeks from today."

"May I go, Uncle Harry?"

He said, with some hesitancy, "I will give it some thought."

That was almost a yes.

"One day I may need to deliver precious cargo to some museum," I commented, hoping to strengthen my chances. "It will be a great learning experience for me."

"It will be a dark day when it is customary for women to travel about without a chaperon, and as long as this old uncle of yours is still alive, you'll be doing no such things."

I had blundered. "Well, I suppose not, but it will still be a great learning experience."

Uncle relented, "I will talk to Professor Hubert and his wife, and then I will decide."

I knew then it would be a "yes," Grace would see to that.

So, I began preparations. The following weeks, I worked longer hours at the museum doing the necessary paperwork of labeling and categorizing items that had recently been brought in from Uncle's site. Restoration was something I would not do alone. The cleaning, scraping and polishing of thousand-year-old objects took skill and patience, and I still had much to learn in that area.

One afternoon, as I was making a journal entry and preparing new catalogue cards for a very old clay vase, Uncle came into the museum. I could tell by the look on his face that something of importance had been discovered.

"I think that I have found it," he breathlessly told Dr. Mehreiz and me.

"Found what?" I asked.

Uncle was shaking with excitement. "Today we hit a hard surface. A stone step. It leads down into a steep cut in the rock."

"Is it possible that it could be a tomb?" asked Dr. Mehreiz.

Uncle gave a triumphant smile. "I would recognize the manner of cutting. There is no doubt in my mind that it is a sunken stairway entrance to a royal tomb." He went on to explain, "Yesterday we discovered a broken box containing a gold leaf stamped with the name of Smenkhkara."

Dr. Mehreiz whispered, disbelieving, "Smenkhkara! Holy Moses, Harry! Are you trying to tell us you believe it's the tomb of Smenkhkara?"

It was believed that Smenkhkara was the brother of King Tutankhamun.

"I would almost bet my life on it," Uncle told him.

It seemed too good to be true. "Oh—Uncle Harry!" I cried with exultation.

Uncle commented, "It could be one of the greatest archeological discoveries of our time."

I realized at that moment I would have to make a decision. Would I stay—or go with Philip?

The following day, after I had given it much consideration, I went to Uncle Harry. "I'll not be going with Philip."

"What's this?" he asked.

"I have given it some thought, and I can't go with Philip to London. Not now! I would not want to miss being part of this discovery for anything in the world."

I was certain he understood, for if he had to make a similar decision, he would do likewise.

He smiled, his eyes aglow with gratitude. "I would have been lost without you."

"I doubt that, but I want to be in with you on this."

Uncle began making plans. "We'll turn one of the chambers into a conservation laboratory and storeroom. I can hire a freelance archeologist and a few other experts to help out. We'll need you to do the cataloguing. I hope you don't mind working on-site."

"Mind! It's what I've been longing for."

"It has its dangers."

"Well—I will be careful."

"We have lots of planning to do before we start out. We'll need a storehouse of special equipment, photographic material, chemicals, and packing boxes of every description."

"Then we need to get started," I said. "I know how to pack for myself, thanks to Grace's help on our last safari to Princess Ihi's tomb. If you will make a list of personal supplies and such, I can do some of the shopping. I will leave the equipment purchases up to you."

"You are sure about this? It's not very glamorous. Most of the time it will be unpleasant, hot, and often lonely. Philip probably has dining out in London's finest restaurants in mind. The sort of things women like."

"Candlelight dinners with Philip can always come later. I don't have to tell you that this is a chance of a lifetime."

He said with some emotion, "It is always what I have longed for: to discover such a find."

"Believe me when I tell you, I don't want to miss this chance. I would not enjoy going with Philip. I would not be able to think of anything but this."

I must have finally convinced him that I preferred to stay. He kissed me on the forehead. "Then we must get started right away. I am meeting with the antiquities service about funding for the expedition. When I return we will begin our preparations."

The next day I met with Philip at one of Cairo's finer cafes. It was a sultry afternoon, so I chose to wear a cool cotton sundress, and I wore my hair twisted up off my neck. We sat outside on the patio at a table for two, shaded by a large, white-and-green-striped canvas umbrella, drinking tea. We were situated in such a place that we could view below us the busy street. The waiter had just refilled our glasses, and I sat silently for a moment watching the passers-by.

I could sense Philip's eyes on me. "You've been quiet this afternoon, Beth," he said, probably wondering why.

I had worried all day about telling him of my change in plans. "I have news."

He leaned forward and took my hand, his soft, brown eyes studying me intently. "Bad news?"

I wasn't sure what to tell him. "Yes—and no."

One of his eyebrows rose inquisitively. I continued to explain, "Uncle believes he has found the tomb that belongs to Smenkhkara."

"Smenkhkara!" he repeated the name almost reverently. "Great Scott! Is he certain?"

"Very. Uncle Harry told Dr. Mehreiz, and me, that they discovered a broken box containing a gold leaf stamped with the name of Smenkhkara. The very next day, as they dug deeper, they came upon a sunken stairway entrance."

He ran a hand through his thick hair. "A man can only imagine and dream of such a find, but to actually be the one to discover it. He must be ecstatic."

"He is."

"And you? You must be as equally excited."

"I am—and this is where the bad news comes in."

His eyes narrowed at me a little, and his mouth twisted perceptively. "You will not be going to London. You have decided to remain here."

"I'm sorry if I have disappointed you."

"Beth, I would do the same. And yes, it will be disappointing not to have you along on the trip, but it would also be very selfish of me to ask you to go. If I hadn't already made the arrangements to deliver the princess, I too would stay."

"You will hurry back? We could use your help."

"You have my word. I will hurry back."

I smiled warmly. "Thanks for understanding. I hope I have not caused any inconveniences by not going: the arrangements and the fare."

He feigned a look of bereavement. "It means that Professor Hubert will share a cabin with his wife instead of me, and I will be left alone."

"Left alone. I don't believe it. If I know you, as I think I do, you'll only be in that cabin to sleep. Probably you will find some pretty girl to spend most of your time with."

"Yes, you are right. I will be spending my time with Princess Ihi."

"I have grown to dislike her."

He laughed. "I may be spending my time taking care of the princess, but my heart belongs to you."

My heart suddenly melted. I could easily fall in love with Philip. "I'll miss you."

He gently squeezed my hand. "I'll hate every minute that we are apart. You must promise me that you will be very careful. Not only do you need to watch out for poisonous insects and vermin, but thieves."

"Uncle is hiring guards, and plans to have the tomb secured with steel gates and padlocks."

"Wise decision. But still, you will need to be very careful."

"I've been meaning to ask you. Did anything show up missing from the princess's tomb?"

His eyes flickered with anger. "The alabaster box."

"Oh—Philip! No!"

"I'm afraid so. Everyone is searching, trying to catch the thief. Dr. Clairborne has been of some help in the search."

I blurted out, "Dr. Clairborne! Don't trust him, Philip!"

He looked surprised. "Why not?"

I did not have enough evidence to explain what I truly thought of Dr. Clairborne. "Well—I don't exactly know."

"Just intuition?"

"He seems so..."

"Sure of himself?" Philip finished for me. "I rather like the chap."

"He seems rather mysterious. Does anyone really know him?"

"Father knows him well enough. I suppose that is why I would never question his character." He eyed me with some concern. "Did he do or say something that has offended you?"

"No, nothing like that."

He suggested, "Personality clashes?"

I did not think that was the reason, but to avoid further questioning I agreed.

"I'll let Father be the judge of Dr. Clairborne. After all, he has known him for quite some time."

I said nothing more concerning Dr. Clairborne. Philip changed the subject by saying, "I will be meeting up with the Huberts at Giza port. You must come and see us off."

I told him that I would.

Philip's eyes then turned mysterious. "I was going to wait until we were sailing under the stars, but since you will not be going along, I'll give it to you now."

He pulled out from his shirt pocket a very small black velvet jewelry case, then handed it to me. "Let's say it's a farewell gift."

"Oh, Philip!"

"Go ahead—open it."

I gingerly lifted the lid, and there on black velvet was a marvelous solid gold pendant watch; engraved on its cover were my initials, and underneath Philip had inscribed: "Forever yours, Philip."

I was overwhelmed. "It's beautiful!" I looked up at him; the smile he gave me was charming.

He took my hand and kissed it. "Something to always remember me by."

"I don't need gifts to remember you."

Four days later, along with Uncle Harry, who believed that women should not travel unescorted, we met up with Philip and the Huberts at Giza port.

I did not like goodbyes—in fact, I hated them. I had dressed for the occasion, wearing a crisp linen skirt and organdy blouse with the pendant Philip had given me pinned above my heart. My outfit was complete with a large-brimmed white hat. I hoped to make an impressive memory. One that Philip would not easily forget.

Uncle Harry and the Huberts stood in deep conversation. Philip and I walked ahead so we could be somewhat alone.

"Don't forget about me," he said. "I promise I'll be back as soon as possible."

We were standing close, and had Uncle not been near, I was certain he would have chosen that moment to kiss me goodbye.

"I will think of you continually."

"You will be so busy with the excavation of Smenkhkara's tomb to think of anything or anyone."

"It will make time go by faster—staying busy."

"For you perhaps. But for me it will seem a lifetime."

"You will be extremely busy too." I reminded him. "The princess will see to that."

"Ah, yes, the princess." He grew somber. "I do wish you were going."

"You do understand? To leave Uncle Harry now, especially when he needs me the most. I will admit I am very excited about the excavation. Smenkhkara's tomb—it is still hard to believe."

He brushed my cheek with a finger and then lightened the mood. "You're going to miss a most incredible journey."

"I usually get seasick."

"Not on this vessel you wouldn't. It's like a floating city."

"Really?"

"We'll board her in London and sail to New York. She's eleven stories high and four city blocks long."

"Incredible."

"That's not all. There's a gymnasium on the boat deck; a Turkish bath; private promenade decks; a dining room so fine you sink knee deep into plush carpet..."

The *Nile Queen* blew its final signal, indicating departure time, and making it impossible to hear more about this fine ship.

"I guess this is it," Philip said a moment later.

I said goodbye to the Huberts, and watched as they walked up the boat's plank.

Philip appeared to be the only passenger that had not yet boarded. Uncle shook his hand and wished him a safe journey, and then asked to be excused so that he could speak with a fellow archeologist that stood not far away. I was left alone to see Philip off.

"If you don't get going, you'll be left behind," I told him.

"I don't like farewells," he said.

"Nor do I."

He set down his luggage, pulled me into his embrace, and then kissed me. "Goodbye, Beth," he whispered into my ear.

I held onto him for a moment, still affected by his gentle kiss. "Goodbye, Philip, and do hurry back."

"You know I will."

The boat's crew began making preparations to push off. "You best hurry!"

He grabbed up his luggage and ran; once he hit the plank, he turned and yelled, "You can read about our voyage in the paper."

"Read about what?" I shouted.

"The *Titanic*," he yelled. "It's her maiden voyage."

Chapter 5

When news reached us that the *Titanic* sank, I was devastated. I refused to believe that Philip was gone. It was just not possible! Philip, who had been so full of life, would have defied even death somehow. I clung to the hope that some lifeboat was missing. "He may be drifting about!" I sobbed to Uncle Harry.

Uncle Harry tried to say words to comfort. He looked at me sorrowfully. "I know this is hard, Beth. I'm sorry."

I began to weep. "But they said the *Titanic* was 'unsinkable.' I don't understand!"

Uncle Harry wrapped his arms around me. "Losing someone is never easy. When your Aunt Margaret died, my heart was ripped in two. I wanted to die. I couldn't imagine life without her." He sighed, and then went on to say, "This is a great tragedy."

"Why would God allow something like this to happen?" I asked, withdrawing from his embrace. "Why!?"

"Perhaps to remind us that life is fragile, and we are only upon this earth for a short time. Men live life carelessly, often not giving any thought to where their souls are destined."

"But why Philip?"

"I don't have an answer as to why it was Philip's time to leave this earth, but I will say that out of all those lost, we know that Philip was ready to meet with God. He believed and obeyed Acts 2: 38 salvation. He was ready, Beth. Paul wrote to the saints at Philippi, to live is Christ, and to die is gain."

This did not comfort me. For weeks I had difficulty eating and sleeping.

Uncle Harry began to worry and thought that I should see a doctor, but I refused. "What can a doctor do?" I asked. "He cannot bring Philip back!"

One afternoon I was sitting out on the back patio, and Uncle Harry came out and announced that I had a visitor. I looked up and there stood David, tall and lean, wearing a white linen coat and trousers, his sandy-blond hair tousled by the wind.

"Hello, Beth."

"David!"

I stood and he gave me a hug.

After Uncle left us to converse alone, I offered him a chair next to mine.

He started the conversation by asking, "How are you doing?"

Tears quickly came to my eyes, but I managed to say, "Not very well. And you?"

I could tell he was having difficulty controlling his own emotions. His blue eyes watered. "It has been tough. Philip and I did a lot together."

I said, "I keep hoping that there has been a terrible mistake." I began to cry.

He put an arm around me to comfort me. "I'm sorry, Beth. I know it hurts."

It was easy to confess my feelings for Philip. "I was in love with him—you know."

I withdrew from his embrace and wiped my tears.

David smiled. "Yeah, and he never stopped talking about you. If that's not love, I'll never know what is." He laughed. "I remember once when we were working at the princess's tomb and he said to me: 'What luck that I found her.' I said to him: 'What do you mean? You can't take credit for finding the princess; it was your father that came across the tomb.' He looked at me as if I had lost all my senses and said: 'Not the princess—Beth.' "

I laughed with David. His visit did me a great deal of good. He shared stories about Philip and the things that they had done together. He said, "Philip would want us to go on with life, Beth; to remember him, not grieve him."

"I know," I whispered. "But it's so hard."

"With time it will get easier."

I remained silent, brooding over the fact that I did not want my life to be without Philip.

David quickly added, "Look—I have some pictures of Philip. I'll bring them over and we'll make a scrapbook of some sort. You can even pick out a few photos to keep for yourself."

It was a marvelous idea and I told him so. It was then that I thought of

Philip's family. "Colonel Whittley must be sick with grief."

"I think he feels responsible. I overheard Colonel Whittley tell Dr. Clairborne that had he been the one to deliver the princess, Philip would still be alive."

"He shouldn't blame himself."

"I guess it is a natural thing to do."

"He had no control over the matter."

David reminded me, "And to think that you came so very close to going yourself."

I considered what he said. True, if Uncle Harry had not discovered the tomb of Smenkhkara when he had, I too, along with Philip and the Huberts, would have been aboard the *Titanic* that tragic night. "It would have been unbearable to have watched Philip and Professor Hubert die." Thinking of the Huberts, I then asked, "Have you heard from Grace?"

He shook his head. "No."

"When I saw Grace's name on the list of survivors without Professor Hubert's, my heart ached all the more. She loved him dearly. Oh—David! How could this kind of tragedy befall our friends?"

He shrugged his shoulders. "I don't know, Beth. It's much like a bad dream that won't go away."

"I'm afraid it is one we will never awaken from," I added.

He took my hand and gave it a squeeze. "We'll get through this together, and if you ever need me, even if it's just to talk about Philip, I want you to look me up. I'll be around for awhile."

"I can't tell you how much that will help."

He smiled. "If you're not busy on Friday we'll start that scrapbook."

"That'll be great!"

He asked, "When will you be going out to Smenkhkara's tomb to work?"

"Uncle Harry wants me to wait several more weeks. He thinks I have grown sickly, when in fact I have only lost a little weight."

"You do look a bit wan, but that stands to reason."

"Uncle Harry has really been wonderful. I know he's really anxious to get me out to the site to begin cataloguing the finds. When we first found out about Philip and Professor Hubert, out of respect for them, he shut down work at the excavation for several weeks."

"Colonel Whittley closed down the princess's tomb also. However, I don't think he intends to work it again for the remainder of this year."

"I must go and see him."

"I believe he is with his family in Highclere."

"Oh—I see. Maybe when he returns then."

"I'm sure he would like that, Beth. Colonel Whittley thought a lot of you."

I had gleaned a certain amount of comfort from David's visit, and before David said his goodbye, we agreed, once again, to meet on Friday to work on the scrapbook. I was anxious, and Friday, which was only three days away, seemed like an eternity. I had only one picture of Philip, so I was eager to go through all of David's photos and choose out which ones I would keep for myself.

On Friday, Uncle Harry was the one to greet David at the door. It was quite a scene.

From his waist up, David was well hidden behind the boxes he was carrying. All that was visible to Uncle Harry and me was a pair of khaki-clad legs and the white-and-brown oxfords he wore.

Uncle Harry eyed him over his reading glasses with a newspaper in hand. "Well!" he exclaimed. "What's this?"

A voice from behind the stack of boxes managed to say, "It's David. I'm here to see Beth."

Uncle Harry took several boxes from off the stack David was carrying and then spoke more cordially, "Hello, young man. Do come in."

"Thank you, sir," said David.

Uncle Harry, now curious, asked, "You walked here like this?"

I could envision the scene now, David precariously walking through Cairo's busy streets, unable to see where he was going due to the stack of boxes blinding his view—a balancing act to say the least. Imagining David in such a plight brought a long-needed smile.

David chuckled. "Oh no, sir, I borrowed a friend's automobile."

I said, coming upon the two, "That was nice of your friend."

David gave a greeting and then we went into the dining area to use the table to sort out, piece by piece, photos and other personal items that had belonged to Philip.

I asked, "Will his family not want to go through his belongings first?"

"Not at all. His mother told me that most of Philip's possessions are at Highclere, and since he and I were best of friends, I was welcome to keep what belongings he had here."

"How nice."

David then added, rather chivalrously, "And now I am going to share them with you. Choose whatever you would like."

"David! How thoughtful."

I was moved that he would make such a sacrifice, for I could take what was most important to him. Perhaps men did not hold sentimental value to inanimate objects, as women were apt to do. I touched the watch pendant that Philip had given to me. I would cherish it forever.

We went through the photos first, and I had quite a stack accumulated for myself, most chosen out by David. He would say, "Here Beth, you'll want to keep this one."

It was when we began to go through Philip's personal items that I became emotional. A gold watch, several rings, a gold tie clip, a fountain pen with his initials engraved on its case.

David said, "You should have this."

It was Philip's class ring. I took it and studied the intricate detailing. Tears glistened in my eyes, for I remembered him wearing it often. "Why did he not have this on?"

David shrugged his shoulders. "I don't know, he must have forgotten to put it on. He was in a hurry that morning."

"I see," I managed to say, and then I thanked David for letting me keep it.

When we began to remove items from the third box, I came upon a hard-back notebook. I cried out ecstatically, "Oh—David! Look!" I thumbed through it quickly. "It looks like a journal."

"It is," he said. "Philip recorded the events that took place at the princess's tomb. The things discovered and what all took place."

As I was flipping through the book, hieroglyphs that had been drawn on one of the pages caught my attention, and below it the interpretation. I read it silently to myself: "Awake from the swoon in which you sleep and a glance of your eyes will triumph over everything that is done against you."

It was the curse that had been found under the princess's pillow!

I was suddenly chilled. "Oh, God in heaven," I whispered. "David, read this." I handed him the journal.

He said nothing for a moment and then reminded me, "As I said, he recorded all that happened at the opening of the tomb."

I could tell he did not want to discuss it.

I continued with it anyway by saying, "I had forgotten about the curse. Until now."

"I know what you are thinking, Beth—and you're wrong."

"I'm not just thinking it, David, but I feel it."

"Philip did not fall victim to some curse. Philip was a child of God! It just couldn't happen to him."

"But who is to say?"

He ran a hand through his hair. "It would be too bizarre. Things like this just don't happen, not in our time."

"Now you are sounding like Dr. Clairborne."

"You must admit he is a logical sort of fellow."

"Opinionated."

"Perhaps to some degree."

"You've been thinking it too—don't deny it. Be honest with me, David!"

"All right. Yes!" he admitted reluctantly. "It did cross my mind. But think about it, Beth, people would label us crazy if we told them the *Titanic* sank because of some ancient curse."

He was right. I did not even mention to Uncle Harry of my thoughts, but what I did do was gather information from newspaper articles concerning the *Titanic*. I was determined to start my own journal, until I had enough evidence to say: "The curse was the cause." Call it crazy...Call it hokum, but some inner feeling was driving me.

By the end of two weeks I had gathered enough newspapers to start my own stand. I began to clip out articles to keep, and burned what I did not need. One article that held my interest stated that Edward J. Smith, captain of the *Titanic*, had acted strangely that April night. It began with the course he steered and the unusually high speed at which he allowed the ship to travel. I thought: *Did Captain Smith also fall victim to the curse? Was he being driven by an unknown force to act irrationally, which thus led to the sinking of the* Titanic*?*

I think my quest to link the curse with the sinking of the *Titanic* brought back some normality to my life, perhaps because it occupied not only my time, but also my mind. I was like a Scotland Yard detective, earnestly searching for clues.

My time spent on research soon ended when Uncle Harry suggested that I come out to the site to work. I agreed that I was ready to do that. So, my weekend was spent preparing for the safari out. I was packing the clothes I would need, when Grace stopped in to see me. I was overjoyed to see her.

She hugged me tightly and then held me at arm's length. "How are you doing, my dear?"

The ordeal had not changed her looks any; she still appeared youthful and lively—where as I felt ancient.

My eyes quickly pooled with tears. "I'm coping," I told her, then I thought how horrible it must be for her, losing a husband that she had been married to for many years. She, too, had lost a very dear companion. Words were not much comfort; I knew that for a fact, but I said truthfully, "I am sorry for your loss."

"Yes," she whispered. "We have suffered the loss of two wonderful men."

I fixed cups of hot tea that we carried out onto the patio. She began to tell me all that had happened that horrible night.

"I wanted to stay by William's side, but he would not allow that. You know how he was, my dear—very stubborn. When his mind was made up there was no changing it. He literally lifted me and placed me inside one of the lifeboats. He said our children and grandchildren did not need to lose the both of us, and that I needed to be here for them."

She could no longer hold back the tears. I went to her and placed an arm around her.

She went on to say, "You should have seen them." She gave me a smile. "Philip was so brave. They were both so chivalrous and noble."

Yes, that was Philip, I thought: *chivalrous and noble.*

Grace went on to say, "You would have been so proud of him. They helped the women and children into the lifeboats."

We cried together and then she took out of her purse a note. "Philip asked me to give this to you."

I took it. It was a note from Philip that read: "Beth, I'm sorry, but I will have to break that promise. Always know this: I love you," then he signed, "forever yours, Philip." I then remembered what he had said the day that he gave me the pendant: "I promise, I will hurry back."

"Oh, Philip!"

"He thought of you those final hours, my dear. He scribbled that note standing on the ship's deck with the band playing 'Nearer My God to Thee.'"

"I'll miss him terribly, Grace."

"I know. And how terribly I will miss William."

We talked of other things. Conversation was centered on her grandchildren. I saw her eyes light up when she spoke of them. They held a special place in her heart, and I knew that Grace would be able to go on with life. She was that sort of person. She would mourn for Professor Hubert for a time, then go on living—taking the bitter with the sweet. I was not sure I would be as resilient.

When Uncle Harry arrived home, he was surprised to see Grace out on the patio chatting with me. He gave her a consoling hug.

"You must stay for supper," he told her.

Grace said, "Only if you will allow me to help prepare the meal. I do enjoy cooking and I have not had the chance to do so for some time."

Uncle Harry smiled. "Well, I know cooking is not Beth's forte, so I'm sure she would love the help."

"Most definitely," I told her. "Do stay, Grace."

She accepted and did most of the cooking. I was the third hand—stirring this and that, or chopping up vegetables. I was fascinated with how quickly she managed to make a lovely meal of lamb chops with vegetable gravy. It would have taken me twice as long to prepare, and would not have been as savory. Uncle Harry definitely enjoyed it.

Later, I told her, as I began to clean away the remains of our dinner, "If you were staying in Cairo, I would insist you give me lessons on the art of cooking."

She informed us, "I'll be leaving in about two, maybe three weeks for London. You must come and stay with me for a little while. I will teach you all that you need to know about cooking. It's really rather simple. It is the way to a man's heart, you know."

"She doesn't know me very well. Does she, Uncle Harry? Teaching me to cook would be a great undertaking."

Grace laughed. "Nonsense! You are a very brilliant girl. You would catch on quickly."

"Beth is being too hard on herself," Uncle Harry told her. "She is really not a bad cook. Just needs some experience."

"That's a polite way of putting it, Uncle Harry."

We laughed.

Grace asked, "Harry, how's the excavating coming along?"

"Well, you know how that goes. The first month is slow going, carefully chipping away at the plaster and stone, being careful not to damage anything, but we are ready to enter the main antechamber."

"You will be helping out at the site, Beth?" Grace asked.

"Most definitely!" Uncle Harry put in for me. "I would not enter without her."

"Then I wish you both the best of luck. I do hope you are taking precautions against thieves. It is becoming quite a problem I hear."

"Yes, it is," said Uncle Harry. "I'm doing everything possible to avoid any robbery attempts."

"William mentioned that the Antiquity Services Department has hired agents to capture the culprits."

Uncle Harry gave a nod. "Yes, Dr. Mehreiz said the same."

I said, "Well, if these agents are working under cover, then isn't it best not to be spreading the news, lest these thieves learn of it?"

"She's right, Harry. I do hope the Antiquity Department is not too eager to tell all."

Uncle Harry took a drink of his coffee and then set the cup onto the saucer. "I'm sure they are only telling a select few. Especially those involved with present excavations. They want to make sure we are on guard."

"Yes, of course," said Grace. "Philip was telling us about the alabaster box."

"A great shame," Uncle Harry commented. "It was an extremely priceless piece. And the jewels it contained probably even more so."

"Do they have any idea who is behind all this?" Grace asked.

"For certain, there is a mastermind behind all the robberies," Uncle Harry told us. "Not just your ordinary thief or tomb robber."

"Not a very intelligent individual would find himself or herself delving into such practices," I blurted out. "Do they not know, as the Bible so plainly puts it: 'Their sins will find them out.'"

Grace laughed. "She has a point. They are being rather stupid."

Uncle Harry said, "Yes, the Bible is foolishness to the worldly wise," and then he added, "But it is just a matter of time and the culprits will be exposed. Let's just hope it is soon, before something else of great value and historical significance is stolen."

"Or they kill someone to get what they want," I added.

"That has not yet happened," said Uncle Harry. "And we'll pray that it never does."

"Do take added precautions while you are out at the site," Grace warned.

"As I said earlier, we are doing everything possible to discourage any robberies," Uncle reassured her. "I have thought that perhaps Beth should remain here until this all blows over."

"You don't mean that!?" I said quickly.

"I do."

"But, Uncle Harry, I have so looked forward to this! I'll go mad if I can't go."

I needed something to occupy my mind. I had to stay busy. It was the only thing that seemed to relieve my grief. He just couldn't leave me behind.

Grace helped by saying, "Let her go, Harry. If you have taken added precautions, I'm sure you will thwart any problems. And if things do become unsettled you could always send her home."

I thanked Grace with a smile.

Uncle relented easily. "Yes, I suppose you are right."

It was getting late. Grace said she must go. After we said our goodbyes, I finished packing and set my luggage by the door. The next morning I was up before Uncle Harry. I was not going to give him the chance to leave me behind.

I had his coffee ready and set the morning paper next to the saucer.

"You're up early," he said, as he sat down and unfolded the paper.

"I'm ready to go," I told him.

I set a plate of hot muffins in front of him. He took one. "I can see that. If only our workers were as eager. We'd get twice as much done in one day."

I smiled. "I didn't want you to leave without me."

"Leave without you?"

"I was worried you might change your mind about my going."

"Now why would I do that?"

"You don't remember what you said?"

"Oh—yes. You staying here until they catch the thieves."

"Yes, that is what you said."

Uncle laughed and then rubbed his bearded chin. "I wonder if I could use that sort of tactic on the workers to help prod them along."

I narrowed my eyes at him. "Don't tell me you said that on purpose, just to 'prod me along.'"

"You have to admit, I won't be waiting on you; more like, you'll be waiting on me."

"Uncle Harry!"

He grew serious. "No, Beth. I meant what I said. I don't like what's going on. I don't want you caught in the middle of it."

"But you will let me go?"

He said nothing for a moment. "I hope I don't live to regret it, but I have not changed my mind. You may go. However, if there is anything that arises that could cause you any danger, I will have to send you home. You do understand that? You must know I am only concerned for your safety."

"Thank you, Uncle Harry. I don't think I could bear to be left here alone—to think."

"Yes, I know. It will be good for you to go and to stay busy."

And busy we were. As soon as we arrived Uncle Harry's foreman quickly approached us. "It is all complete," he told us. "We are ready to tear down the sealed wall."

Uncle Harry smiled. "A job well done, Ahmed."

Ahmed gave a toothy smile.

Uncle Harry then introduced us. "Ahmed, this is my niece, Elizabeth." Then he turned to me. "Elizabeth, our foreman, Ahmed Abduleh. He'll be in charge of the workers and whatever else I turn over to him."

I said, "Ahmed, it is a pleasure to meet you."

He was, of course, Egyptian. He was of medium build and looked to be in his late forties. He acknowledged me with a nod, then said slowly, in perfect English, "It is a pleasure to meet you. Your uncle speaks very highly of you."

I smiled at Uncle. "I am his only niece, so he has no others to compare me to."

Ahmed laughed. "Yes, he says you keep him busy enough."

I laughed with Ahmed. "I see."

Uncle Harry cleared his throat. "Don't give me away, Ahmed."

Ahmed said, "Then I say no more. I need to keep my job, I have seven children to feed."

"Seven!" I repeated.

He smiled showing sturdy teeth. "Yes, and they keep me busy trying to keep them all fed."

I could only imagine such a task.

I followed Uncle and Ahmed down the steps that led into the tomb. The torch flame flickered as we descended into the dark ground, producing images of ghostly figures dancing against the ancient walls. At the far end of the passage was the plaster-covered doorway stamped with the priests' seal. The seal, Uncle told me, was definitely the name of Smenkhkara.

Uncle Harry chipped away at the plaster and stone with an iron rod until there was a hole the size of a man's fist.

"Light a candle, Beth," came Uncle Harry's anxious voice.

I did, with trembling hands.

Uncle Harry put the candle through the hole to test for foul gases. It was safe—the flame remained lit. He chipped away a little more plaster until it was large enough to peer through. He put the candle back inside, it flickered as hot air escaped from the chamber. The flame steadied, and for the first time in over three thousand years, light permeated the inky blackness.

"Can you see anything?" I asked Uncle Harry excitedly.

A few seconds passed. "Yes," he finally told me. "Come and see for yourself."

I peered through the hole and once my eyes adjusted to the dim light, I was able to make sense of the mysterious dark shapes in the room. "Such marvelous things," I gasped. There were gilded wooden animals, statues of different shapes and sizes.

I tore myself away from the vision. "Uncle Harry! This is unbelievable!"

Uncle Harry said, "Ahmed, have a look."

Ahmed peered through the hole, and after several minutes had passed, he said, "You have found a great treasure."

"His life belongings," Uncle commented. "After all, the Egyptians did believe they would need their belongings in the afterlife. Remember Ahmed, God's Word tells us not to lay up earthly treasures that will perish, but heavenly treasures."

Ahmed replied, "Yes, for where your treasures are there will your heart be also. Seek God first and his kingdom, for it is everlasting."

With a raise of my brow, I glanced at Uncle Harry.

"We are having Bible studies in the evening."

"That's wonderful," I said.

"Well, this is all that we will do here for today," Uncle Harry told us. "We will need to erect our tents, and tomorrow we will set up Beth's work station. When all of our staff arrives, we will tear the wall down and proceed.

After my tent was erected, I set up house. I placed a water basin next to the tent pole where a mirror hung. I had a comfortable cushioned cot to sleep on. A spirit lamp, on which to brew my tea, sat on the small round table beside very large floor cushions. Basically, it was set up similar to the one Grace and I shared at the opening of Princess Ihi's tomb.

Immediately my thoughts went to Philip. I remembered him holding my hand as we descended into the princess's tomb. I shut my eyes and could vividly see his smiling face. The pain of losing him was fresh again.

Anguish enveloped me, and I cried for a time.

Before lunch I freshened up, splashing water on my tearstained cheeks. My eyes were slightly swollen; I knew it would not go unnoticed by Uncle Harry.

"You've been crying, Beth," he said with concern, as we sat under a canvas awning to eat our lunch.

"So much here reminds me of being with Philip at the opening of Princess Ihi's tomb."

"Perhaps it was too soon to bring you out," he said, compassionately.

"No—Uncle Harry, it would have been worse to remain in Cairo…alone." I quickly changed the subject. "Exactly what is on the agenda?"

"We'll need help," Uncle Harry told me without hesitation. "Do you realize to repair just one royal robe embellished with hundreds of jeweled sequins could take two to three months alone."

"What do you plan to do?"

"I have notified the British Museum. They have the best Egyptologist staff, and the best archeological photographer in the business."

"I'm glad you did not ask Mr. Marvin Adams to do the photographing."

"I'm not interested in hiring those eager to make a dollar by putting my niece on the front page of some newspaper. I want professionals that will work honorably."

"Good!"

"I have also notified a preservationist to help with all the delicate items that will be extremely fragile. We'll also need a specialist to decipher hieroglyphs. We'll want to unravel the endless subtleties of the ancient Egyptian language. By the time we are finished I am sure we will add other specialists to our list. You, of course, will do our cataloguing. And there will be plenty of opportunity for you to learn a few other useful things."

"This is exciting!"

Uncle Harry's eyes shone brilliantly. "In just a few days, Beth, we'll enter a room that no one has entered in over three thousand years. Think of the antiquities we will find.... The historical value alone will exceed many other discoveries."

When the photographer and preservationist arrived, both from the British Museum, the sealed wall was quickly torn down, exposing the treasures in the antechamber.

Uncle Harry was the first to enter the chamber and I was next to follow. We carefully stepped into the room, lest we accidentally step onto precious things and crush them. I felt like an intruder in someone else's home. One would expect foul odors, but instead there was a faint smell of sweet perfumes and oil—I was amazed.

The photographer and preservationist stood back waiting for Uncle Harry's instructions. At first no one spoke, the flame from our candles moved crazily about as we tried to take in the wonders before us. We saw exquisitely carved chairs, elaborate beds and a regal throne overlaid with gold and jewels. I stood next to a huge gilt couch carved in the shape of a strange animal—part crocodile, part lioness. As I ran my hand along the back of it, Uncle explained, "The great goddess Ammut, who devours the souls of the wicked."

To our right, as if they were standing guard, were two life-sized statues of royal guards. A pair of beaded sandals lay on the floor; they looked to be in perfect condition. Uncle Harry tried to pick up one; it crumbled to dust, leaving him holding a handful of beads.

Horrified, Uncle Harry then advised, "We best not touch anything." He turned to the preservationist, Jim Riley. "Some of the objects will need to be conserved on the spot."

Mr. Riley, who was a short but stocky-looking fellow, informed us, "We can pour melted wax on the other sandal, and once it has hardened we'll be able to pick it up easily enough."

Uncle Harry nodded his head and then proceeded. "This is just the beginning."

I looked around the room again, taking in all the objects. Several brightly painted chests lined the wall. I was fascinated with the delicate alabaster vases. Cluttered against the opposite wall I saw pottery wine jars, baskets for fruit, stools and chairs.

Uncle Harry ran his fingers along the uneven surface of one wall. Between the two statutes was another sealed area. "This sealed doorway probably leads to the burial chamber where we will find the real treasury. We'll begin work on this one later. We'll need to clear the antechamber first. We'll take this a step at a time. Go slowly. That is a must. You saw what happened to the sandal—I don't want that mistake repeated."

They agreed.

The photographer, Theodore Madison, or Teddy, as he preferred to be called, was next with his job. He set up the camera tripod and added large torches to give sufficient lighting for photographing.

Mr. Madison was not much older than myself. His hair was a nice shade of brown and he sported a well-trimmed mustache. His keen eyes were dark brown, and he always seemed to look at everything with interest. He seemed a gentleman.

James Riley, the preservationist, began to study the objects in the room, noting how best to handle each piece. After two hours of being in the tomb, we were ready to ascend to the living.

After two weeks of tedious work, I began my job of cataloguing each piece, which Uncle had taught me to do with extreme care. First Mr. Madison would take an on-site photograph of each object before it was removed from its original location, and then Uncle Harry would make a line drawing on a five-by-eight-inch card and record all measurements, noting any damage or loss of any part of the material. Mr. Riley would do the conservation spot work, and then the object would be transported to the laboratory. Finally, my job was to record a brief description of each object in a preliminary "journal of entry."

The excavators worked their way around the antechamber, and piece by piece objects were brought into the lab. I encountered marvelous objects. What an exciting job I had! When an elaborate chest was brought to me, I became ecstatic. It was a superbly crafted wooden chest made of cedar with retractable handles, and was inlaid with ebony strips and inscribed with hieroglyphs. Unfortunately, our man to decipher hieroglyphics had not yet arrived. The closer we came to the opening of the burial chamber, the more anxious I became for his arrival. I wanted someone there that could decipher any cursed tablets that may be found within the chamber.

I admitted to myself that the thought of a cursed tablet being found frightened me. I had already made up my mind that if one was found, I would need to convince Uncle Harry to put all the antiquities back to their original locations, and to seal up the tomb. Perhaps in doing so we could counteract any cursed tablet found. Somehow I knew that would be a task not easily achieved. Uncle Harry did not believe cursed tablets held any powers. "Greater is he that is in me, than he that is in the world," Uncle Harry had once quoted to me.

"That's true, Uncle Harry," I whispered to myself. "But what about things not of this world?"

Chapter 6

A week had gone by before Uncle Harry finally received a telegram from the hieroglyphics specialist, Mr. Richard Montgomery. According to the telegram, he was to arrive in Luxor on the next train. It would be a relief to have someone on-site that could immediately decipher any cursed tablets found within the tomb.

I had been cataloguing a bronze cat inlaid with gold and silver, representing the goddess Bastet, when Uncle Harry came into the lab to inform me that he was going to Luxor to meet Mr. Montgomery. He asked if I would like to go. I told him that I was behind on my work and if he did not mind, I would stay and finish cataloguing the items that had been brought into the lab late yesterday afternoon. He said he would be gone for most of the day and if any problems should arise that Ahmed was not only efficient, but also very capable of handling any unforeseen difficulties. I assured Uncle Harry that I would be fine. I kissed him on the cheek and he left me to do my work.

An hour must have passed, or so it seemed. When one is involved with work they enjoy, time has a way of slipping by quickly. I had just finished cataloguing an alabaster vase, when I realized the watch pendant that Philip had given to me was not pinned to my white blouse.

I thought over what I had done that morning. I distinctly remembered attaching the pendant to my blouse. I checked the pockets of my khaki split skirt—they were empty.

Panic rose within me and I began to tremble. It was too precious to lose. How could I have let this happen? I must not have hooked it properly.

I searched the floor. It was not there. I went back to my tent and searched.

Still nothing.

The tomb! I had gone down with Uncle Harry into the antechamber before breakfast. He asked that I make a journal entry of several gold objects that were to remain within the chamber behind the padlocked gates.

It must be there! I thought.

What was I to do? If I did not go after it now, the workers might kick it around and bury it in the sand. Worse yet, step on it and crush it.

I knew what had to be done. I would have to go down into the tomb and find it.

I did not want to go alone. I searched for Ahmed. One of the workers said he was about half a mile away, supervising the transportation of one of the wooden crates that housed a priceless wooden chest. Ahmed would not be available and I was not about to ask one of the workers to go down with me. They were all strangers to me. Mr. Madison was busy developing his film and according to the sign he had posted, he was "not to be disturbed." I was not sure where to locate Mr. Riley.

I can do this alone, I told myself. *All I need to do is light a candle and go down into the chamber, check the floor by the wall that I bumped into, and hopefully I will find it there. It should only take me a total of twenty minutes. Twenty minutes,* I said to myself. *I can do this.*

I went for the spare key kept hidden in my tent to unlock the padlock. Uncle had given it to me in case he lost the other. I then made my way to the tomb. Once there, I noticed the two large torches set in poles outside the tomb entrance. I took one and lit it. It would give more lighting than a candle—that thought was comforting. Candles had a way of giving off an eerie glow.

As I began my descent into the tomb, I clutched the torch with both hands as if my life depended upon it—most certainly, if it went out I would die of fright. I proceeded slowly, which was not to my advantage. It would have been better to go quickly, giving no thought to where I was, but my feet would not allow that. So, I continued at a snail's pace down the dark, narrow passageway that led into the antechamber.

Often, one's greatest enemy is oneself. I began to think of bizarre possibilities. One, the pendant had been taken by some unseen hand, and now I was being led by the spirits, to be a victim of a curse that was yet to be discovered. Another, the mummy would come to life and walk the chambers, seeking revenge on those who plundered his tomb—I was one of them.

How frightening these thoughts were. *I must think on other things,* I told myself. I began to quote Philippians four and eight: "Finally, brethren, whatsoever things are true, whatsoever things are honest, whatsoever things are just, whatsoever things are pure, whatsoever things are lovely, whatsoever things are of good report; if there be any virtue, and if there be any praise, think on these things."

I was still afraid.

The twenty-third chapter of Psalms was more appropriate: "Yea though I walk through the valley of the shadow of death, I will fear no evil: for thou art with me..."

I was deep into the passageway, but had not yet reached the end of the tunnel, when I was certain I heard a noise from behind. My heart raced wildly and a suffocating terror enveloped me. Oh God! I should not have come here alone. But it was too late to go back, to change plans now. And whatever, or whoever, was in the tomb with me was drawing closer.

I imagined it to be spirits—spirits from the ancient world.

I turned the corner and pressed my back firmly against the wall. When the sound came again, I shut my eyes tightly, waiting for some unknown being to overtake me, to devour me, to make me a victim of some ancient Egyptian curse.

I was going to faint.

Suddenly, and before I had time to do just that, the torch was yanked out of my hand.

"What are you trying to do? Kill yourself!" came an acrimonious voice.

My eyes popped open and there stood Dr. Clairborne!

"You should never use a torch until all the chambers have been tested for poisonous gases," he quickly reprimanded me.

I could only gape at him, my breathing uneven. Finally I said, rather angrily now, for he had truly frightened me. "What are you doing here?"

He looked down at me somewhat annoyed—I think. "What am I doing here!" he repeated. "What are you doing down here alone.... Does Harry know?"

He had a lot of nerve asking me these questions, when he should do the explaining! No one was allowed to enter the tomb without permission from Uncle Harry. I, of course, was the exception.

I was shaking, he noticed, and said more cordially, "I'm sorry if I frightened you. Have these chambers been tested for foul gases?"

My fear quickly turned to anger. "Yes, Dr. Clairborne, they have been tested. I was doing quite well until you nearly scared me witless!"

"Quite well indeed," came his cynical tone. "You'd have killed yourself using that torch down here, if these adjoining chambers had not yet been checked."

I was not going to argue with his reasoning; after all he was a toxicologist. I simply said, "Now, if you will excuse me, I will proceed with what I had set out to do."

I turned to go, but he took hold of my arm, stopping me from doing so. "I think not!" he said.

"Let go of me!"

"On one condition," he said. "You tell me what it is that is so important that you would brave coming down here alone."

"Why should I?"

"Because, otherwise, I will escort you straight back up to the living—even if I have to do so forcefully. Now, what are you doing down here alone?"

I could see I had no choice but to tell him. "I've lost my pendant. I'm certain it must be down here."

His eyes narrowed perceptively. "A pendant?" he repeated.

"That is what I said."

"Obviously worth millions."

"Hardly that."

"No?" he feigned thoughtfulness. "What then, that it could not wait until you had an escort."

"Why would I need an escort? Hardly anyone around that could do me any harm. Unless, Dr. Clairborne, I should be leery of you. Now, let go of me!"

I tried to free myself, but his grip tightened.

He warned, "It can prove to be very dangerous in the tombs; things are often unstable. And again, never come down here with a torch until all these chambers have been tested first."

"Yes, so you have said. Now please, let me go!"

He was growing annoyed, I could tell by the set of his jaw. "Very well," he said with diminishing tolerance. "Where did you lose your pendant?"

"I believe in the antechamber. I was with Uncle Harry this morning to make journal entries of two gold objects. I bumped into a wall. It must have come loose at that time and slipped off."

"Very well, we will look for it together."

I tried to appear braver than I really was by saying, "You needn't bother. I am capable of doing this alone."

He eyed me with impatience. "I am not leaving you down here alone. Now, either we proceed together, or I shall escort you back to your tent."

He was sounding more like Uncle Harry: that women should not walk about unescorted. I suppose I was genuinely relieved that I would not have to continue on alone.

He led the way into the antechamber, and I followed close behind, his broad shoulders blocking most of my view. Being close to him made me take note of his height and next to my five-foot-four-inch frame, I guessed his to be six foot two. I noticed that he was carrying a leather satchel; the strap went diagonally across his back, from right shoulder to his left side. I had seen Uncle Harry carry the same, often to place little treasures in.

The satchel made me all the more suspicious of him. Just what was Dr. Clairborne doing here? Had he come to steal away some small treasure? Earlier, he had eluded the question as to why he was here.

"Just why are you here, Dr. Clairborne?" I asked with growing curiosity.

He said nothing, but continued walking forward.

I continued to press him. "Uncle Harry did not mention your coming. It seems strange that he did not say something to me this morning regarding your arrival."

"I cannot answer as to why your uncle failed to inform you of my arrival, Miss Woodruff."

"Then Uncle Harry did ask you to come?"

He stopped so abruptly that I nearly bumped into him. He turned to face me, his smoke-gray eyes held daring amusement. "Why the inquisition?"

"Well—I just find it unusual that Uncle Harry did not mention it."

I was growing nervous under his scrutiny. His lip curled up at one corner, almost as if he found what I had to say humorous.

"You don't trust me," he said, still finding the situation amusing. "I have yet to understand why. I have practically saved your life twice now."

His comment caused me to feel ashamed, for what he said was true. "Yes, and I am very grateful for that. Truly!"

"Yet you find me a scoundrel?"

"I did not say that!"

"I can see it in your lovely green eyes, Miss Woodruff."

"That is absurd, Dr. Clairborne."

"Is it?" he asked, with a certain amount of gentleness.

I was never a good liar—besides, lying is a sin. So, I said nothing, and averted my focus from those gray eyes that held me in question to the inky blackness of the antechamber.

He said, "Perhaps once we get to know each other better you will be able to consider me a friend."

He was being very gentlemanly, and I hadn't the heart to be rude or unkind by saying something that would question his character, especially if in fact he was guileless.

I gazed up at him. He seemed sincere. "I would like to consider you a friend, Dr. Clairborne."

I was being truthful, however, a "friend" is one that is trustworthy. He had yet to prove he was a man that bore such fruit.

He said, matter-of-factly, "Then, let us get back to finding your pendant, instead of wondering why I am here."

He turned to continue leading the way into the antechamber. He had skillfully taken charge of the conversation. I still did not know why Uncle Harry had asked him to come out to the site, or what he was doing in the tomb!

As if he could read my thoughts he asked, "Just where is Harry? When I saw that the entrance gate to the tomb was unlocked, I thought perhaps he would be down here. You were the last person I thought I would find wandering about in the grave. Especially alone."

"He went into Luxor to meet with the hieroglyphics specialist, a Mr. Richard Montgomery."

"He'll be back today?"

"He said he would be back before late afternoon."

Dr. Clairborne said no more, but when we entered the antechamber he asked where I thought the pendant might be. I pointed to the corner wall.

He knelt down closer to the ground and began to search. I walked about the antechamber, retracing the steps I had made earlier that morning, but my search was futile.

What if it is not here? The thought made me ill.

At about that time, Dr. Clairborne stood. "I believe this is your pendant."

Elated and relieved, I rushed to his side. "Oh—how wonderful!"

He brushed off sand particles, and then popped open the cover. For a moment the ticking of the watch was all that was heard. I saw him glance at the engraved inscription on the bottom of the cover, which read: *Forever yours, Philip.*

His eyes riveted to mine for a moment, as if, perhaps, weighing out my past relationship with Philip. "It's still ticking. No harm has come to it," he said, as he handed it over to me.

"I really appreciate your helping me to find it. It is priceless to me," I said, my voice wavering.

"Obviously, to brave coming down here alone," he said with a certain amount of compassion. "And I am sorry about your friend."

I was feeling too emotional to respond. He must have sensed this, for he gently took me by the arm and led me out of the antechamber, back up the passageway and out into the open.

After he slid the torch I had taken back into its pole, I thanked him again for his assistance and then asked if he planned to wait on Uncle Harry. He informed me that he would.

"Please join us for lunch." I pointed to the tent where we took our meals. "Over there."

The tent had a canvas top to protect us from the sun, and was open on all sides to allow the air to circulate more freely. During our meals, netting was lowered to keep out insects and sand particles.

He squinted in the direction I pointed. "Thank you, I'll do that." He then asked, "Where are you headed?"

Again, I pointed. "My lab."

The lab was not far from the tomb. Uncle Harry wanted objects from the tomb to be easily transported, and the less distance from the tomb to the tent that had been erected for that purpose, the less likely any accidents would occur. However, Dr. Clairborne felt the need to walk with me the short distance, and when we arrived there he asked, "Where is Ahmed?"

"Not far."

"You should be careful," he then felt the need to say.

"Careful?" I repeated.

"I am surprised Harry left you alone."

"But I am not alone."

"It appears that you are."

"Appearances are not always what they seem. As I said, Ahmed is not far, and then there is the photographer and journalist about."

"Someone should have been around to stop you from going into that tomb alone. You could have been hurt and no one would have known until you showed up missing."

I felt chagrined and was growing tired of defending my actions. "You're right, I should not have gone into the tomb alone," I said, hoping to appease him. "However, Dr. Clairborne, others should not be held responsible for my actions, nor should I be looked after as if I were but a small child."

"In the desert, one must always consider the safety of others, and you have yet to learn of its ways."

"Truly, I am no expert when it comes to desert life, but I will learn."

He gazed at me thoughtfully, as if he wanted to say more, but thought better of it.

"Then you will meet us for lunch?" I asked.

"Thank you—yes. What time?"

"Twelve-thirty."

"I'll be there."

He departed, leaving me to do my work, and after making several journal entries, I stepped outside the tent to take a short break. I noticed then that Dr. Clairborne had erected a tent not far from Uncle's and mine. *So,* I thought, *he is not just here for the day to wait on Uncle Harry's return. It appears that he is planning to stay for a while.*

I felt a little uneasy about this. After all, I was still trying to piece together Dr. Clairborne's involvement with the tomb robberies. I wondered then if I should tell Uncle Harry of my suspicions.

"Hello," came a resonant voice, interrupting my thoughts.

It was the photographer, Mr. Madison, and like most men prepared for the desert, he was dressed in khaki trousers and a white shirt. His aquiline nose was sunburned from being out in the open for several days, photographing whatever.

I smiled. "Hello, Mr. Madison."

He glanced over toward Dr. Clairborne's tent. "Who is he?"

"An American toxicologist, Dr. Maxwell Clairborne."

"A toxicologist. Interesting. Why is he here?"

"Your guess is as good as mine."

He thought about it for a moment, and then said, "Poisons and toxins. I suppose those are some concerns to take into consideration when opening the tombs."

I remembered the torch incident. "Yes, he seems very concerned about foul gases."

"Does Harry feel there may be problems with that?"

"You'll have to ask my uncle. I really don't know much about it."

"Well, I guess it's good for us then, that Dr. Clairborne is here."

"Yes, I guess it is," I said, but did not entirely mean it.

He smiled. "I thought it would be good to get a few pictures of you at work."

I looked down at my attire. My white blouse was smudged, and loose strands of hair had escaped the braid wound at the nape of my neck. "Only if you will let me tidy up a bit."

He glanced at his watch. "Can you be ready in fifteen minutes?"

"I think so."

I quickly went to my tent, splashed water on my face, changed my blouse into a fresh crisp white cotton shirtwaist, straightened my hair and was back at the lab by the allotted time. Mr. Madison was patiently waiting.

He was leaning on the tent pole and straightened his lithe frame when he saw me coming. "You look splendid!"

I laughed. "Well, hardly that. But I will blend in quite well with the surroundings—plain and hot."

"More an oasis," he complimented.

We went inside the tent and he began to explain how I should pose. He took several pictures of me working at my desk with a very old statue that I was about to begin work on. After he had taken the necessary photos, he then suggested that we do a candid pose.

I was sitting on a stool facing the tent door and Mr. Madison was in the process of showing me how to pose.

"Turn your shoulder slightly this way," he said, as he positioned them for me, his hands firmly on my forearms.

This was how Dr. Clairborne found us. He stood at the tent door looking at me rather reproachfully.

Inwardly, I cringed. I could only imagine what it must have looked like: Mr. Madison standing a breath away, his hands firmly on my forearms. Very intimate! Why could Dr. Clairborne not have come upon us when I was posing at my desk?

Why did I care what he thought, and to prove it so, I straightened my back and looked away from his penetrating smoke-gray eyes.

"Yes, that's it," Mr. Madison praised. He placed a finger under my chin tilting it upward, then stood back and took the picture.

"Photos for the *London Times*, Miss Woodruff?" Dr. Clairborne teased.

I smiled as I alighted from off the stool. "So, you read the article too?"

"Bitten by the curse. Quite a story—wouldn't you agree?"

"Oh, yes! Indeed it was." I laughed.

I then made the proper introductions. "Mr. Madison, this is Dr. Clairborne. Dr. Clairborne, this is Mr. Madison, the photographer from the British Museum."

They shook hands.

"Please, call me Ted. Things here are too unconventional for formalities—besides, the three of us may be working close together for some time."

Dr. Clairborne found that amusing. "Yes, quite 'close.' The name is Maxwell, friends call me Max."

I did not appreciate Dr. Clairborne's barb. I knew to what he was referring: the "close" scene with Mr. Madison's hands upon my forearms. My eyes narrowed in his direction, which only proved to heighten his amusement. All of this went unnoticed by Mr. Madison.

"Well, Mr. Madison, I do believe it is time for lunch," I said.

"U-uh-uh," Mr. Madison scolded. "You must call me Ted."

I could feel myself blush. "Yes, of course—Ted, it is."

That was how it all came about, my addressing Dr. Clairborne as Max. He knew I felt uncomfortable dropping the "mister" and "doctor" from their names. I could clearly see the humor dancing in those gray eyes of his.

When Mr. Madison excused himself—in my mind that is how I will continue to refer to him, for he was not a friend that I should be on familiar terms with…as for Dr. Clairborne?

Dr. Clairborne then said, "Well, it appears that you have acquired an admirer."

"You are referring to Mr. Madison?"

"Teddy," he reminded me.

"Ted," I corrected. "And I will only call him thus when he is present. He is hardly an admirer."

Dr. Clairborne laughed. "Oh, I don't know. I think he enjoyed working 'close' more than you may want to admit."

I could feel my face grow warm. "Would you please stop that!"

"Stop what?"

"Oh, for Pete's sake, Dr. Clairborne! He was only taking a picture!"

Suddenly he grew serious, his eyes gazing intently into mine. What he did next surprised me.

He took hold of my hand, and began to study my fingertips. "You did not mean what you said," he then told me.

"I don't know what you mean."

"Come, Beth," he said emphasizing the use of my name. "I believe you said that you would consider me a friend."

That is what I had told him in the tomb. "Yes—of course."

His eyes gazed deeply into mine. "Then what is with the Dr. Clairborne?"

"What?"

"You must cease from calling me 'Dr. Clairborne,' when we have agreed to drop the formality. What is so hard about addressing me as Max? Of course, if you did not mean what you said, then..."

"I don't know what that has to do with it."

A dark eyebrow rose, and a smile formed. "It has a lot to do with it. How can a friendship form between us if we stay on unfamiliar terms?"

I was drawn to the warmth of his hypnotic smoke-gray eyes. I think he was aware of what effect he was having on me. I am certain he was probably inwardly laughing at my naiveté.

I jerked my hand free from his show of friendliness, as he would call it. "This is silly!"

His smile remained. "Is it? What is so silly about nurturing a friendship? Unless of course you find me repulsive."

"Why would I find you repulsive?"

His eyes narrowed thoughtfully. "I haven't figured that out yet. Maybe you should fill me in."

He was hardly "repulsive." Matter-of-fact, he was extremely good-looking, and I think, at that very moment, I was more perturbed with myself for having such feelings toward him. Could I befriend a criminal? Was he a criminal?

I felt cornered. "I hardly find you repulsive."

"Well, then, that's a step in the right direction."

Was it? I wondered. I preferred having my guard up.

"Now that that is settled," he finished. "I'll escort you back to your tent."

"Dr. Clairborne"—I quickly corrected my error—"Max."

He smiled, showing perfect teeth. "It might take some getting used to."

Indeed it would!

I continued, "One thing that we need to come to an understanding on is that I can manage to walk to my tent unescorted. It's not far, you know."

"Just the same, I'll walk you to your tent."

He did, and once we arrived he thoroughly scanned the lab interior.

"Everything looks okay," he assured me.

"I don't get it?" I told him.

"Snakes, scorpions—lions."

"Lions!?" I blurted out.

He then spoke out the true reason for his concern. "Thieves."

"Thieves," I whispered back.

"You will need to be watchful."

"Uncle Harry and I have already discussed that."

"Good." He then advised, "You should learn how to shoot a gun."

I looked at him incredulously. "What would I do with a gun?"

"Use it if you must."

"I could never shoot a man!"

"You might change your mind if the occasion calls for it. And if for no other reason a gun can be useful as a signaling device if you ever need a means to call for help."

He was probably right. "All right. What do you suggest I do? I haven't a clue as to what type of gun to buy; not ever having done so."

He smiled. "I have just the gun for you. You may borrow it."

"You're so thoughtful. Then, I suppose, you will also need to teach me how to shoot it?"

His smile broadened. "Most definitely."

The lessons were going well, and Max praised my ability on how expertly I handled the gun in such a short amount of time. After about a month he felt that I was a fair enough marksman, so the lessons ceased. I actually hated to see them come to an end. I enjoyed time spent with Max. My suspicions concerning his involvement with the robberies vanished. His vigilance for my safety managed to dissipate any doubts of his untrustworthiness, which had, at one time, been a constant reminder not to befriend him. I was seeing a new side to his character, and although he was a man not to be reckoned with, he was also a gentleman.

One evening I discovered another characteristic that I thought him not capable of. As our party sat by the campfire, indulging in conversation, the sinking of the *Titanic* was brought up. Uncle Harry was not present to guard me against the pain the topic caused, but Max was quick to discern it.

He said, "We had friends aboard. Beth may find the topic yet painful."

Only a sensitive person capable of feeling for others would have made such a comment for another.

Apologies were made and the conversation was then centered on the discoveries found in the tomb that day. After ten or fifteen minutes had passed, I excused myself and headed for my tent. I was feeling out of sorts. Mention of the *Titanic* brought back the pain and anguish I had felt upon first hearing of it, and I wanted to be alone to cry it out.

Max caught up with me before I entered my tent.

"Are you all right?" he asked, his voice gentle and laced with concern.

My back was to him and he could not see the sorrow that I knew was etched on my features. I wanted to hide behind a mask of pretense, to show him I was strong, and that, like Grace, I could go on with life.

Because I said nothing he turned me to face him and although it was dark, the stars gave enough illumination that he could immediately see the pain that was tearing at my heart.

His arms circled around me as he drew me into a compassionate embrace. "It's all right to cry, Beth."

I did—into his shoulder.

"Were you in love with him?"

I could only nod my head. I felt his hand gently stroking my hair.

"Losing someone is the hardest test we will ever have to face upon this earth. My wife and son died during childbirth."

Oh heavenly Father! I thought. It was no wonder that he was sensitive to the fact of losing someone—he'd lost two.

My own grief was now forgotten. I stepped out of his embrace. "I'm so sorry. Truly, it must have been a horrible time. How long ago?"

"It will be five years this month," he said.

I felt drawn to him. I suppose because, like myself, he'd lost what was dearest to him.

"Does the pain ever go away? Do you even want it to?" I asked.

He gazed up into the starry sky. "My wife and son were gone, the pain was all I had left. I think for that reason, I did not want to let it go."

"I think I understand."

He gazed down at me. "If it helps, I can say that with time healing comes."

"That is what I've heard."

Nothing more was said, but the silence between us seemed appropriate.

After several minutes, he offered, "Let me fix you a cup of tea. It will help you sleep."

"Tea?"

He smiled warmly. "A special blend."

"Are you going to drug me again, *Dr. Clairborne?*" I asked, emphasizing his professional name.

"Only by the use of natural remedies."

By the time he returned with the tea concoction, the water was ready for two cups. For the sake of propriety we sat outside the tent on folding chairs next to a small fire he had built. I brought out the teacups and the teakettle.

He prepared the tea, I poured the water and then we drank.

We conversed about the wonders of the Nile, and after a half hour elapsed, I was feeling very relaxed—the tea had worked quickly.

Max asked, "How do you feel?"

"I'll sleep like a baby."

He stood to go. "I'll leave you to do just that."

I stood and gave him a hug. "Max, I want to say thanks for being a friend."

Before I could back away from what I thought was a friendly hug, his arms encircled me.

Something was happening here that I was not ready for. My heart was racing to his touch. He drew me closer, and I could feel the warmth of his breath on my cheek. Philip's memory was too fresh. I quickly pulled away.

He seemed reluctant to let me go.

"Goodnight, Max," I said. I turned and walked into my tent. Tomorrow, what had happened would be forgotten.

Chapter 7

Clearance of the antechamber took eight weeks, and used 1,760 yards of cotton wadding and 25 bales of calico. The antiquities were crated up with extreme care and then transported to the river en route to Cairo. Armed guards from the Egyptian army were provided by the Antiquities Service Department to help protect the precious cargo. Uncle Harry often traveled with them, and I was left under the protective care of Ahmed. I was also aware that Max was very attentive when it came to my being looked after.

I was not seeing much of Max; he was staying busy helping Uncle Harry prepare for the opening of the burial chamber, and I was occupied with journal entries. I had wondered if he was avoiding me. As for myself, I thought it best to keep some distance between us. I did not want to nurture anything more than a friendship with him. I had convinced myself that my heart still belonged to Philip.

I could hardly keep up with their progress, but the journalist, Mr. Bruce Ingram, helped me out when things became overwhelming. He was great when it came to writing descriptive notations for each object brought into the lab. Mr. Ingram was an elderly gentleman, in his late fifties, widowed, and the father of five children—all of which were married and providing him with grandchildren. Like Uncle Harry, he could not bring himself to marry again, his work occupied too much of his time. He did a lot of writing for *National Geographic*, so traveling was always on his agenda. Here he was in Egypt, filling such a mission.

It had been one of those days when the work was piling high, and the heat was unbearable. Mr. Ingram was busy typing up his latest manuscript, and I was left alone to do the journal entries; and for the third time that afternoon, items had been brought into the lab that had been mishandled—I was suddenly beside myself. This had to be stopped!

I asked one of the workers, "Where is Ahmed?"

He said something in broken English, and I decided then to search for Ahmed myself. I stormed out of the tent and over to the tomb.

"Ahmed!" I cried out, as I stepped down into the entrance of the tomb where the workers were busy preparing to tote out the last objects that remained in the antechamber.

I called out again, "Ahmed!"

His turbaned head turned my way. He seemed surprised to see me.

"Yes—what is it?"

I was still overly distraught. "We have a problem!"

He was alert. "A problem?"

"These workers need to be more careful. This is the third time this afternoon that objects brought over to the lab have been mishandled. Two small arrows have been broken. They must understand that just because an object is small it is no less significant. You must make them understand!"

His dark eyes smoldered. In their language he began to yell at them. "Careless! Careless mongrels!"

Tension was growing.

"What are they saying?" I asked Ahmed, a bit bewildered.

"They are saying: What does a woman know? And that you are the careless one."

"What!"

They all began to accuse me, pointing fingers and saying what, in their language, I did not know.

I was so angry I could not even speak. Uncle Harry and Max came in at that time, with the workers pointing their accusing fingers.

"What's going on?" Uncle Harry asked. "Beth, are you okay?"

"No, I'm not okay!" I told him, tears of frustration beginning to pool in my eyes.

"Ahmed?" came Uncle Harry's deep voice.

"Your niece says the workers have been careless."

I spoke up. "Two very small objects have been broken. And I know for a fact that they were intact inside the chamber. This is a serious matter, Uncle Harry!"

"Indeed!" Uncle Harry agreed. "Ahmed, see what you can do about this.

Tell them that if it happens again they will lose their jobs."

"Yes—of course," Ahmed said to Uncle Harry.

Uncle Harry changed his mind. "Perhaps it would be better if I talked with them."

Ahmed nodded his head agreeably.

Uncle Harry said to Max, "Would you take Beth and get her something cool to drink. Help her to calm down a bit."

Max gently took me by the arm and escorted me to the open tent where we took our meals. I sat on one of the canvas chairs; he stood over me, his smoke-gray eyes assessing my disposition. His jet-black hair was combed back neatly. He looked fine in a clean pair of khaki trousers and a white chambray shirt that had a soft and slightly weathered look to it. He had shaved that morning and the smell of his aftershave still lingered.

I was acutely aware of his closeness.

"They really got you riled," he said with a tinge of amused interest. "A bit foolish of you though, to try and take them on single-handedly."

"I was not trying to take them on 'single-handedly,' as you put it. They should all be fired from their jobs!"

His brow rose to my heated comment. "That's rather severe—don't you think?"

"Hardly!" I was quick to disagree, my face growing hot with indignation. "They accused me falsely!"

"Yes, I heard."

I again went into a rage. "How could they be so careless? Two arrows were broken. Yesterday, they looked to be in perfect condition. Mr. Riley had finished his spot preservation work.... It should not have happened!"

"Harry will make sure that it doesn't happen again."

I was trembling slightly to the aftereffects of my anger. The incident had really gotten to me. Max went to a chest on the opposite side of the tent and then came back with two bottles.

"Here, drink this. Maybe it will help."

He placed one of the bottles into my hand. It was wet and cold, two combinations that were scarce in the desert.

His grin widened at the delighted expression on my face.

"Coca-Cola!" I yelled out in exaltation. "Where did this come from? And cold!"

"I know the right connections," he told me.

"I'll say," I laughed and then took a drink. "This is wonderful!" And before

I realized my error, I said, "I could hug you for this."

"Best not," he said soberly.

Remembering our last hug, I immediately regretted saying those words. I could feel the heat rush to my face. "Oh, Max, I—"

"You've been avoiding me."

I did not know what to say.

He was watching me carefully. "I will not apologize for something I did intentionally. I knew exactly what I was doing, Beth, and for that reason I won't apologize."

I thought: *What he did—he did intentionally? Had I read more into that embrace or was it merely a show of compassion—or friendship? I was not a worldly-wise individual. What did I know when it came to relationships?*

I simply responded by saying, "You did nothing wrong that you need to apologize."

He gave thought to what I said. I could feel his smoke-gray eyes probing deeply. "Then there is only one other reason why you would go out of your way to avoid me."

He was probing too deeply. I did not want him to know my feelings for him.

What were my feelings?

"I don't know what you mean?"

He then concluded, "You are afraid?"

"Afraid of what?"

He smiled too confidentially. "Of what feelings may be aroused when I touch you."

I could feel my face go red. I hated that I blushed so easily. "We agreed to be friends, nothing more."

Uncle Harry came in and our conversation ended.

"Well, I hope you have cooled off some," Uncle Harry said to me. "I have never seen you so upset, Beth. You were madder than a hornet."

"The Coke has done wonders," Max put in.

I smiled at Max. "It was a very pleasant surprise. Thank you."

Max said, "My pleasure." And as if to confirm my last statement he added, "From one *friend* to another."

We had both been very vulnerable that night. He had talked of his wife and I of Philip. Lonely hearts can cause people to act strangely at times.

Again, his probing eyes were studying me, as if he could read my thoughts.

I looked away. "Uncle Harry, I do hope that nothing else will get broken."

"They'll be more careful. And as for you, young lady, I do believe you need a break from all this. What do you think, Dr. Clairborne?"

"What?" I voiced loudly.

"Best not get her too riled, Harry, we'll have to give her another Coke."

I smiled to his remark. "I'd have given you the treasure of Tutankhamun for that Coke."

Max whistled between his teeth. "Did you hear that, Harry?"

"Hmmm," Uncle Harry said with a certain amount of humor. "Her condition is worse than I thought."

"What's this about needing a break?" I asked. "You know I love my job."

Uncle Harry eyed me over the rim of his spectacles. "You may love your job, but that does not mean it won't frazzle you from time to time."

I thought woefully, *Because of my confrontation with the workers, Uncle Harry was going to send me home!*

"Don't look so stricken," he said. "We will all be taking a break for a couple of weeks."

"Why?"

"The British Museum will be sending a few of their bigwigs for the official opening of the burial chamber. We will not continue any further until they arrive. So we will wait it out at home."

I thought this over for a moment. It was the museum that was partially responsible for the funding of the expedition. Of course, Uncle Harry would have to do as they asked.

"I see," I said flatly.

"She doesn't sound very enthused," Max said, still grinning at me as if he were still amused with the afternoon's events.

"I am anxious to see what treasures are sealed behind the walls of the burial chamber," I told them.

Uncle Harry nodded his head. "A wondrous sight. You can count on it."

"We cannot even peek?" I asked.

Uncle Harry and Max exchanged looks.

"What's going on?" I wanted to know.

"You could let her go?" Max then voiced.

"It could prove to be dangerous," Uncle Harry answered back.

They continued their conversation as if I were not even present.

"Dangers lurk everywhere, Harry," Max stated. "We can take extreme caution."

Realization then came. I looked at them incredulously. "You two have already planned to look into the burial chamber and you were going to do it without me!"

"Where's that other Coca-Cola?" Uncle Harry teased.

Max laughed.

"I don't believe this!" I gazed directly at Uncle Harry. "Of course, you will let me go in with you?"

Uncle Harry rubbed his chin, thinking it over carefully.

"I'll make sure the chamber is breathable and safe before she enters," Max put in.

"All right," Uncle Harry agreed. "Beth, no one else is to know of this. We will go down after all have retired for the night."

It was agreed that I would accompany them. When Max came for me I was ready. It was dark, but in the moonlight he looked me over from head to toe.

I stuck out my booted foot. "I have them on," I whispered.

He smiled and whispered back, "You're learning."

We met Uncle Harry at the tomb entrance and then descended the stairs without the assistance of candles. Uncle Harry thought it best not to give off any light until we reached bottom, lest someone should see the glow and make an investigation. Max held onto my hand as we descended down the stairs. Inside, visibility was nil, not even the moon or stars illuminated the entrance steps.

Once we reached bottom, it was safe to light a torch, now that all open chambers had been tested for foul gases. I was sandwiched in between Uncle Harry and Max as we walked down the narrow passageway and into the now-empty antechamber.

On the north wall marked the entrance to a third chamber—which Uncle Harry assumed was the burial chamber. Max had us stand aside, in the event that the wall had some sort of ancient booby trap within its confines; then he took a fine-toothed saw and carefully cut a hole in the bottom corner of the plastered wall for us to slip through. Later, they would replace the cut-away piece and reseal it with putty. With minimal light in the chambers, and the putty made of clay, it would appear as if no one had yet entered. Hopefully, the officials from the British Museum would know no different.

Immediately, after Max removed the piece he had cut, hot air gushed out of the burial chamber. He then tested for foul gases—all seemed well. Uncle Harry wriggled through; Max did the same, leaving me to stand alone in the antechamber, waiting for their approval to enter. When I was given the okay, I slipped through carefully.

I stood next to Max, by the hole, my eyes taking in the marvelous sight.

Before us was a huge gilded shrine.

"Oh my!" I sighed rapturously. "It's beautiful."

Max was watching me closely. I think he was more interested in my reaction to the treasury of the burial chamber than the magnificence of the gilded shrine.

The shrine bore the original undisturbed seal, the seal of Smenkhkara. It had been untouched since the king was laid to rest nearly three thousand years ago. Uncle Harry said the dismantling of the shrine would be a mammoth undertaking.

Besides the shrine, our focus of attention went to a large pylon of gilded wood with carrying poles, and upon the top lay a life-sized image of the black Anubis dog, carved from wood, and with a covering of black resin. The dog had inlaid eyes of calcite and obsidian set into gold, and a large collar also of solid gold.

The Anubis dog was, to the Egyptians, a part of their myth and belief, ritual and custom, associated with the dead. They believed that Anubis was guardian of the burial chamber and of the king's canopic equipment.

On the south side of the chamber lay black shrines and chests, all closed and sealed; a number of model boats with sails and rigging all complete.

It was a hurried survey of the burial chamber, but we knew it was a room filled with fantastic things, and with our curiosity now satisfied, we went back through the entrance and into the antechamber.

To my relief, I saw no cursed tablet.

Uncle Harry and Max replaced the cut-out piece of plaster and then sealed the wall with clay putty. With that job complete, we ascended from the tomb, said goodnight, and went to our tents.

Max followed me to mine.

I broke the silence first: "What do you expect to find inside the shrine?"

He spoke softly, as not to awaken the others. "Perhaps a sarcophagus of alabaster. Inside that an ordinary coffin of wood, then a second of finely chased silver, inside this, a coffin of thin wood, but richly gilded. We should also find richly ornamented vessels in which the heart and other internal organs are preserved."

I boldly asked, "I have, for some time, been curious to know your part in all this."

He smiled. "You are curious about a number of things. One day it may get you into trouble."

"Or keep me out of it."

"That's not likely. But if you must know my part, then I shall explain. Not only do I want to do a study of the amulets that we shall find on the great pharaoh, but I will also assist with the autopsy of the mummy. I know something of it and will assist the professor of anatomy from the Egyptian University in Cairo."

"I'm impressed."

"Are you?"

"Of course."

"You are easily impressed."

"You are being modest. Not everyone is as intellectually versatile as you are."

"Autopsies are a part of the medical profession."

"Then the medical profession must be one of versatility."

"Not so much the profession as that of the many functions of the human body. The physician must have a broad understanding of the science and art of diagnosing, treating, curing and preventing disease, relieving pain, and improving and preserving health."

"As I was saying, it is a profession of versatility. Not everyone, *Dr. Clairborne*," I said in good humor, using his professional name to emphasize his calling, "has the capacity to undertake such a vocation. It's a gift, really. I believe God has given to man such abilities in order to care for his creation."

"I'm glad to see that your opinion of me has changed somewhat over the last several months…from a scoundrel to a gifted person. I would say our friendship is making headway—wouldn't you?"

I smiled, for I knew that my opinion of him had changed drastically. What would he think of me now, if I told him what I had thought of him then? A criminal!

"You remember the night I was bitten by that horrid insect?" I asked. "I heard voices outside my tent, and when I went out to investigate, I saw you and another man conversing in a clandestine sort of way. What I overheard made me speculate."

"What did you hear?"

I shrugged my shoulder. "It is not important now."

"But it made you speculate?"

"Yes, I suppose it did…and then when the robbery happened…well, you can easily guess my assumption."

"Easily," he said rather flatly, as if to agree that my imagination had gotten the better of me.

"You would have thought the same."

He seemed annoyed. "You know me so well."

"Are you trying to make me feel guilty for assuming that you were a part of the robberies?"

"No, but I hope that bite on your leg will be a reminder not to meddle into other people's affairs. Especially if it could prove to be dangerous."

"You talk as if I am some silly school girl—eavesdropping."

His jawline tensed. "I will tell you again, Beth, do not meddle into such matters...you'll get in way over your head."

He was angry!

"Meddle?"

"Whatever you overheard, and whatever you saw that night, I want you to forget it!"

I became alarmed. *Why would I need to forget it?*

Again, doubt crept in, and mystery shadowed his character. Did I truly know him?

I thought I did.

I said, "I don't understand."

"There is nothing for you to understand. Nor will I explain. Just forget it."

I wanted to ask him *why*, but I said nothing. I so desperately wanted him to be the man that my imagination had made him out to be, yet, here again was a reason not to trust him.

My heart wanted to believe that he was a man of Christian character: good, kind, trustworthy, loyal; yet my mind was warning me that he was a man of dark and mysterious secrets, capable of sinful ways. I was torn between the two—good or evil?

Perhaps I would see things differently with tomorrow's sunrise—one usually does. Something about the night can often make one feel desperate, lonely and afraid; but when the darkness of night disappears, and a new day arises, those feelings will oftentimes dissipate with it.

I hoped that mine would.

I think he sensed my inner turmoil, for he then tried to reassure me.

"Trust me with this, Beth," he said. "I am only thinking of your safety."

"Yes, of course," I responded curtly. "You have been very vigilant where my safety is concerned...and I do thank you. I did not intend to be a bother."

He ran a hand through his hair in a frustrated sort of way. "It has not been a tiresome task, if that is what you are thinking. I happen to care about you."

I said nothing. Just what were his feelings for me?

"Beth," he whispered softly and then to heighten my emotional battle, he gently placed his hands upon my forearms, pulling me closer to him.

It was frightening that I could so easily enjoy his nearness.

He continued, "Please try to understand the seriousness of the matter. Promise me you will not involve yourself in things you do not understand?"

His grip tightened. "Promise me."

"I would not intentionally involve myself with danger."

"Somehow I don't believe we share the same definition of danger. Wandering outside your tent to eavesdrop is asking for trouble. You may decide one day to listen in on the wrong conversation with the wrong people and find yourself in more trouble than you can handle."

"I think I have learned my lesson. I don't intend to wander alone outside my tent, nor anywhere else for that matter."

"You will promise me that no matter what, you will not get involved with trying to find the culprits behind these robberies?"

"I promise not to seek out danger, nor will I meddle into matters that are none of my concern. I'm here to help my uncle, not to play Scotland Yard."

He seemed satisfied with my answer. He removed his hands from my arms, but remained close. "I will hold you to that."

We said good night. Max waited outside my tent until I gave him the okay that all was well within my own. No unwanted creatures or monsters were hidden in the corner.

I had difficulty falling asleep. My thoughts were on Dr. Maxwell Clairborne. I told myself: *I must not jump to conclusions about him. He is a good man.* That is what I wanted to believe. Yet, I sensed he was not telling me all…he was keeping or hiding something from me. But what could it be? And why? Why would an honest individual have to keep hidden, or be secretive about his goings-on? A verse came to mind that I had read earlier in the day: *For God shall bring every work into judgment, with every secret thing, whether it be good, or whether it be evil.*

Then as quickly, another verse came to my mind: *A good tree cannot bring forth evil fruit, neither can a corrupt tree bring forth good fruit. Wherefore by their fruits ye shall know them.*

Just who are you really, Dr. Maxwell Clairborne?

Chapter 8

We left the tomb under the protective care of Ahmed, and by the week's end Uncle Harry and I arrived home early in the day. My first objective was to soak, for a good long while, in a tub of hot sudsy water. It was luxurious to say the least, and after I emerged and put on a cool cotton chemise, I lay on my bed under the whirling of the ceiling fan. I slept until the afternoon.

Beside French doors that opened to a verandah was a round table on which I kept a spirit lamp for warming water; content to remain in my room for a while longer, I awoke and had tea there. Newspaper clippings that I had collected of the *Titanic* stood out against the whiteness of the laced tablecloth. I picked up the one with a large photo of the splendid ship centered under the headline, "Unsinkable." The article gave details of her pomp and grandeur. I studied her sleek frame—grand she was. Whoever would have thought that her voyage would have ended thus?

Over the previous months my quest to link the curse with the sinking of the *Titanic* had been put aside, but now that I would be home for several weeks I could devote some time to it again. As Max had once pointed out to me, time does heal the pain of losing someone, yet deep inside remained that desire to know more. Why did it happen? And just what circumstances took place that brought it all about? I would continue to search it out until all reasons were exhausted.

I met up with David on several occasions, once at the museum. He and I talked for a good while. He was back to his jovial self; being the sort of person that would divulge in cheerful conversation and avoid unpleasant topics. I suppose I could label him an optimist. I, on the other hand, would be his opposite—a pessimist. I find it difficult to go beyond the facts. Perhaps it was my lack of faith. The book of Hebrews does state that: "Faith is the substance of things hoped for, the evidence of things not seen." Yes, I lacked faith, and there was no doubt about it, David's outlook on life always brightened my day. I invited him to have supper with Uncle Harry and me. He agreed, and arrived punctually the next afternoon with a bouquet of flowers held together by a pink silk ribbon—in his other hand a box of chocolates.

I gave him a kiss on the cheek. "Don't tell me you have connections too? You must enlighten me on how to arrive at such accomplishments: chocolates and flowers."

David smiled boyishly. "Just let me know your heart's desires and I will see that you get it."

"I'll give you my list next week," I teased.

Uncle Harry had hired a cleaning lady to do the rigorous chores; he wanted me freed up to do the more important things, which consisted of archeological journal entries and the book work. The cleaning lady, Mrs. Bilgas, also cooked our evening meals, which I think was Uncle Harry's true reason for hiring her on, for I was no cook. So, for the evening I was free to entertain David without the encumbrances of putting together a meal and so forth.

We sat out on the patio until dinner was to be served.

"It's pleasant here," he commented, as he relaxed on one of the rattans.

I gazed around at the simple setting Uncle Harry and I had been resourceful enough to put together. "It lacks the loveliness of an English garden, but I think we did well enough considering the climate here."

"It's not just that," he then remarked soberly. "There is a tranquility here. Not just out here on the patio, but when I step through the doors of this house." He smiled. "Probably sounds foolish."

I quoted: "Peace be within thy walls, and prosperity within thy palaces. For my brethren and companions' sakes, I will now say, peace be within thee."

He made no comment, but seemed thoughtful.

I informed him, "That is what Uncle Harry quotes to those who say the same. I believe that you will find that Bible verse written somewhere in the book of Psalms."

"I admire his walk with God."

"He is as men should be."

"Yes, but many choose not to be."

I shifted my position to better see him. "Do you ever wonder why people prefer to live unrighteously?"

He shrugged his shoulders. "No, I have never really dwelled on it much. I guess some will always choose the pleasures of sin for a season, rather than to serve God for eternity."

"But is there really pleasure in sinning? Sins have consequences that I care not to reap. Adultery destroys families. And here, if a man steals or kills, they hang him. One reaps what they sow. And then the most tragic of it all is where those that do not know God will spend eternity. No one is exempt from death and we will all stand before God."

"Ah, but the devil is a great deceiver. He leads people to believe that God does not exist. Look at Darwin's theory."

I tried to remember what I could of it, then replied by saying, "That evolution is by natural selection—basically nothing to do with God."

"That's right. We are just here."

"What a depressing thought, that mankind is just existing with no purpose to life, or the one hereafter. I am glad that I know different. Jesus said, 'I have come to give you life and that more abundantly.'"

Our conversation ended when Mrs. Bilgas announced that dinner was ready to be served. We went into the dining area, took our seats, said grace and then delved into what Mrs. Bilgas had prepared for us. Uncle Harry opened the conversation—David was too busy with his plate of food to do so.

"How are your studies going?" Uncle Harry asked as he buttered his dinner roll.

"Quite well," David answered between bites of food.

Uncle Harry continued. "Will you be here much longer?"

"My studies will end this quarter, and then I will head back to London."

"We'll hate to see you go. You must come spend several weeks with us at the site before you leave."

"Oh yes—David, you must!" I agreed excitedly.

David stopped eating. "Say—that would be splendid, sir!"

Uncle said, "Then we'll expect it."

"Yes, sir! Wouldn't miss such an opportunity."

Uncle then told him, "We have plenty of tents, so don't bother to carry out any gear."

David's smile broadened. "That's good, considering I haven't any of my own. What I use all belongs to the school."

As pie was being served Uncle Harry made his second invitation—one which even I was unprepared for.

"There's to be a grand dinner party next weekend at the Cairo Museum for the bigwigs from the British Museum; you must plan to join us."

I went into a mild state of hysteria. "Uncle Harry! Why did you not tell me? I'll have to find a dress!"

"The telegram just arrived today."

"Where will I find a dress?"

Uncle Harry seemed confused. "You haven't any?"

"Not for a grand dinner party!"

"I see," was his only comment.

David's suggestion was outrageous: "Make one."

I laughed, imagining what such a dress would look like. "I can't even thread a sewing machine."

David said, "I thought all girls knew of such things."

I smiled. "Do I live like all girls?"

His eyes narrowed in contemplation. "I see your point. I suppose not."

"No—I don't. I can tell you anything you need to know about archeological tools, and even how to use them, but don't expect me to know much when it comes to cooking and sewing."

Uncle Harry looked concerned. "Perhaps Mrs. Bilgas could help you in those areas."

"What is this?" Mrs. Bilgas asked upon hearing her name as she entered the room.

Now Mrs. Bilgas was an extraordinary woman, and no doubt she had successfully taught all five of her daughters how to cook and sew—I knew this because all five were married, and in Egypt a man did not marry a woman that could not do so. After all, that a woman is capable of taking care of a husband and a good number of children, and feeding them properly is, to most men, of utmost importance.

Uncle Harry said, "I'm afraid, Mrs. Bilgas, that I have failed where my niece is concerned."

Mrs. Bilgas looked me over. "What is this?"

"Uncle Harry thinks because he has not had me properly tutored on how to cook or sew that my life is in ruins," I told David and Mrs. Bilgas.

David and I laughed.

"You no want a husband?" she asked sternly.

"No—not at the moment."

"Then who is this young man?"

David and I looked at each other and smiled. I suppose to Mrs. Bilgas he was dining with us because he was a prospective choice.

"He is a good friend."

She looked surprised. "I never hear of such. A girl not wanting a husband, not wanting babies."

I reassured her, "Oh, someday maybe."

"Someday!" she repeated quickly. "No man will marry an old maid that cannot cook or is too old to have babies."

"In my country," I went on to tell her, "men and women marry because they fall in love, not because the woman happens to be a good cook, or he needs someone to produce his children."

"You have strange ways in this country of yours."

I said to Uncle Harry, "If it will make you feel better, when we are home, I will help Mrs. Bilgas in the kitchen."

"Mrs. Bilgas," said Uncle Harry, "will that be okay with you?"

"That will be okay." She gave Uncle Harry a pat on the arm. "You no worry. I will teach her to cook, then you can find her a husband."

I could see that Uncle Harry was holding back a laugh. "Thank you, Mrs. Bilgas."

Mrs. Bilgas had a certain look of determination kindling in her dark eyes, and I had a feeling that I was about to be her greatest challenge.

The following day, Mrs. Bilgas assured me that she was as capable as any dressmaker, and that I should go to market, pick out a nice bolt of silk fabric, and she would transform it into a lovely gown.

I decided to give Mrs. Bilgas that opportunity. So, my plans were to go to market, pick out the fabric, and then drop off a parcel Uncle wished to give to Max. It was addressed from the Metropolitan Laboratories.

I had taken special pains with my appearance, telling myself that I might run into an official from the Metropolitan Museum; they were due to arrive in at any time. Uncle Harry said they could have a mind to just pop in on us. I thought it best to be prepared to serve tea at a moment's notice.

But as I chose my violet chiffon dress, designed for the comfort of casual wear, I admit I had Max in mind. He had not seen me wearing anything other than dusty khakis. Would he consider me attractive?

I studied my reflection. I was not exceptionally beautiful; my hazel eyes, which were now a shade of violet, were too large and my nose too prominent.

I had a look of what Uncle Harry called "willfulness." I suppose that was due to my high, arrogant cheekbones. My golden hair was my glory—long and naturally curly. Today, I had it pulled up into a barrette, leaving the back tresses to fall to my waist.

I took one last look at my reflection, pinched my cheeks, picked up the parcel and placed it inside my satchel, and then I headed out for my excursion. I had decided to do my shopping first.

The market was lined with booths of different shapes and sizes. The vendors were openly displaying their wares below the awning of their tents. I began to browse casually from one to the other. I found a lovely red silk scarf embroidered with gold and bought it. The fabric I chose for my dress was a beautiful bolt of black chiffon with flecks of gold shimmering throughout its entirety. I also chose a bolt of black organza to serve as an underlining. Together, the pieces would make a very elegant evening gown. I hoped that Mrs. Bilgas would not be upset that it was not silk, as she had recommended.

I gave the vendor the denariis for the fabric, she bundled it up in brown paper, and I put it inside my satchel. I now made my way to Max, to deliver the parcel.

It was not a long walk, and within fifteen minutes, I stood directly across the street from Max's apartment.

I was feeling a little nervous about being with him in a more intimate setting.

I crossed the street and went through an enclosed entrance that led to a heavy wooden door. I bravely rang the doorbell. A gentleman opened the door—a valet perhaps. He was an elderly man, tall and thin, and probably American.

"I am here to see Dr. Clairborne," I told him.

He asked, "And you are—?"

I realized my error. "Oh, pardon me, I am Miss Woodruff, Professor Harry Woodruff's niece."

He stood silently for a moment, as if wondering what to do with me; I thought it best to state my business: "I have a parcel from the Metropolitan Laboratories that I am to deliver."

He opened the door wider. "Please come inside."

I stepped into a large vestibule where masculine scents of wood and leather faintly aromatized the air.

"If you will please wait here," he instructed.

I nodded my head that I would.

Being curious to know more about Dr. Maxwell Clairborne, I began to study the interior. To my left was an open room where artifacts and a variety of books were meticulously arranged on a shelf against one wall; a burgundy leather sofa and two high-back matching chairs filled the room. Artifacts were everywhere—mostly Egyptian, a few from India. Some, perhaps, even from the darkest Africa. His collection was as impressive as Uncle Harry's.

Adjoining this room was another room, separated by a door that stood open. I stepped a little closer to peer in. I saw a desk, a few chairs and....

Oh God! It couldn't be! The dim lighting had to be playing tricks on me. But no—there it was! There could not be another like it. It was the alabaster jewelry box that had been stolen from Princess Ihi's tomb!

My mouth went dry and my heart began to pound painfully. *Max had the alabaster box! He was behind the robberies, as I had first suspected!*

I felt sickened. I could not face him now. The walls began to close in on me. I had to get out! All I could think to do was to run. Run as far away as possible.

I set the parcel down and then ran out the door. *What a fool I had been to befriend him—a criminal!*

By the time I reached the market area I was breathless, my heart was still pounding frantically, and tears blurred my vision. I mindlessly mingled with the people, not really going anywhere, or seeing anything or anyone. I was just there, wandering.

A good thirty minutes must have gone by, when I was brought to a sudden halt by a pair of two strong hands.

"Good heavens—Beth?!"

I looked up into a pair of concerned blue eyes. "David!" I whispered, grasping his shirtsleeves.

He looked around, as if searching for what may have caused my turmoil. "What's happened?"

I could say nothing as tears, once again, began to flow.

He looked about. "Over here," he said, guiding me to a table near a refreshment stand.

I sat down, wiping the tears from my cheeks.

"What happened?"

"I've been such a fool."

His mouth skewered up. "We all are at one time or other."

"But I knew...I let him deceive me."

David's eyes narrowed contemplatively and then anger flitted across his features. "You should not go about unescorted. Did some chap try to take advantage of you? If he did I'll—"

"No—no, it's not that." I covered my face with a hand and then sighed heavily before continuing. "I don't know what I'm going to do."

David took hold of my hand. "Look, I think you better explain all this. Maybe I can help."

"Do you remember the alabaster jewelry box that was stolen from Princess Ihi's tomb?"

He nodded. "Yes, I remember. The one with all the jewels."

"I found it."

"What?"

"Dr. Clairborne has the alabaster box."

"Dr. Clairborne!?"

"I knew from the beginning that he was behind the robberies, but I let him deceive me into thinking that he was not."

"Are you sure about this? That's some heavy accusation."

"I saw it for myself—in his apartment. Uncle Harry asked me to go there to deliver a parcel. While I was waiting I saw it."

"But are you sure? I mean, maybe he has one similar."

"Come—David," I said tersely. "There would not be another one like it."

He thought it out for a moment. "No, I suppose not."

"I'll have to tell someone."

"You must tell your uncle."

"No!" I quickly disagreed. "I mustn't. If he even suspects that I know something, or that I might be in any kind of danger, he'll ship me back to London."

"Who then?"

"I don't know. I know that there are agents that are working on the case, but who they are I don't think anyone really knows."

"Maybe we can find out."

"How?"

"I'll ask around. There has to be a way to get a message delivered. I'll do what I can."

"It is the right thing to do? To report it?" I asked, unsure of myself.

"Of course it is the right thing to do. And it is what you should do," he encouraged.

"I almost feel traitorous."

"You shouldn't. He is the one that is being deceitful."

His eyes squinted perceptively as he gazed off into the distance. "Dr.

Clairborne," he said thoughtfully. "I never would have guessed it."

"Well I did!" I said vehemently, now angry with myself for ignoring the evidence, "but I was too much a fool to believe it."

"Guys like that are professionals. They build up your confidence in them, and then when the opportunity arises, they snatch things right out from under your nose."

"Like the alabaster box."

"I'm afraid so."

I thought: *What great lengths people will go to, to get what they want.*

I was suddenly very tired. I pulled the satchel strap across my shoulder and then stood. "I would really like to go home now."

"I'll walk you there," he quickly suggested.

We did not converse until we stood facing each other at the doorstep to Uncle's home.

He asked, "Say—are you going to be all right?"

I sighed heavily. "Dr. Clairborne had become a friend to Uncle Harry and me. It is very disturbing to know that he was not the man that we made him out to be."

"I understand."

I said nothing more.

He said, "I suppose I will see you at the dinner party?"

"Yes. And David, I'm glad you were at the market today. You were a Godsend. I really did not know where to turn."

"Don't worry, Beth, I will find out who you need to contact about Dr. Clairborne and the alabaster box."

"Thank you, David, I truly appreciate it."

We said our goodbyes and I went to my room. Although I was tired, I knew that my mind would not let me rest. So, I picked up my Bible and began to read. I found, that in times of distress, it was a great comfort.

I read aloud: "Hear my cry, O God; attend unto my prayer. From the end of the earth will I cry unto thee, when my heart is overwhelmed: lead me to the rock that is higher than I."

"Oh God," I prayed. "My heart is truly overwhelmed. Please lead me, for I cannot lead myself."

I began to cry, for truly my heart was grieved to discover the truth concerning Dr. Clairborne.

Chapter 9

The room chosen for the dinner party was decorated exquisitely, and although Egyptian artifacts still lined the museum wall, candle lighting and a long table covered with heavy lace changed the room's atmosphere into one of divine elegance. Under the glow of the candles the table sparkled with imperial plates and diamond-bright crystal goblets like jewels in a case. If my inner turmoil had not been so intense, I would relish the event to its fullest, placing it somewhere at the top with the discovery of the tomb of Smenkhkara. But that was not the case, for undoubtedly at some time during this memorable affair, I most certainly would come in contact with Dr. Maxwell Clairborne.

Because I did not want to place myself in a situation where I would have to converse alone with Max, I spent the last several days worrying over how best to avoid him. If he were to inquire of me why I left his apartment so hastily—what was I to say? That the hour was getting late?

How ridiculous!

What dangers would confront me if he knew that I had seen the alabaster jewelry box in his apartment? But then, perhaps, he had already come to such a conclusion, for his valet would have told him that I had dropped off the parcel; therefore, I could not pretend that I had not done so.

I was standing with Uncle Harry, conversing with Dr. Mehreiz, when Max came into the room. He stood near the entrance next to large double doors, scanning the already growing crowd of those who had been invited to the party. He looked honorable in his black tuxedo. Handsomely sophisticated. It was hard to believe that he was behind the tomb robberies—possibly even the mastermind.

I was determined not to let his presence unnerve me.

Before I was caught looking his direction, I shifted my focus back to Dr. Mehreiz, who was sharing with Uncle Harry and myself an intriguing story, one which I now had difficulty concentrating on, for I knew that Max had spotted us.

Thank the heavens that Mrs. Bilgas was a marvelous seamstress. My gown was elegant and provided me with a certain amount of confidence. The black organza was formfitting, covered by the sheer drama of gathered chiffon at my waist. At least I could show an outward display of poise. I would not let evil doings frighten me, nor cause me to cower behind a mask of indifference. I would, most certainly, stand for what is right, no matter the cost.

Uncle Harry would be enraged if he knew what I was planning to do. He mustn't find out!

As I presumed he would do, Max headed toward our small gathering, which now consisted of myself, Uncle Harry, Dr. Mehreiz, and another gentleman who had just introduced himself as Dr. Karon.

Dr. Karon was, as I learned later, a radiologist that worked with the British Museum. He being a middle-aged gentleman of medium height and stocky build, and cloning the look of one highly educated by sporting a well-trimmed mustache and wire-rimmed glasses. He was noted for his experiments based on the relationships between the shapes of the pyramids and the physical processes within. This, he said, was observed by the reaction of organic matter.

"For example," Dr. Karon said, as Max included himself into our small circle, "a fish placed inside a modeled pyramid, built, of course, to scale, lost two-thirds of its weight within thirteen days. Another experiment showed that the windpipe of a sheep shrank by one-half in six days, and in forty-three days an egg had wasted away from fifty-two grams to twelve grams. And what was to our further amazement, these did not mold or smell."

Max asked, as he made himself part of the conversation, "Do you believe that the educated men among the ancient Egyptians had knowledge concerning the application of energy?"

"It is hard to believe that the few select Egyptian priests knew of modern science. But indeed I believe they were well educated in these matters."

The conversation was a little over my head. *Who cares if an egg wasted away to twelve grams, and a sheep's windpipe shrank within days—doesn't everything that rots eventually shrivel up to nothing?*

I noticed Max looking me over with some amusement. Why did I always have the feeling that he could read my thoughts?

Quite annoying!

"Did you not have a colleague that also did an experiment with a razor blade?" Dr. Mehreiz then asked.

"You are speaking of Karl Drbal," Dr. Karon told him.

"Yes, yes—I believe he is the one. Can't say that I remember much about him."

Dr. Karon went on to tell us, "He used the physical impact of the pyramid shape to develop what we gentlemen use daily, of all things, a razor blade sharpener. Out of cardboard he built a model pyramid, placed the cutting edge of a dull razor blade crosswise to the east-west axis onto a piece of wood a third as long as the pyramid, then he covered the base and gave it exposure to normal daylight. Thus within six days the blade was sharpened."

I suppose this was quite a discovery.

Max did not seem too impressed with Dr. Karon's theories either, for his focus was on me. His gray eyes held no humor, and a muscle twitched at his jawline.

He knows, I thought. *He knows that I saw the alabaster jewelry box! What will he do?*

I looked about for a means of escape. I needed to get away from his penetrating stare. I knew that he wanted to make eye contact. I had once heard it said that one's eyes are the mirror to their soul. What did he want to discover by looking into mine? *That I loathe him? That I know of his doings?* It was then that David came into the room. I was genuinely relieved. He could be my reason to escape.

I said, after Dr. Karon had finished with what he was saying, "Will you gentlemen please excuse me? A friend of mine has just arrived."

I was, of course, graciously excused, but only after Dr. Karon made the comment that it was a pleasure to meet the loveliest archeological assistant in the field. This was easy for him to say, since I was probably the only woman that he knew in the field of archeology anyway. However, I thanked him for his kindness, and then made my way to greet David. I could feel Max's eyes following me across the room.

David's greeting came with a tender smile. "Trying to escape from the lion," he whispered into my ear, indicating a nod toward the direction I had just come from, the "lion" being Max.

"Where have you been?" I scolded.

"Sorry I'm late, but I had a very important meeting."

"You?" I said, knowing very well that nothing could be as important as the party.

He went on to prove otherwise: "Perhaps I'm mistaken, but I thought you were quite eager for me to get you certain information?"

The agent! I thought quickly. I gaped at him for a moment before speaking. "Are you serious?"

"I told you I would."

"Well, yes, but—"

"You did not think that I really could?"

"No, that's not it. I know that you are very efficient, but it's just that I didn't expect it so soon."

He leaned closer, and then whispered, "I have all the information you need."

"You must tell me."

"Not at this moment."

"Why not?"

He indicated a hand toward the table. "We're getting ready to eat."

"At a time like this, that is all you can think about—is food?"

His smile was conniving. "We are playing a different game now, my dear. We must act the part."

"Should I call you Sherlock?"

"Seriously," he then advised. "If we were absent from the banquet, would we not look suspicious to a certain gentleman?"

I looked in Max's direction. "I think he knows that I saw the alabaster box and that I suspect him."

"Then that is all the more reason to be careful. We can talk later."

David and I took seats opposite Uncle Harry. To my surprise, Grace was seated next to Uncle Harry.

"Why Grace! How wonderful to see you!"

She smiled. "I was invited to the party and I knew that Hubert would not have missed it for anything in this world."

"I'm glad you're here," I told her. "We must have lunch together before you leave for London."

"I know just the place," she informed me. "How about Monday—say one o'clock."

I agreed, and before the meal was served, Dr. Mehreiz went down the table and made formal introductions. I would never be able to remember every person by name. A few individuals stood out and would be easy to recall. I made it a point to note the VIPs, for one the director of the British Museum, Dr. Nathaniel Corinth, his wife Opal, and their lovely daughter, Helen.

Helen was seated next to Max. I discovered later that they were already acquainted. Unlike myself, she was very sophisticated. Dark curls were arranged perfectly on top of her head. Her resplendent brown eyes were set apart by a slender nose, and her full red lips curved naturally upward. Glittering sequins lined the bodice of her midnight blue gown. She looked to be about six to eight years my senior, and was the epitome of high society. I bet a hair was never out of place. I wondered if she were as snobbish as she appeared, then was chagrined with myself. How could I be so quick to judge her character? It was not Christian to do so. Perhaps it was jealously that caused me to think of her in that way.

This thought became disturbing—*why would I be jealous? I was not in love with Max!?*

It was not until after the meal, which was a delicious pineapple-glazed baked ham and rice pilaf, that I found myself face to face with Dr. Maxwell Clairborne. David had been dragged away by Uncle Harry, which left Grace and me to converse alone.

Max came up behind me, stealthily, I suppose. Grace smiled up at him.

"Why—Dr. Clairborne," she said to him sweetly. "How nice to see you again. Look, Beth, it is Dr. Clairborne."

I turned, looking up. I was sure the smile he wore was that of triumph, or that of being wickedly cunning—maybe both.

"Hello, ladies," he said, the smile still in place.

"Dr. Clairborne," I said as cordially as possible. "How nice to see you."

Again, he could easily read me. I was certain he knew that I was anything but pleased.

"Grace," he began, "would you mind if I stole this young lady away from you for but a moment."

She was probably thinking that this was some sort of romantic interlude. Her smile widened.

"That would be perfectly all right," she told him. "You two go along, there are a few friends of Hubert's I wish to speak with."

Grace left us, and before I had time to object, Max took me gently by the arm and ushered me through French doors and out onto a secluded balcony.

He wasted no time. "You want to tell me why you have been avoiding me or shall I do it for you?"

My heart began to pound frantically. If only I had followed Uncle Harry and David, I would not be in this uncomfortable predicament.

"What do you mean?" I asked nervously.

He still had hold of my arm, and stood closer than I liked. With a finger, he titled my chin upward, forcing me to gaze into his intent gray eyes. "What's going on in that pretty head of yours?"

How ludicrous! He wants me to confess?

"You ran from my apartment without saying goodbye." He gave an acerbic laugh before continuing. "No, actually, before even saying hello. And tonight you have been avoiding me as if I have the plague."

I looked away from his condemning gaze.

"Why did you leave my apartment, Beth, and in such a hurry?"

"It was getting late." Inwardly, I grimaced. I had given myself instructions to not say those exact words. How stupid of me! "I—I mean," I stuttered, sounding all the more guilty. "I was to meet with someone—I was running out of time."

Oh God! I'm lying!

He said nothing for a moment and then spoke rather flatly. "I think we both know that is not the truth. You don't lie very well."

My dander was up. I looked back up at him, not wavering. "You're right, Dr. Clairborne. I'm not a very good prevaricator," I said, choosing that word instead of liar. I went on, "Nor am I accustomed to dealing with people who are not what they seem!"

His eyes narrowed speculatively. "And you are referring to—?"

"You!"

He nodded slowly, then said, almost as if humored by my remark, "Me?"

"Yes…you!"

"Please explain."

"Do I really need to? You know for yourself what you are about. Is that not so?"

The tension between us thickened. His square jaw stiffened, and his eyes narrowed dangerously. "I do believe I told you not to meddle into things that you know nothing about."

"Really! How thoughtful of you." Then I said a trifle heatedly, "Turn a blind eye. Is that it?"

"You don't know all the facts, Beth."

"What is there to know?"

"As you have made it so perfectly clear…perhaps things are not as they appear."

"That is what some would prefer others to think. However, facts are facts and cannot be hidden." I then quoted: "'For nothing is secret, that shall not be made manifest, neither any thing hid'"—I thought of the alabaster box—"'that shall not be known and come aboard.'"

I felt a surge of confidence.

He looked away, almost as if suddenly deflated. "I can see that you are not easily fooled. Then I shall leave you to whatever conclusion you like."

He turned and stalked away, leaving me to stand alone on the balcony.

I took a deep breath. The confrontation with Max was over. He was aware that I know of his doings. Probably he wanted to give some sort of explanation. A justifiable reason as to why he had the alabaster box, and why he had a part in the robberies. What reason could there be? It was wrong to steal. Even if the President of the United States wanted the Egyptian antiquities for American museums that would be no reason to commit such atrocities. Wrong is wrong. Stealing is stealing. Murder is murder.

Lying is lying, my conscience then told me. "God forgive me," I then whispered to my heavenly Father.

My thoughts then went back to Max. *Would Max go as far as to commit murder?*

I hoped not.

"There you are!"

It was David.

"I've been looking all over for you," he said.

"You are not soon enough. I just had a most interesting conversation with Dr. Clairborne."

He whistled between his teeth. "Say, I'm sorry."

"It doesn't matter…he knows."

"What do you think he will do?"

I really did not know. I gave my head a negative shake.

"You don't think he would harm you in any way, do you?" David asked soberly. "I think you better tell Harry about this."

"I can't tell Uncle Harry! David, you know that! He would ship me to London sooner than I could get all my clothes packed."

"Gee—that would be a desolate situation: a woman without her wardrobe."

He was joking, but then grew serious. "Better with no wardrobe, than lying dead somewhere."

"Dr. Clairborne would not murder me!"

"Perhaps not Dr. Clairborne himself, but—"

"David! He wouldn't do that! Nor would he hire some thug to do it. He just—"

I did not know what to think anymore concerning Dr. Clairborne.

"Look," I then said calmly, "let's forget about Dr. Clairborne for right now and talk about who and how I'm supposed to get in touch with this agent. We'll let him take care of all this. I've had my fill of it."

"Right," he said, pulling out of his pocket the needed information. "You'll be talking with the head man himself. His code name is Moses."

"Moses," I repeated. "Do we know him?"

"I don't think anyone really does. It could be your Uncle Harry."

I laughed. "Uncle Harry! That would be a switch of character. The solemn and reserved professor, Harry Woodruff, an undercover agent."

I gave it some thought. "David, you're right! If he were using the code name Moses he would have to be Christian. Uncle Harry's a Christian, and he loves the books of Moses. It can't be Uncle Harry. I can't talk to Uncle Harry about this!"

"That would be a tough break. What are you going to do?"

I thought about it for a moment, but was still not sure what to do. "I'll have to take it a step at a time. Where am I supposed to meet this Moses?"

He handed me the paper, I read it aloud: "The Cairo Museum!"

"Shhh—"

I then whispered, "David, the museum? That's not being very secretive."

"Perhaps he doesn't want it to appear secretive."

"Yes, of course."

Again, I studied the note, which read: "Tomorrow. Two o'clock, in the library. You will ask for the book on Thutmoses."

David then informed me, "You are to go alone. Will you be all right with that?"

"Certainly."

"Well, if you change your mind, come over to the hotel and have me paged by one of the bellhops and I'll go with you."

I laid a hand upon his arm. "I'll be fine. Thanks, David, for setting this up."

"Any time," he said gallantly.

I folded the note neatly and then placed it inside the black satin purse I carried. "Let's go inside."

David offered his arm, I took it and then he led the way toward Uncle

Harry, who stood with several others. After David and I joined the group, Max and Helen did likewise.

Helen said to me, "I was hoping to have a chance to talk with you personally. You've become quite a feminine figure with the women's rights movement."

"Really? I can't imagine why."

"Freedom to do as you please," Max said tartly. "Helen is a great advocate for women's rights. Isn't that right, Helen?"

"Most assuredly. Women must stick together on these issues. We should be allowed to vote. We should have equal job opportunities. I'm sure you agree? You certainly have found a place in what has always been considered only a man's profession."

"I haven't really given it much thought," I told her. "Uncle Harry has always been very liberal where women are concerned. Except, of course, when it comes to traveling about. He feels that women need to be escorted. And there are times when I understand why."

"Good common sense," Uncle Harry interjected.

She then said, "But you have accomplished what many women only dream to ever achieve: working successfully outside the home. Tell me, do you face discrimination on the basis of your gender?"

I smiled. "No. Not here."

"That's splendid," she said.

"Ladies," Uncle Harry spoke out. "The Bible does say that women are to be keepers of the home, and men the providers. Women may one day regret their insistence for equal rights when they have to juggle working outside the home and taking care of a family."

"You are so right, Harry," Grace put in. "When you marry and have a family the chores never end."

"There are some things that women need not be involved in," Max stated.

He was looking at me.

Helen laughed. "Forgive Max. He believes women are weak and defenseless, and they belong in the home."

"Not entirely," Max said. "But there are certain dangers that women need not subject themselves to."

Again, he was looking at me. *Was this a hidden message, perhaps?*

"That doesn't make sense, Max." Helen laughed. "Should rock climbing only be for man's enjoyment, and because it is 'dangerous' women should not be allowed to enjoy it also?"

Dr. Mehreiz said, "Here we are talking about women's rights when one of the greatest archeological finds has been discovered. May I be so bold as to change the subject? Dr. Clairborne, when do you intend to do the autopsy on the mummy?"

I was glad that the conversation took a turn. Max seemed intent on conveying to me some sort of hidden message. Probably, that meddling would put me in danger? That I needed to back off?

I was set to do what I thought right. Tomorrow I would most definitely meet with Moses.

Chapter 10

The Cairo Museum library is a very large room that contains every book available on Egyptian history and other such books that, through the years, had been donated by international scholars and universities. Books and journals of Egypt's earliest travelers and treasure seekers also add to the library's extraordinary selection. You can obtain information on where men like Napoleon Bonaparte and Richard Pococke had gone in the valley, and what they observed. Students who visit from various countries often use the library as a means to obtain a better understanding of hieroglyphics, and what life must have been like some three thousand years ago, during the reign of the great kings. Although Uncle Harry is a marvelous teacher where archeology is concerned, I too, have found the library to be a useful source of information on the mighty pharaohs, and the numerous dynasties that have long since been buried under the sands of Egypt.

As I walked past the library's large mahogany bookshelves, weighted with hardback volumes, I was not sure what events would need to transpire in order for me to achieve my mission. First, I was to ask the man behind the counter for the book on Thutmoses. And then I would be given further instructions as to what I must do next in order to converse with the mighty Moses himself.

I looked about. The library was empty except for the man behind the counter and a woman and child seated at one of the tables overlooking a book.

I walked up to the counter, and then said, "Please, sir, I need to see the book on Thutmoses."

The man to whom I spoke was a short man and wore wire-rimmed glasses.

On any one of my visits to the museum, I had never seen him before. His balding head gave away his age. He was probably fifty-something. I was not sure of his nationality, but he was not Egyptian. Perhaps British, German, French. In Egypt, a diversity of nationalities is not an uncommon sight. You could say it is made up of a cosmopolitan and polyglot crowd of individuals, from royalty to American tycoons and politicians.

Over his wire-rimmed glasses, he looked me over. He was to ask, *Thutmoses III?*—which he did. I was to say *Thutmoses I*—which I did. Thus completing our interchange.

The book was ready. He handed it to me, then said, "You will find what you are looking for on page fifty-three."

I thanked him for his assistance, went to one of the tables and sat down as if to peruse the book.

I looked about to make sure I was not being watched, then turned to page fifty-three. Written on a plain piece of white paper with black ink, were further instructions. After I read what I must do, I scanned my surroundings. Certain that I was not being watched; I took the note and shoved it into my purse. I returned the book to the man behind the counter, and then headed out to do as I had intended—which was to speak to the man called Moses. I would tell him all that I knew concerning Princess Ihi's alabaster jewelry box and the evidence leading up to its disappearance.

I adjusted the brim of my white hat to shade my eyes from the glaring sun, and I ran a hand down the banana yellow, soft cotton sundress I wore to smooth out any wrinkles. I was now ready to meet with Moses at King Tut's Cafe. I was informed that he would be seated at a round table overlooking the street. I was to ask the waiter for a Mr. Smith.

Smith—How original!

King Tut's Cafe was about a block and a half away. The thoroughfare was busy with shoppers and vendors, and children playing in the street, knocking a ball around with a stick. I marveled at how expertly they weaved in and out of the maze of people, dodging dogcarts and other such contraptions without causing some serious mishap.

It was when King Tut's Cafe came into view that I felt I was being watched—maybe even followed. *Who?* I wondered. *Only David and those connected with Moses knew of my meeting today. What if information had leaked out to the wrong people, and somehow they knew that I was to meet with the man in charge of exposing their operation? Would they slay Moses and myself, there at the cafe, and then call it a religious skirmish of some sort?*

I did not know how these people worked. So, in my mind, such ominous behavior was possible.

What should I do?

A vendor's stall was close, so I chose it as a means to better evaluate my situation. I stood there feigning interest in the merchandise being sold. Occasionally, I would look up to see if I could catch eyes watching, but not a soul seemed interested in what I was doing.

Was my imagination at work?

Perhaps. I decided to cautiously continue on.

As I drew closer to King Tut's Cafe, I could vaguely make out the form of a man seated at the designated round table on the balcony. I assumed it was Moses, and the closer I drew, the more like the age-old Moses he appeared: a man with a gray beard, and wearing dark attire. *Where did they dig this man up from?*

Of course, they would want Moses to be an average-looking individual. But this man was conspicuous in a different sort of way: he looked to be as ancient as Egypt.

I was about to enter into the cafe, when, out of the corner of my eye, I noticed a man standing not far away. I felt his eyes upon me, and when I turned to look his way, he disappeared from view, but not before I had a chance to catch his height and hair coloring. I was certain it was Dr. Clairborne!

So I was being followed. And by Dr. Clairborne himself!

What a chain of events!

Why—if Maxwell Clairborne did confront Moses, Moses would not even have the strength to beat him with his cane, old as he was.

I could thank God that Moses was not Uncle Harry!

Continuing on as planned was not possible. I did not want to put this gentleman, Moses, in any sort of danger. I would never be able to forgive myself if my careless actions caused any sort of unpleasantness to befall him.

A booth lined with fruits and vegetables was set up next to the cafe. I went there and chose a few apples. I wanted to appear as if I were out shopping. So, after the vendor gave me my apples in the brown bag he had placed them in, I went to the next booth and did the same, but this time I perused the merchandise and went on my way. I had decided to go to David, tell him of the situation, and have him once again get a message delivered to Moses.

The hotel foyer was bustling with activity. Since the discovery of the Valley of the Kings, the once-tranquil Egypt was turned into a city overrun with curious archeologists, treasure seekers, and vivacious journalists eager for a story that would win them the Pulitzer Prize. I was presently maneuvering through such a conglomeration of people, and my goal was to reach the front desk without bumping unceremoniously into others.

I asked the clerk behind the desk to please page David Carter—which he did, and in a matter of minutes David was standing beside me.

"Say, are you okay?" was his greeting.

"I'm fine," I told him. "But we need to talk."

He led me out onto the open verandah where white-cloth-covered tables were set up and spread far enough apart to allow for some privacy. He chose a table, called for a waiter, ordered our tea, and then waited patiently for me to divulge whatever I had come to discuss with him.

I told him, in hushed tones. "I did as told."

"And?"

"I was being followed."

His eyes narrowed and his jaw muscled twitched. "You really shouldn't be doing this. Your uncle—"

"This really is not so complicated, David. I just need for you to get another message through to this Moses."

"What exactly happened?"

"I felt I was being followed, and before I entered into the cafe where I was to meet with Moses I spotted Dr. Clairborne, off in the distance, watching me. He disappeared from my view, but not before I got a brief glimpse of him."

David rubbed the back of his neck, as if tension was building there. "I don't like this."

"If I can just get a message through to Moses, to let him know what happened."

He sighed heavily. "If anything happens to you, you do realize it would be my fault."

"Your fault!"

"For letting you do this!"

"David," I said soothingly. "All that I need to do is get a message to Moses. I must tell him that I was being followed and had to abort the meeting. He'll arrange for another rendezvous, and then we can forget about all this."

"All right! All right! Write the note and I'll drop it off."

His hand lay on the tabletop, I gave it a squeeze. "Thanks!"

"I must be daft!"

"Don't be silly."

I dug through my purse for pen and notepad. After I wrote the note, I tore it off, folded it and then handed it to David. "You are doing a great service."

"A great mistake, more likely."

"Really, this is for the cause of science and archeology. Once the thieves are caught and this black market operation put to a halt, you will be rewarded for your involvement."

"I don't see how. And I can only imagine the wrath your uncle will pour out on me for letting you get yourself involved like this."

"Well, Uncle Harry will be pleased."

"I doubt that."

"He might be angry at first, but when he sees that no harm has come to me, what can he say?"

"He'll say," David lowered his voice as he spoke, "'Never step foot near my niece again, young man.'"

I laughed at his antics. "Oh, David, he'll say no such thing."

With some reluctance he shoved the note into his shirt pocket. "I have a feeling I'm going to regret this."

"As soon as you hear something, please come to the house."

"Okay, but if this becomes too dangerous, promise me you will tell your uncle—he should know."

"I promise," I told him. "It's not going to become too dangerous. Moses will take care of everything, so you needn't worry."

"Right," he said, as if he did not really believe that to be so.

It was customary that Uncle Harry and I dress formally for supper, and I had chosen a dreamy, cream-colored charmeuse blouse, adorned with a figural cameo, portraying the myth of Leda and the Swan. My straight, ankle-length skirt was made of silk and linen—a cool combination. My hair, which was springy with curl, I wore down, but held back with a large, ornate barrette. My reflection mirrored femininity. I was hoping David would pop in with news of Moses. Two nights had already passed without any word from him and I was becoming anxious.

As supper was soon to be served the doorbell rang. I rushed to get it, certain that it was David. He knew what hour we dined, and being hospitable, he also knew that we would ask him to stay and eat with us.

In great haste I flung open the door, like some silly schoolgirl who had been impatiently waiting on her beau. I blushed crimson when I realized that it was not David, whom I had expected. My smile quickly vanished, and I gasped, "Dr. Clairborne!?"

One dark eyebrow shot up, then he briefly scanned me. "Max is the name. Obviously, you were expecting someone else."

"Yes—I mean no. Not exactly," I stammered ridiculously on.

Uncle Harry's voice then boomed, "Max, do come in." Then he turned to me. "Beth, I have asked Dr. Clairborne to dine with us tonight."

Just lovely, I thought.

I stepped aside, allowing Max to enter.

Uncle then continued, revealing his purpose for the invitation. "I want Max to take a look at that amulet we discovered in the tomb."

"I see," was my reply.

Max said to me, "I hope you don't mind?"

The constitution of proper etiquette came into force, and I answered by saying, "Of course not," but inwardly, I felt uneasy.

Max, on the other hand, looked relaxed. I gave him a thorough examination. He wore a dressy white linen shirt and black trousers. His dark hair was neatly combed back, revealing what many would consider an intellectual forehead. A strong, square jawline indicated that, indeed, he possessed a stubborn nature…one which I had confronted oftentimes enough. But his eyes I could never quite figure out. They seemed to hold an inner peace.

Again, I could not help but wonder: *What did I really know about Maxwell Clairborne?*

One thing was certain: he had Princess Ihi's alabaster jewelry box. The one Philip said had been stolen!

I did not realize I was still scrutinizing the good doctor until he looked my way.

Caught!

His eyes held mine for a moment, and then he said, quite gentlemanly, "You're sure I won't be intruding."

Uncle was quick to reassure him. "Nonsense! We love having guests for dinner. Is that not so, Beth?"

Congenially I replied, "Why yes—of course."

We entered into the dining room, which, for the sake of convenience, was open to the kitchen. Uncle Harry and Max stood waiting for me to take my seat, however, after Mrs. Bilgas had prepared our dinner, she went home to her family. So naturally, I was left to put the meal on the table.

It is customary that gentlemen remain standing until the women are seated. But, I thought it silly that Uncle Harry and Max remain thus, just for the sake of propriety, while I carried out the task of bringing our meal to the table. So, I insisted that they go ahead and be seated—which they did. I successfully poured the tea into the glasses without spilling a drop onto the white tablecloth and then I went into the kitchen to get our meal out from the oven.

While I went about my task of mindlessly taking out the hot casseroles from the oven and placing them onto the stove top, Uncle Harry and Max began to converse about various objects that had just recently been found in the tomb. I could hear them quite clearly from where I stood.

The large casserole dish I removed first. It contained a roast in succulent gravy, relished with carrots and potatoes. Next were the hot vegetable casserole, and then the peach cobbler.

As I was removing the cobbler, the hot pad slipped, causing me to burn the underside of my wrist. When I let out a painful yelp, Max and Uncle Harry came quickly.

"I'm fine," I told them.

Max said, "Let's have a look."

"I'm fine, really."

Gently, Max took my arm and began to look over the area that I had burned.

How stupid of me to be so clumsy!

Uncle Harry went for the first aid kit, while Max still held onto my hand.

"I think this can wait until after dinner," I said, even though the burn was very painful.

His eyes came to rest on mine. "You don't have to be brave, Beth. I know it must hurt. A blister is already rising."

"Well, if it would help, I suppose I could cry," I said, making light of the situation.

His smile was genuine. "I would hate to see you cry, but if it would make you feel better—"

Uncle Harry entered, carrying the first aid kit. "Here we go. Now let's get you fixed up."

He gave Max the job of "fixing me up," then they both insisted that I take my seat while they finished putting the meal on the table.

"A small burn hardly makes me an invalid. I can finish doing this," I told them. But they completed the job anyway, ignoring my protest.

After the meal was underway and we had already tired of discussing the tomb, Max said to me, "I saw you at market the other day."

The tea I swallowed went down wrong. I sputtered while he continued on: "I was late for a meeting, otherwise I would have stopped to see if you needed help carrying your packages home. I hope that you will forgive me?"

I had no packages!

I looked at him from across the table—pale faced I'm sure, wondering if he were not making excuses, or trying to discover whether or not I saw him spying.

"Quite all right," I said, still trying to figure him out. Then stepping out boldly, maybe foolishly, I said, "I do remember someone watching. Was that you, then?"

With nonchalance, I stirred more sugar into my tea, waiting for his reply, as if it did not matter. I could play this game too.

"Perhaps," he said neatly. "But then, not many beautiful English women walk alone in the marketplace, I'm sure many eyes were watching."

"Walking alone," Uncle Harry interjected.

I was sure to hear it from Uncle Harry over the not-being-escorted issue.

I was right. Uncle Harry then said, "You shouldn't go to the market alone, Beth, or anywhere else for that matter. Take Mrs. Bilgas the next time you need to go to market."

I gave Max a narrowed look. "You used to not mind my going out alone so much, Uncle Harry."

"Times are becoming a little uneasy around here, with the tomb robberies. It's probably best that you take Mrs. Bilgas the next time you need to go to market."

"She appeared to be on some sort of mission, Harry," Max audaciously commented.

"What!" I blurted out.

"A mission?" Uncle Harry asked.

"I was shopping. That is always a task."

What was Max trying to do? Get a full confession out of me, right here in front of Uncle Harry!? Or just make me so uncomfortable that I will never do it again!

He continued his investigation. "For a moment I thought you were about to step into King Tut's Cafe for lunch. Have you ever eaten there?"

I eyed him, with some impatience. "Yes, I have."

"Great place."

Uncle Harry asked, "You would have lunched alone?"

I answered Uncle Harry, but still had my eyes on Max. "Of course not," I said truthfully. "But we should go there some time, Uncle Harry. It is a wonderful place to eat."

"Mrs. Bilgas does just fine."

"Mrs. Bilgas?" Max asked.

"Our cook and cleaning lady," I said. "The one whom you can thank for this delicious meal."

"Yes, it is delicious." Then he surprised me by saying, "What a brilliant idea, Harry, to hire someone to do the chores around here so your niece has time to help you out with the more important things."

I suppose I sat gaping at him for a brief moment. Did he really consider what I do important? Did he actually think it more important than tending the house?

"Indeed!" Uncle Harry put in. "The paperwork is at times monstrous."

I said to Max, "I was under the impression that you find it distasteful for women to work outside the home? I believe Miss Corinth said that you see women as weak and defenseless, and that they belong in the home.'"

Max said, "I believe I also said, not entirely. A woman should be home to care for her children and the needs of her family. However, if she happens to be unmarried with no children to care for, I see no reason why she can't use her mind and talents in other areas. Learning should not be selective."

Uncle Harry said, "The world will be in a sad state when women start leaving their children to the constant care of others, so that she can hold down a job outside the home."

"The voice of a prophet," Max said. "Let's hope the world never comes to that."

"Amen!" Uncle then added.

After the meal we sat in the living area, where a sofa and two chairs were placed, Uncle Harry's wooden desk, and several bookshelves that were packed tightly with all sorts of literature. I poured coffee from a carafe while Uncle Harry went for the amulet. Max and I were left alone.

He was seated at one of the high-backed upholstered chairs watching me, as if trying to decide something.

I broke the silence, asking, "Would you like cream and sugar?" I held up his cup of coffee.

"No, thank you. I drink it black."

I handed him the cup. He thanked me, and then I stirred cream and sugar into my own cup.

It was then, before Uncle Harry returned to us, that Max said to me, "Beth, don't go out alone. Even to the market. I'm not concerned about the issues of propriety as much as I am concerned for your safety."

"My safety! The market is hardly a dangerous place."

How could I meet up with Moses if someone accompanied me? But then, he would know that. Was he trying to keep me from meeting up with Moses?

He said, "It's not your common thief that I am worried about."

"Then—what are you worried about?"

"The men behind the tomb robberies," he then told me. "And you are a prime target."

Uncle Harry came into the room. Max said to Uncle, "I hate to bring gloom upon the excavation, Harry, but I was just telling your niece that with the situation of the tomb robberies, she could be in more danger than either of you realize."

Uncle Harry's brow furrowed. "What have you heard?"

"I've not heard anything. But I do know these men will stop at nothing to get what they want, and with Beth being a woman, and having access to the tomb…well, it just naturally makes her an easy victim. Beth is the only other person besides you, Harry, that has access to Smenkhkara's tomb."

Uncle Harry set the square velvet case that contained the amulet onto the desktop. He sighed heavily. "I can't say that I have not given that some thought. These men probably realize that I would willingly exchange Beth's safety for any priceless object that we would ever find within that tomb."

"Uncle Harry," I blurted out, "do you really think they would go as far as that?"

"Men with no convictions never cease to surprise me. Their consciences are seared. Nothing bothers them. Yes, Beth, some men will go to great lengths to acquire wealth and power. We may very well be dealing with such men. I should send you to London with Grace."

"Please don't!" I cried. "Uncle Harry, I'll be very careful, and I won't go anywhere alone again."

Max stepped in, saying, "Perhaps there is another way."

The room became very quiet, and Max now had our full attention.

I asked, "What do you mean by 'another way'?"

Uncle Harry then voiced, "Another way for what?"

Max set his cup down onto an oval coffee table, which sat on top of a very large, white lamb's wool rug in front of the two high-backed chairs. He seemed to be weighing out just what to say—or how best to put it.

Max explained, "If the workers know that Beth has the only duplicate key to unlock the padlock to the gates of the tomb, then you can be certain that those involved in the robberies have the same knowledge. I suggest that you put some other person in charge of Beth's key and make it a known fact."

Uncle Harry thought it over, then blurted out, "Yes, of course! And I know just the person."

"You do?" I asked.

"Well—who else," Uncle Harry said to me, "but Max."

This couldn't be happening!

"Uncle Harry, I don't think this is necessary," I said, trying to sound indifferent. "Why—it would put Dr. Clairborne's life in jeopardy instead of my own. He might not appreciate that."

"I will gladly do it," Max quickly asserted.

"Really," I continued to object. "I don't think this is necessary."

Max wore an amused smile. "Perhaps she doesn't trust me with the key, Harry."

Uncle Harry laughed. "More like she'll be trusting you with her life."

Max looked at me. "I think she knows she can trust me with her life."

He was referring to the bug bite and the time in the tomb when he so gallantly yanked the torch from my hand, exclaiming that foul gases could still be within the adjoining chambers.

Uncle Harry said, "If one can trust another with his or her life, then trust is never in question."

I should be able to trust Max, I thought, confused. *So, why didn't I? It all goes back to the alabaster box. Why did he have it? The man is a paradox!*

"Beth, you go for the key," Uncle Harry said. "Max and I will take a look at that amulet."

I went to my room while Uncle Harry and Max looked over the amulet. The key was stashed in the bottom of my lingerie drawer. I took it out and turned it over in the palm of my hand, thinking: *This could very well be my life, and I'm putting it in Max's hand.*

I clutched it tightly. My heart was telling me to trust him, but my mind was still full of doubt. One thing was certain, if anything in the tomb showed up missing, he would be the first suspect. Yet, he would know that. Was his true reason for doing this for my protection only?

When I returned to them, I was reluctant to give up the key, so I gave it to Uncle Harry, who then handed it over to Max.

"I have a friend who is a journalist for Egypt's *Morning Post*," Max told us. "I'll have him write up a story. That will be the quickest way to get the word out that the key has changed hands."

Uncle Harry gave him a light slap on the shoulder. "I don't know how to thank you for this. My mind is at ease already."

Max smiled. "I'm glad I can help."

It was then that the doorbell rang. I welcomed the distraction. "I'll get it," I told Uncle Harry.

David stood on the doorstep, hands in the pockets of his trousers.

"David!"

"Can we talk?" he asked.

"Not inside," I then whispered. "Dr. Clairborne is here."

He grabbed my arm and pulled me out the door, shutting it behind me. We walked away from the house, so as not to be heard.

"I've been waiting for you," I told him.

"These matters are not always easy," he explained. "This time it took some real effort to get your message into the right hands without being apprehended or carried off to some underground hideout."

I did not have a clue as to what he was talking about. "What did you find out?"

We stopped walking; he turned to face me, serious. "I don't like this, Beth."

"Just tell me."

"Moses wants you to meet with him tonight."

"Tonight!? How am I supposed to do that?"

"This is the part I don't like. Two men will meet you out back tonight. They will then escort you to Moses."

"Oh," I said flatly. "I see what you mean."

"Why not wait, Beth, for a better time. I can get word back to Moses that you prefer speaking to him in public, and during daylight hours."

I thought of the key. "No, I need to talk with Moses as soon as possible. Dr. Clairborne now has the duplicate key to the tomb."

"What!?" David all but shouted.

"It was all so clever how he managed to do it. Yet, David, I am almost convinced he did it for the sole purpose of protecting me."

"Be careful, Beth. Guys like that are professional con artists."

"Yes, I know that there are men capable of deceiving others into believing anything that they want them to. It's just—Oh, I don't know…anyway, I think I should meet with Moses tonight, and get this over with before something happens."

David said nothing for a moment, but looked off into the distance. He sighed heavily before saying, "You know your uncle would disapprove of this."

"It'll be okay. Uncle will never find out."

"All right. But if you are not back by morning, I'm going to tell Harry everything."

I nodded my head in agreement. "That will be fine. Now, exactly what am I supposed to do? Tell me again."

"Your uncle does retire before midnight—I hope."

"Yes, he usually goes to bed around ten-thirty."

"Around midnight, you are to wait for two men, dressed in black, out on your back patio; they will escort you to the hideout. You'll speak to Moses personally, which I have been informed, has never been done before. And when your rendezvous is over, the two men will see you home. You are to wear dark clothing."

"Got it!"

"Are you sure you want to do this tonight?"

"Positive."

"I suppose I won't be able to change your mind?"

"I need to do this, David."

He said nothing, but looked off into the distance.

I laid my hand upon his forearm. "Thanks. Would you like to come inside for awhile?"

"I would love to, but I'm to meet up with an old chap."

"Then I will see you tomorrow."

"Bright and early. I want to make sure you make it home okay."

"I'll be fine, David."

I went back inside. Max and Uncle Harry were once again studying the amulet; they looked up when I entered the room.

Uncle Harry asked, "Everything okay?"

"Yes, of course. It was David. He was passing by and decided to drop in for a few minutes to say hello. He couldn't stay long."

Uncle Harry gave a slight nod. "I see. Pleasant young man."

"More coffee, Dr. Clairborne?" I asked, picking up the carafe by its handle, ready to pour.

"Yes, thank you."

"Uncle Harry?"

"No, I have had enough. Thank you."

I was pouring Max a second cup of coffee, when the doorbell rang, but this time Uncle Harry went to answer it. Again that evening, I was left alone with Max.

Max was sitting on the edge of the wooden desk, looking comfortable. I closed the distance that was between us, and then handed him the cup of coffee.

"How's the wrist?" he asked, taking hold of my good hand before I could distance myself from him.

"Fine," I said. "It's no longer painful. Thanks to you."

We were eye level, and I was close enough that I could see the darker flecks of gray in his eyes. His nearness was disturbing.

"I've enjoyed the evening," he said.

"I was hardly the perfect hostess." I lifted my bandaged wrist, indicating that it was the cause of my imperfection. "And if I did not thank you properly, then I must say, it was very kind of you to not only bandage my arm, but to help serve out the meal."

He gave me one of his charming smiles. I was finding it hard to remember that he was not to be trusted…or so I thought.

Uncle Harry came in and Max let my hand drop.

"Well," Uncle Harry said. "It looks like we'll be back out at the dig by the end of next week."

He waved the telegram that had just been delivered. "It's from the members of the Metropolitan Museum. They are ready to proceed with the opening of the burial chamber."

I bubbled over. "That's great news! I was worried they would drag this out for months."

Max said, "It is apparent that we are not the only ones anxious to see what treasures are behind the sealed wall."

"You will be there, Dr. Clairborne?" I asked.

"Of course. Have you forgotten? I now possess the duplicate key to the tomb."

How could I forget?

Chapter 11

It was eleven o'clock before Uncle Harry finally retired for the night. When the clock struck midnight, I was out on the patio, donned in black and shrouded by the darkness, waiting for the two men that would escort me to the place where I was to rendezvous with Moses.

My hair was still curled and held back by the ornate hair barrette. The black dress I chose to wear had a tight bodice and full skirt made of chiffon, with a cotton-linen underlining of the same color. It was the only black dress I owned that was appropriate for covertness. I also wore a heavy black shawl for warmth; the nights can often be chilly. And, of course, I did not forget to put on my boots.

My escorts appeared five minutes after the hour, and were so darkly clothed from head to toe that they appeared as dark silhouettes against the night. As they neared, all that could be seen was the glistening of their eyes. They did not speak, but motioned for me to follow them. The taller one led the way, the other followed behind me.

All was going as planned.

It was not a short trip. We walked for some distance through the dark and secret alleyways of town. When we came to the edge of the desert, I was placed upon a horse with one of my escorts behind me; his arms came around me in order to hold onto the horse's reins. We traveled away from Cairo to a desert place. I would never remember how I had arrived, nor find my way home if I would need to. I suppose that was the intent.

Upon reaching our destination, they led me to an underground dwelling that was well lit. I was not afraid, for I was certain that Moses had to be a man of good character, for he bore the name of the great patriarch of the Old Testament. However, I was uncertain as to how to explain what I knew about the alabaster box. That Max could possibly be involved in the tomb robberies was still difficult for me to believe, so I had decided earlier to tell Moses only what I had heard and seen. I would not point a condemning finger at anyone—especially at Max.

A long, narrow hallway led us to a room heavily equipped with several desks, chairs, tables, and various office necessities. I did notice against one wall artifacts on top of a long table. I wondered what they were doing there. Perhaps these were items that had been stolen and then retrieved by the underground operation.

One of the escorts entered into an adjoining room; I was left standing with the other. After several minutes had passed, the one came out of the room and motioned for me to enter from whence he had emerged.

I did as instructed, the door closed behind me and my escorts shut out. I was now left alone with a man in the room.

He was sitting on the edge of a desk, dressed in denim pants and sports shirt. His arms were folded across the expanse of his chest, and he was observing me with a sardonic half smile on his lips.

This had to be some sort of joke!

My heart stopped and my throat went dry. For that man was Dr. Maxwell Clairborne!?

He said, almost as if amused by my presence, "Welcome to my abode, Miss Woodruff."

"Dr. Clairborne!?" I said in disbelief.

I scanned the room quickly. He noticed and said, "If you are looking for Moses, I hit him over the head and stuffed him into the closet."

He, of course, was not serious?

He went on, "That is what you were thinking? Is it not, Beth?"

I blinked nervously. "I don't know what to think."

He said nothing, but did look somewhat annoyed. "Then I shall sum it up for you."

A gentleman came into the room. It was the man I had seen at King Tut's Cafe—I was certain of it! The one I had thought to be Moses. Only, this time, he did not look so ancient.

The man said, "Excuse me, I did not realize you were with someone."

"Come on in, James," Max said.

He did and then handed Max a file folder. "The folder you asked for."

Max took it and thanked him. He left the room, leaving Max and me to converse alone.

I asked, "He was at the cafe?"

"Yes, in my place. We have to be careful what we do in public. I wanted to be sure you were not being followed."

"I see." It was all very clear to me now, but I asked anyway, "You are Moses?"

"You find that hard to believe, being the diabolical person that I am."

I bit down on my bottom lip, for that is what I had thought of him. I said quietly, "I have grossly misjudged you."

I wanted to cry. I could feel the tears of shame pooling in my eyes.

He said nothing for a moment, but continued to study me.

I went to him, quickly closing the space between us. I wanted to look into his eyes, to feel his nearness, to mend, somehow, the breach that I had caused in our friendship.

I stood very close to him. "You must loathe me."

He said nothing. I gazed into the depths of his smoke-gray eyes. "I'm so sorry. Can you somehow forgive me? You must believe me when I say that I did not come here to make accusations against you personally."

"Why did you come here?"

"To only tell what I know."

"What you thought you knew, Beth, is that I had stolen the alabaster box. That is why you ran from my apartment. You believed that I was involved with the tomb robberies, and perhaps, that even I was the ringleader behind it all."

"You were involved in the robberies, just not in the way that it appeared. What else was I to think or do?"

"Why could you not just trust me?"

In desperation I grasped his shirtsleeves. "Oh Max, how I wanted to. I was devastated when I saw the alabaster box in your apartment. I didn't want to believe you were capable of such deeds. Yet, the facts were unexplainable. What would you have thought if it was I who had the alabaster box? If it was I who was being so mysterious?"

"I am a better judge of character than to believe that you would commit such acts."

I was growing angry now. "Not all of us are as gifted as you, to so expertly judge another. You should have explained yourself, if you knew that I was thinking such things about you! Why did you not explain?"

The tears came then and I wanted to hit him. I tried to push away, but his arms came around me preventing me from doing so. "You needn't cry, Beth," he said.

"I always cry when I'm angry."

I stepped away from him; this time he let me go. "I'm ready to go home now. Please," I told him curtly.

"You are not going anywhere—yet! I think we still have some issues to discuss."

"I have nothing else to say."

His eyes narrowed my way. "We are going to talk. You don't realize the danger you have placed yourself in. I thought I told you not to meddle."

"I—I had no choice!"

His jaw tensed. "You had no choice?" he repeated angrily. "This could have been solved easily enough had you remained at my apartment and confronted me about your suspicions. No, instead you let your imagination get the better of you, putting your life in danger and everyone else's, for that matter—including David's."

"I did not mean to put anyone's life in danger!" I countered evenly. "Besides, everyone involved in this is in danger no matter what I do. So don't even try to make me feel guilty!"

"I am trying to make you understand the danger," he said, teeth clenched. "I asked you not to get involved."

"I could not keep hidden what I thought I knew. It would have been wrong of me."

"Why did you not go to Harry with this?"

"I was afraid he would ship me to London with Grace. Besides, what have I done that is so dangerous—really? I am not trying to seize the culprits' single-handedly. I came here to talk with Moses so he could take care of doing that!"

"Oh yes, you have come to tell Moses about the dastardly Dr. Clairborne." He spread apart his arms. "Well, here I am. Tell me."

I cringed. I felt the traitor.

The room was growing warm. I removed my shawl and draped it over a chair. I must now eat humble pie. The only way to repair what damage I had caused was to be honest with him by revealing my innermost feelings.

I slowly walked around the room as I spoke. "The first time I met you, I thought that you were an eccentric individual in your dust-covered khakis, appearing the lion tamer with that leather whip you kept coiled and attached to your belt. You seemed mysterious to me and even more so when, on the night that the alabaster box was stolen, I overheard your clandestine meeting outside my tent. I heard bits and pieces of the conversation. I wondered what you were up to then. I did not reveal, at that time, what I had overheard. Everyone seemed to trust you but me. However, the better acquainted we became, the more I realized that you were not the nefarious individual that my mind had first made you out to be. You were kind and caring. How could I not trust you?"

I now glanced his way. He was watching me closely, attentive to what I was saying.

I continued, "You really cared about my well-being and my safety. You helped me to find the pendant that I had lost in the tomb. You were there when the pain of losing Philip was almost more than I could bear. You shared your own feelings over the loss of your wife and child with me. Eventually all the suspicions within my mind, concerning your involvement with the robberies, vanished.

He said nothing, but waited. The room was too quiet. *If only I knew what he was thinking.*

"So," I then went on to say, "your friendship is very important to me. More than you may realize."

I was becoming emotional, the quiver in my voice revealing it to be so. I took a deep breath and then continued, "But when I saw the alabaster box in your apartment, I was devastated. I went home and cried. I thought that my suspicions had been right after all, and that you were involved with the robberies. Perhaps, for some unknown reason, these robberies were, to you, justifiable. For the cause of archeology—or something noble."

I went to him then, so that I could look into his eyes and he into mine. "You must understand one thing. Although my mind was telling me all the facts pointed to you, my heart was telling me otherwise. But I had to talk to someone about it. I could not go to Uncle, and Moses seemed the right person."

He said, "You should have listened to your heart."

"Is it all so bad—really? Here I am talking to you, now. Is that so different?"

"Friendship is based on trust, and you did not trust me."

"Who can truly know the heart and mind of another? The Bible tells us that we don't even know our own."

His eyebrow quirked, for my reply was indeed truth. Who could argue against the Word of God?

"I'm not going to hold this against you," he said. "You had good enough reason to be suspicious of me. I do regret that you did not confide in me sooner.

I gave a sigh of relief. "I can only ask for your forgiveness. I cannot undo my wrong, or the trouble that I have caused. Will you please forgive me?"

"Of course."

I threw my arms around his neck. "Thank you."

He did not respond.

Stepping back, I realized that even though I had been pardoned, I undoubtedly had damaged any future relationship with him. Would he now tell Uncle Harry of my involvement?

He said, "There is one thing I will need to ask of you. It is important that you tell no one that I am Moses…that includes David."

"Yes—of course. But there is also one thing that I need to ask of you in return."

He waited. I fidgeted with the collar of my dress. "Please don't go to Uncle Harry with this."

His response came after much deliberation. I'm not exactly certain what he was weighing out. Perhaps, that I was due Uncle Harry's strong hand of correction.

He looked down at his wristwatch. "It's getting late, I best get you back home."

He was not going to give me an answer! "You're going to tell Uncle Harry!?"

He reached for my shawl, but I snatched it away. Anger took precedence over common sense, and foolishly I said, "I'll see myself home—thank you very much!"

How stupid of me to say such a thing.

He laughed. I glowered.

"I think not," he said. "I intend to personally escort you safely back home."

It was my good fortune that he was not going to let me wallow in my own foolishness. For certain I must learn to tame my tongue, before one day paying for its unruliness. I would have wandered for days—lost. And who knows what lurks in the desert besides brigands. I could easily imagine creatures of all sorts. I remembered the poisonous bite on my leg and gave a shudder. Yes, indeed I was fortunate that I did not, at this time, have to reap the error of my words. But I would not give Max the satisfaction of knowing that I felt thus.

We came out of the underground cavern…or perhaps it was some sort of ancient tomb. Max had donned a black cloak to better conceal him, and had mounted one of the horses. He reached down to help me mount, and once I was securely seated in front of him, he motioned for the larger of the two escorts, who had also mounted a horse, to follow.

Now, knowing the true Maxwell Clairborne, the arms that came around me to hold to the horse's reins were comforting, strong and capable. I easily relaxed against him, all worries vanished, except for the lingering fact that he would tell Uncle Harry what I had done.

Max set the pace. It was not too hurried, I think on my account.

He asked, "Are you doing okay?"

"I'm fine."

We continued on for about half an hour, until Cairo came into view. We dismounted and walked the remaining distance to the back patio of Uncle Harry's home. Max walked me to the door.

"I'll wait until you are safely inside," he said.

"Max," I began, "if you tell Uncle Harry what all has transpired he will most assuredly send me to London. You must realize how I would loathe leaving him and the excavation."

He was not quick to reply, but when he did it came in whispered tones. "Whatever Harry decides, you must remember it is for your good."

"Then you are going to tell him?"

"I think it best."

I tried another tactic. "You will reveal who you are."

"He already knows who Moses is."

"What!? Even he has kept this from me."

He seemed a little agitated. "There was no need to tell you. You must understand the fewer that know who is behind the operation the more successful it will be."

I said nothing, hurt that the two men that I cared deeply for had purposefully kept important information from me.

He must have sensed my feelings and said, "It was for your protection."

No longer able to hold back the deep feelings that even I was unaware of, I blurted out, "Had I known about it all, I would have been spared much heartache."

"Heartache?" he questioned gently. "You must believe me when I say I would not do anything to cause you heartache."

I felt tears coming again and tried to suppress them. "It was just a game to you," I whispered heatedly. "I can see it did not matter that I had grown to care about you. My feelings were of no consequence as long as your—your operation was successful!"

"That's not true."
"Well, you have proven otherwise!"
I turned quickly and unlocked the door. "Good night, Dr. Clairborne."
"Beth—wait," I heard him say before I quietly shut the door between us.

Chapter 12

At Giza port, I stood silently, clutching my small carpetbag, while Uncle Harry, Grace, and the Corinths gaily conversed with one another. Mr. Corinth was saying something about the British Museum's foundation stone of King Edward VII galleries. He was dressed for travel wearing a crisp white linen suit. He looked the wealthy businessman with a stiff white hat atop his head and smoking a Balmoral handmade cigar. Physically he was not heavy, which I think made him appear younger than his actual years. Mrs. Corinth was his complement, being a petite woman, and I would guess a good ten years younger than her husband. She wore her dark brown hair up Gibson girl style. Their daughter Helen was the perfect result of their union. She stood by them, her black hair in a neat French twist, and her navy suit emanating her social status.

I was in no mood to listen to their idle chatter. The wide-brimmed hat I wore was useful for shadowing my disinterest. It was impossible for me to pretend that I was happy about leaving Cairo. Matter of fact, I was sick at heart.

I had begged and pleaded with Uncle Harry not to send me away. He and Max had spent hours conversing over what best to do with me—my opinion mattered little. Uncle Harry had almost convinced Max that he could keep me safe enough until one of the workers was found dead. His decision then came quickly: "It's best that you leave until all of this blows over," he had explained, "then I will send for you."

"It could be a year before that happens, if not longer," I had pointed out. But he would not relent. He had decided I must travel with Grace and the

Corinths to London.

So, I am neatly packed and ready to sail away—or more like sail out of the way, I thought with much reluctance. Of course Grace was thrilled that I would be staying with her. She had many plans for us, and I was sure that I would enjoy my visit. Yet, I knew that I would undoubtedly long for Cairo, and my mind would constantly be wondering what all was transpiring at the dig. I would also worry about Uncle Harry's safety. He, too, would be in danger until the persons behind the robberies were apprehended.

I gazed off into the distance and saw Maxwell Clairborne coming toward us!

How could I escape him?

I did not want to talk with him. I was angry that he had told Uncle Harry about all that had transpired, and even though he had presented it inoffensively, I was still brooding over the fact that he had mentioned it at all.

I looked about and noticed a refreshment stand not far off. A group of people had just disembarked and gathered there. I could momentarily lose myself in the crowd until time for us to board ship.

I glanced down at the pendant watch, the one that Philip had given to me; it was attached to my white French-pleated shirtwaist. We had thirty minutes before departure time.

"I'm going for something cool to drink," I whispered into Uncle Harry's ear.

He gave a nod of his head and I was off.

I stood in line with the others, trying to hide myself in the crowd. After five minutes had transpired I was the next one up at the counter.

"A lemonade please," I told the young man.

While he was preparing my drink, I dug into my purse for the necessary coins. I handed him the coins and he gave me the drink. I turned, bumping unceremoniously into Max.

"There's a bench under the shade tree," he said. "Why don't we have a seat there."

"I really haven't the time," I remarked coolly.

"Ah—but you do," he then informed me. "We were told by one of the porters that there's a forty-minute delay. You really didn't think you could hide from me, did you? Perhaps you could have done so without the hat. Nice hat, but you stick out like a beacon."

I looked around. Indeed, amongst the foreigners, donned in their native attire, I looked the English tourist. I said nothing as he took me by the arm and led me to the bench.

He was the first to say, "You're still angry with me."

I sipped on the lemonade.

He continued, "I was hoping we could part on good terms."

Uncertain as what to say, I continued to sip the lemonade, feigning interest in a group of children playing tag.

He brought his face closer to mine, forcing me to look into his eyes, and he said again, "I was hoping we could part on good terms."

"What do you consider 'good terms'?"

He straightened in his seat. "Well, a friendly goodbye would be nice. I know that you're upset that I told your uncle about your involvement, but you must understand it was necessary. There are lives at stake here and yours was one of them."

"I don't see as to where I was in any present danger."

"And you don't know the half of what has been going on."

"Perhaps not."

He tried to console me by saying, "You'll be back soon enough."

"That is easy for you to say. I am not looking forward to leaving. I shall worry myself sick wondering if Uncle Harry is okay. You can't possibly think that I'm going to enjoy this?"

For a brief moment he looked away, then his eyes came back to rest upon me. "No, of course not. But you don't know what a relief this is for Harry that you will be safely distanced from the danger." He waited a moment then added, "And it is a great relief for me too."

What was he trying to say? That his concern went deeper than that of a friend?

The smoke-gray eyes that were deeply probing into mine caused my heart to speed up.

I looked away, not wanting to read more into what he said than what was meant. "I appreciate your concern. Truly, I do."

"Well—I would say that's a step in the right direction. Then I am no longer considered the ogre?"

I smiled. "I didn't say that you were an ogre."

"You didn't have to. I could see it in your expression."

My smile deepened. "I was very angry with you."

"The fiery daggers that shot out of those beautiful eyes of yours left me wounded for days."

I laughed and then said with a certain amount of sarcasm, "I'm sure you lost an infinite amount of sleep over it."

"Actually, I did lie awake wondering if you would ever speak to me again."

"For how long? Five minutes?"

He grinned.

"That's what I thought."

"I don't want you to leave Cairo and travel thousands of miles from here still angry with me. Can we call it a truce?"

I thought of Philip. I had said goodbye not knowing it would be a lasting goodbye. So much could happen, and both Uncle Harry and Max's lives would be in perilous situations. Life, I knew, was too fragile to let anger and bitterness consume one's heart. I would never forgive myself if I left them both in such a state and something horrible happened to one of them. Yet, I did not want to give in so easily to Max's charms. I would not be leaving Cairo if he had kept quiet about what I had done.

"It's not fair, you know," I said.

He looked puzzled. "What's not fair?"

"You and Uncle Harry are sending me safely away, but I will worry incessantly about you both."

He seemed unduly delighted. "Then you wouldn't rather see me dead."

I frowned in disgust. "Where do you come up with such thoughts? Honestly, you would think that I have been sending you hate mail or something."

He laughed clamorously. "Or something is right. Like I said, if looks could kill."

"What nonsense!"

He took my hand. "Then is it a truce?"

"Yes, of course."

He smiled, showing perfectly white teeth against a handsomely tanned face. He was looking too pleased.

"I'm not happy about this, you know," I said, wanting to make sure that he clearly understood my feelings of irritation. "And just because we have called it a truce does not mean that I'm okay with your telling my uncle about all that I had done."

"Honestly, Beth, you make me sound like a snitch. It was not just a matter of letting Harry know how you managed to get involved. But whether you realize it or not it placed you in danger."

"So you have said. And just what are you and Uncle Harry about!? Why is it okay for you two to get involved and I must be sent away?"

"Must we go over this again? It is because we are dealing with dangerous men here, and no woman need be involved."

"I see. Gender roles?"

"Don't tell me you're a suffragette?"

"There are some issues concerning women's rights that I agree with."

"Such as?"

"Well—" I hesitated, "that she should be able to make her own decisions, for one."

He seemed amused. "Yes, indeed! And that, of course, is the issue: that you should be able to make your own decision on whether you go or stay."

"And what is so wrong with that?"

"Nothing, if that decision is the right one."

Under my "beacon" of a hat, my hazel-green eyes narrowed at him. He certainly could be domineering. "Oh, I see. A woman has a right to her own decision as long as that decision does not interfere with that of her husband, or father, or brother, or the male species in general. That is truly giving her the right to choose, Dr. Clairborne," I remarked with a certain amount of annoyance.

"I don't entirely see it that way. Truly, you do see me as an ogre. I would never rule with an iron hand over my wife. Have you never heard of compromise? It's not such a bad thing. Decisions between a husband and wife should be agreed upon. However, there are some things that a man must do in order to protect those he loves. Harry did not make this decision lightly, nor did he make it to show his authority. It was made to keep you safe. That is not so hard to understand."

I gave a heavy sigh and looked away. I knew that what he said was right. I just did not want to give him the satisfaction of knowing that I agreed with him.

Pride is a bad thing. It comes before a fall—I think. And I may fall pretty hard if I allow pride and stubbornness to rule over what is right.

I finally made myself say, "No, it is not hard to understand. What you say is true."

"That's more like it."

"Don't be too brassy. You don't know how difficult it was for me to say that."

"Oh—I think I do."

I could see Uncle Harry waving at us from where we sat. I waved back to him.

"Obviously," I said, standing, "we must be getting ready to board. Uncle

Harry is signaling for us to join them."

We returned to the small group, and goodbyes were made. My farewell to Uncle Harry was brief, lest I break down and cry. Uncle Harry, I think, was on the verge of tears as well. He told Grace to take good care of me. She assured him that she would.

Helen kissed Max on the cheek, and with a silky voice, said, "Goodbye, darling. It was such fun to see you again. Do come and visit us like old times."

Like old times, I thought. *Just how involved were they? And did it really matter?*

After Helen released him and he glanced my way, I smiled as if amused by her unreserved show of affection. Having not yet said goodbye to him, I put out my hand, and as if he were just a mere acquaintance, I said, "Goodbye, Dr. Clairborne, and what a great pleasure to have met you."

He gave my hand a punishing squeeze, and his eyes sparked with dangerous humor. "The pleasure was all mine, Miss Woodruff. How dull Cairo will be without you."

I knew to what he was referring. He was thinking that he would have less to do now that he would not have to keep a watchful eye on me. So, I wittingly countered with, "You are a man of unlimited resources, Dr. Clairborne. I'm sure my absence will not even be noticed."

It was then that David appeared.

"Sorry I'm late," he apologized. "Something unexpected came up."

"We are getting ready to board," I told him.

"I was worried I wouldn't get to see you off," David said. "You will write?"

"Of course," I told him.

He gave me a farewell hug. I turned to Uncle Harry. "Do take care of yourself, Uncle Harry."

Holding to my bag, I walked away before they could see the tears that came.

We stood at the ship's rail until Uncle Harry, Max, and David were no longer visible. I think Grace sensed my despair, so she said, "Come along, dear, let's go to the cabin and put our things away, then we'll go and find a nice spot on deck to sit and have some refreshments."

Mr. Corinth then said, "Please join us for lunch."

Mrs. Corinth added, "Oh—yes, please do."

"We would love to," Grace told them.

We left them with plans to meet in the dining area at noon. I followed Grace down the red-carpeted corridor which led us to a cabin equipped with twin beds, two night stands, a bathroom, and a closet in which to hang our garments. Though cramped, the room had its comforts. We put our things away and then went up on deck as she had suggested.

Once we settled ourselves on lounge chairs, I asked Grace, "Will you be glad to finally be home again? I thought perhaps you were planning to make Cairo your permanent place of residence."

"Oh, I could never do that. England will always be home. How I have missed it. My last sea voyage was devastating. A living nightmare, you could say. I suppose that is why I have not traveled home up till now. When I heard that Harry was sending you off, I suggested that you travel with me." She reached over and gave my hand a pat. "I know you don't want to leave Cairo, but you will never know just how much it means to me to have you for a traveling companion. I hope that somehow I can make it up to you."

My heart went out to her. It had not even crossed my mind that she would fear traveling by sea again. "Oh Grace, I have been so inconsiderate. I had not even given it any thought as to how you must feel about getting on ship again. It must be frightening."

She smiled. "At the moment I don't feel any panic, but when the sun goes down, things might seem a little different."

"Grace, if I would have known sooner…"

"I could never have taken you away from the excavation. Away from the excitement and the thrill of what is happening there."

I gave a moan.

"I have reminded you of what you will miss. I'm sorry."

"No—really, it's quite all right. I would have traveled home with you, regardless of my desire to stay, had I known you did not want to get on ship alone."

"Yes, I know you would have made the sacrifice. You have a good heart."

"Do you think so?"

She laughed. "Someone has told you otherwise?"

"Well, not exactly. It's Dr. Clairborne. I somehow manage to think wrong where he is concerned. I have a habit of misjudging him. Or he makes me so mad I have to repent over the anger I feel."

Both of her eyebrows rose. "Oh, I see. Tell me, which young man has your heart fallen for? The one you promised to write, or the one you said a cool farewell to?"

Her question took me by surprise, and I felt myself grow warm. "I don't believe either. David is like a sweet older brother. He watches out for me—that sort of thing. But Dr. Clairborne, I do believe he sees me as a nuisance."

"I doubt anyone would see you as a nuisance."

"Oh—Grace, I could tell you how I have managed to be a constant problem for Dr. Clairborne. Of course, I never intended to be."

"Harry has told me some of what has been going on. We met for lunch one day. The day after he had decided to send you away. He really was very heartbroken that he had to make that decision."

"Yes, I know. But Dr. Clairborne is certainly relieved."

"I think he too cares about your safety."

I said, with obvious austerity, "He feels it his duty to make certain that I am out of the way. He told me not to meddle and I had managed to do so. Not because I wanted to. It just happened."

"I'm sure Harry and Dr. Clairborne are doing what they feel is best for you. I'm not blind, and the years have given me some insight. I would venture to say that Dr. Clairborne has his eye on you. Could there be more to your relationship than you are willing to admit?"

I gave her question considerable thought. I knew that with Grace I could be open. "Perhaps, at one time we were slightly attracted to one another, but I managed to put a quick end to it."

"You did?"

"Yes."

"There is someone else?"

Poor Grace, she believed I could not exist without a romantic tie.

"No," I said slowly. "There is no one else."

"But Dr. Clairborne is a wonderful man. What happened?"

I smiled. She so wanted to be the matchmaker.

"I believed him capable of being behind the tomb robberies." I turned to her sad eyed. "Oh Grace, when he found out that I had such thoughts about him, it hurt him so deeply. Although he may have forgiven me for thinking thus, I feel it permanently damaged any future relationship I could have had with him."

"Did you want to pursue a relationship?"

I gave a shrug. "I really can't answer that. I still miss Philip terribly. I'm not ready for a romantic relationship with anyone at the moment."

"But why do you suppose Dr. Clairborne bothered to seek you out before you departed?"

"So we could part on 'good terms,' is how he put it."

"He did not have to come and see you off—you know. Nor did he have to seek you out so you could part on 'good terms.' Don't give up so easily if he wishes to nurture a relationship with you. You might live to regret it."

I looked off into the distance.

"As they say," she went on to explain, "time has a way of healing."

Standing not far off, I noticed Helen with a gentleman. "Look," I said to Grace, "Helen has already managed to find a means of entertainment to help her time aboard go by faster."

Grace smiled. "She does manage to attract the gentlemen."

"She is rather lovely."

"Outwardly…yes."

"Do you know her very well?"

Grace sipped on her tea before answering. "Not well, I suppose, but the inner circle keeps me informed about what goes on in the lives of the influential."

"Her relationship with Dr. Clairborne, was it a serious one?"

Grace tilted her head. "They were seeing one another—often."

"What happened?" I wanted to know.

"I heard that Dr. Clairborne stopped seeing her because of their strong differences in religion. Evidently, she does not believe in God."

I was flabbergasted. "How can one not believe in God!? He is infallible."

"Hard to believe, I agree."

"I did not realize that Max had such strong convictions."

Grace said, "I believe Dr. Clairborne is a man that lives his life in accordance with the Word of God. He is strong enough to stand for what he believes in no matter what he may have to give up or face in order to do so."

I was fast learning that to be true about him.

Grace and I spent the morning hours on deck until it was time to meet the Corinths for lunch.

As we were being seated to take our noon meal, Mr. Corinth told us, "Helen has asked that she be excused from joining us. She has been invited to dine with a friend. She did not have the heart to turn him down, as he is traveling alone."

Evidently she had hit it off quite well with her new gentleman friend. They were seated together at a corner table, engrossed in conversation.

"That is very considerate of your daughter," Grace politely told Mr. Corinth.

Mrs. Corinth said, "I believe it is the gentleman to whom we must give the credit for being considerate. Poor Helen was bored to distraction until Mr. Rogers came along."

"Do you know him?" Grace asked.

"Just," said Mr. Corinth. "He is a financier."

I was not sure just what labeled a man a financier. It had to be something impressive, I'm sure, or Mr. Corinth would not be looking so pleased that Mr. Rogers had chosen his daughter to share lunch with. *Amazing,* I thought, amused. *How men, upon being newly acquainted, immediately inquire of the other's business affairs. I suppose to a man that is of utmost importance: one's social status in life. And to a father, he wants to make certain that the man his daughter marries will be able to take on the financial responsibility of a family.*

I said, "Hopefully, time will go by quickly for us all. I know I am wishing it for myself. Can't say that I am much of a sailor."

Mrs. Corinth asked, "Do you get ill?"

"Only when the waters are rough."

"We'll trust that doesn't happen," Mr. Corinth added.

Grace said nothing. I sensed that she was once again remembering the smooth seas aboard the *Titanic* when it hit the iceberg. Whoever would have thought that on a tranquil night a ship would sink?

I tried changing the subject by asking, "Mr. Corinth, are you often at the museum?"

Mrs. Corinth gave a diminutive laugh, and then answered for her husband. "Goodness—no!" She laid a well-manicured hand upon Mr. Corinth's arm. "My husband would suffocate if they kept him confined within the museum."

He clarified the question. "I do a lot of traveling."

"Yes, of course," I said, remembering that he had taken the time to travel across the seas to Egypt. "It must make your job very interesting to be able to do so."

"Indeed," he agreed.

Grace said, "And one of the advantages of being the wife is, you get to travel along."

Mrs. Corinth smiled. "It has made life very interesting. I did not do any traveling until I married Nathaniel."

"You have been to the museum, Miss Woodruff?" Mr. Corinth asked.

"As a child, Uncle Harry took me."

"You will have to tour it during your visit."

"I will definitely do that."

Mr. Corinth went on to inform me, "The British Museum's international standing and its key role in displaying the world's and nation's heritage makes it one of the most visited public buildings in London."

"He's very proud of it, as you can see," Mrs. Corinth told us. "He is partly responsible for much of its newly acquired arts and antiquities and now to add Egyptian artifacts to the collection. He will be knighted for his achievement by the queen herself."

"To preserve history is reward enough," he stated modestly.

"Uncle Harry would agree," I told him.

Mr. Corinth said, "Harry Woodruff is a brilliant man. The excitement he must have felt when the realization came that he had discovered the tomb of Smenkhara. It must have been quite thrilling for you both. The historical value alone is astronomical."

"Something every archeologist dreams of," Grace put in.

"It's a pity," he then went on to say, "that such artifacts are to be shared with the Cairo Museum. If I understand Harry correctly, the critical issue is the division of the spoils."

I said, "Well, it is at times a matter of dispute. The Antiquities Service usually picks the finer treasures to remain as property of the state."

Mrs. Corinth commented, "Oh, that is a shame for such beautiful things to be housed up in a place where not many people can view these amazing finds."

"I have given it some thought," I told them both. "How would we feel if foreigners came to our country and uncovered treasures that belonged to our ancestors? I daresay we would not want them to be carried away."

"Indeed," Mr. Corinth burst out. "However, we appreciate and value what has been left by our predecessors.

Grace said, "Men will always seek for treasures to bring them wealth. Our past can prove that to be true. If I remember my history correctly, thanks to Queen Elizabeth and her royal buccaneers, our country was once labeled a nation of pirates."

Mr. Corinth remarked, "Yes, but for a good cause. Take any country's wealth and you take her power. Spain needed to be defeated, and confiscating her gold and ships aided us greatly."

"Most certainly it did," Grace added. "Thank God for bold men that defied Spain's launch against England. Who knows what would have become of our country had they not."

As we ate our meal, Mr. Corinth continued to discuss the treasures of the tomb. He worried that the Antiquities Services would choose the more significant findings to remain as property of the state. I assured him that Uncle Harry would do his best to acquire some very fine pieces for the British Museum. This did not seem to ease his mind, for he continued to fret over the matter.

After lunch Grace and I decided to go to our cabin for a rest. We both enjoyed reading, so we spent several hours engrossed in our novels. The motion of the ship soon put us to sleep, we napped for another hour, then rose and freshened ourselves before going back up on deck to lounge or play shuffle board. Our afternoons, for the entirety of our journey, were spent in this way.

We took our evening meals with the Corinths, and Mr. Rogers became a familiar figure with us.

Once, when Helen had taken ill, and the others had retired for the evening, including Grace, I went up on deck to get some fresh air. I was leaning on the rail, thinking how marvelous God's handiwork really was. I gazed up at the stars, the moon, and then looked down at the dark waters. I suddenly thought of Philip being swallowed into such depths. Where was his body now?

I could only imagine horrible things, so I shut my eyes against it. This was the state I was in when Mr. Rogers found me.

"Are you okay?" he asked, concerned.

Tears had already formed, but I managed to hold them back. "Mr. Rogers!" I said, a little startled.

"Something has upset you?" he then inquired.

I could not deny it. "Yes, a memory."

He too leaned on the ship's rail, his hands clasped in front of him. "I'm a good listener. If you would like to talk about it."

I did not feel compelled to pour out my heart, but I did give him a reason. "We had friends aboard the *Titanic*."

"Yes, Helen told me about your friend. I'm sorry for your loss. It was a great tragedy."

"A horrible tragedy."

"One that will not be forgotten."

"No, Mr. Rogers, not even time will be able to erase it."

After a moment he said, "May time serve to ease your pain, Miss Woodruff. You have my heartfelt condolences."

"Thank you, Mr. Rogers."

He changed the subject by asking, "Helen says you have a very interesting career. Have I heard correctly...you are an archeologist?"

I gave a laugh. "I do suppose you could say that is my line of work, but I owe it all to my uncle. If it were not for him, I daresay our present society would not have made it possible for me to choose such a career."

"Times are changing. I think women should be given certain rights."

I smiled and quirked an eyebrow to his liberal viewpoint. "Then you are part of the select few. Most men prefer to keep their wives at home."

"But there is a time for everything—is there not? And you, Miss Woodruff, may wish to remain at home with your children rather than work."

"You are probably right. When I marry and have children, then the time will come to remain home and care for them. I would not want it any other way."

"Ah—you see then; there can be a happy medium. A balance, you could say, to this social dispute over whether women should remain at home or pursue careers."

"Not everyone sees it so neatly, I'm afraid."

"No," he laughed. "The human race prefers to make life complicated."

I smiled and looked toward the sea. After a few moments passed I asked, "Mr. Corinth says that you are a financier. What brings you to Egypt?"

He did not answer immediately and I thought perhaps I was meddling a bit too much into his private affairs.

He pulled out a cigar from inside his tan suit coat, lit it, and then leaned an elbow on the ship's rail, all the while not taking his eyes off me. They were shrewd eyes—a vibrant blue like the sky on a clear, cool day. His slender, but not too long nose gave him a debonair look, and his round chin softened the lines of his face. He was tall, but not as tall as Maxwell Clairborne's six foot two. Etiquette compelled me to say, "I apologize for being too forward, Mr. Rogers."

He inhaled deeply on the cigar and then released the smoke. "There is no need to apologize. I find it interesting that you would ask."

"And why is that?"

"Business matters usually bore women. But you are not like other women—are you, Miss Woodruff?"

"I am myself. Perhaps my social graces are not always intact."

"There is nothing wrong with your 'social graces,' and I find your inquisitiveness stimulating."

"If that is a compliment—then thank you."

He went on to say, "Egypt is a marvelous place. I believe it was Herodotus that said, 'Concerning Egypt itself I shall extend my remarks to a great length, because there is no country that possesses so many wonders, nor any that has such a number of works that defy description.' So you see, although I am here on business, personal time was also spent to see the marvels of Egypt."

"I gather you know something of Egypt's history."

"It is not wise to do business in a foreign country and not know something of their culture."

"That is true. You do a lot of foreign travel?"

"When the opportunity arises. My business takes me to many different places. I believe it was the American President Roosevelt that thought it necessary to balance the interest of powers that could challenge or curb U.S. influence. Business is not so different from political affairs. It is better to have a balance of interest where money is concerned. To invest into one financial power is not wise."

"Well—you would better know that than I."

He laughed. "And you would better know a genuine artifact from a fake. I could easily be fooled. Tell me, what do you think of this?"

He pulled out from his suit pocket a small scarab crafted with gold and jewels. It was exquisitely made and worth more money than Uncle Harry or I could acquire in our lifetime.

I asked frankly and quite amazed, "Where did you get this?"

"From an old man selling souvenirs."

"Please—may I have a closer look?"

He handed it to me and said, "I can tell you I paid its worth in gold and precious stones. That I knew to be genuine."

I continued to study the piece, and I was certain of its authenticity. It looked to be from the nineteenth dynasty. I realized the scarab should not have left Egypt without first going through the Antiquities Services, who then would have confiscated it. The only way Mr. Rogers could have acquired it was through the black market.

I then inquired, "You say you purchased this from an old man?"

"Yes, a peddler of sorts."

"At market? Did he have a booth?"

"No, he approached me somewhat covertly in the hotel lobby. I was reading a paper when he asked me if I would like a souvenir. He showed me several items. Most of it junk. This piece he pulled out of a pocket from inside his tattered jacket. It was wrapped in a very fine cloth, whereas the other pieces were all from one bag."

"Mr. Rogers," I began slowly, not certain how to tell him he had been innocently involved in an illegal transaction.

He sensed my hesitancy. "What is it?"

"This is no fake."

I gave the scarab back to him. He held it in the palm of his open hand, as if studying the piece for the first time. "You really think so?"

"I'm certain of it."

His eyes came to mine. "And—that is not good?"

"The Antiquities Service would not think so."

"Hmm—I see. I would be arrested for smuggling."

"And questioned. I'm afraid your visit would have ended in a most unpleasant way."

"What would you suggest that I do?"

"Keep it in your pocket and show no one else."

"Should I not turn it over to the authorities?"

"Presently, not even they can be trusted. Best to keep it and say nothing. I venture to say you did pay handsomely for it. If you turned it over to the authorities you would not receive a penny of your money back."

"I see what you mean. Well then, I shall take your advice."

With that much said, he put it back into his suit pocket and then inquired of me, "I heard that there are agents trying to put an end to those involved in the tomb robberies. Would you know how to get a hold of one of them? The least I could do is inform them of what all transpired at the hotel with the old peddler. If they want the piece back then perhaps the Antiquities Service Department would be willing to reimburse me for it."

"That's possible."

"I would not want to lie awake at night feeling like I had acquired the piece through deception. If you know what I mean."

"That is very noble of you, Mr. Rogers. I do understand. What I can do is inform my Uncle Harry of what happened. He can get word to the Antiquities Department and we can let them handle it from there."

"I would detest bothering your uncle, he is a very busy man. Are you sure there is no one you know that I could get a hold of personally? An agent or someone that works with the underground operation?"

I did not have the liberty to divulge any information about what I knew concerning Max and the underground operation. No matter how innocent Mr. Rogers was in this situation, I had promised Max I would tell no one. So, I went on to explain, "It will be no problem for Uncle Harry to give you advice on exactly how to handle this, nor to talk with the Antiquities Department. Matter of fact, he will be thrilled that you have some information to give them concerning these thefts. Every piece of information will help them uncover who is behind all this. I will tell Uncle Harry to not give your name in case their offer to buy it back is not acceptable with you. I would not want you to be harassed in any way."

He smiled. "That sounds splendid. You are quite the businesswoman, Miss Woodruff. If you are sure it is not too much trouble for your uncle, then I will greatly appreciate his assistance."

"Uncle Harry will be glad to help."

He gave me a card on which was written his name and address. "You can reach me there or leave a message with the housekeeper."

"Yes, I will do that. And Mr. Rogers, thank you so much for being open with me. This information may tremendously help those involved in solving these crimes."

"I certainly hope so."

Politely, he offered, "It is getting late, let me see you to your cabin."

There we said good night.

How clever Helen was after all, to catch such a fine man like the admirable Mr. Rogers.

Chapter 13

Grace's home was splendid, nestled away on the English countryside. It was quite a setting: meadows sprinkled with wildflowers and poppies nodding in the breeze. On one side of the home, deep green ivy grew on the stonewall Tudor. Grace told me that it was a home well managed by a butler, a housekeeper, a gardener and several maids…all of whom, with her children and grandchildren, stood at the front entrance to welcome us.

We arrived directly in front of this fine gathering. Jonathan, Grace's youngest son, brought the automobile to a halt. He leapt from the car and ran around it to assist us. "Well, here we are, ladies," he said as he opened the automobile door for us.

Jonathan was a handsome man, I would say near the age of twenty-eight. He was tall, lean, and his hair the shade of maple. He had a bubbly sort of personality and I imagined that he could never sit still.

The children ran to us first, and because I was so near Grace, I too became a part of their cocoon. They shared hugs and kisses, and then Grace told them to stand still so she could properly introduce us.

"This is Martin," she said, holding a fine-looking ten-year-old boy by his shoulders. "Adeline," she said pointing to a freckle-faced little girl about age seven. "Victoria is standing next to Adeline." Victoria's perfect features brightened at the mention of her name. She looked to be about eight or nine, and her hair was almost raven-black. Grace continued on, "The twins, Mary and Margaret."

The twins were five-year-old girls dressed alike in daisy-yellow pinafores. Neat golden braids fell across their shoulders and were tied off with yellow ribbon to match their dresses.

Grace informed them, "This is my very dear friend Elizabeth Woodruff. You must treat her very kindly, as she is to stay with us for some time."

Victoria spoke out softly, "Can she be our friend too?"

I said brightly, "Well, of course you can." I then took hold of her hand to prove it to be so.

I was then introduced to Mary and Martha's parents: Jonathan, I had already met. He introduced me to his wife Vanessa. She was a petite woman with auburn hair. She had a round face in which were set lovely golden-brown eyes.

Grace's daughter Christine was the exact image of a younger Grace. She was enchanting, tall and slender. A very heavy golden braid crowned her head, and her eyes were hazel-green, similar to my own. Her husband, Andrew, stood next to her tall and straight. They were not much older than thirty. Adeline was their one and only, but if my calculations were correct, there would be a new addition to the family within four to five months.

Martin and Victoria belonged to Grace's eldest son James and his wife Catherine. James reminded me of his father, Professor Hubert, who was of average height and stocky build. When Grace introduced us, he expressed his gratitude that I had been his mother's traveling companion.

Victoria inherited her perfect features and raven-black hair from her mother Catherine. She smiled warmly and wished my stay a pleasant one.

I was introduced to the servants: the butler and housekeeper, Mr. and Mrs. Simms; the maids, Jane and Liza; and the gardener, Mr. Smithy. Each gave us a very warm welcome.

We went into the house, the children running and leaping ahead of us, no doubt excited that their grand-mama was home. She had also informed them that she had gifts for each of them, and once we were settled into the parlor she would distribute them accordingly.

The parlor was a charming room with an Aubusson rug with big white lilies and neo-classical furnishings of muted hues.

We sat comfortably while Liza brought in an Ascot-shaped chintz teapot and teacups patterned with roses, daffodils, tulips and wisteria—a sunny and fresh combination fitting the jubilant mood of both spring and summer.

Liza poured the tea, I took mine with cream and sugar, and then she said to Grace, "The children were beside themselves this morning—they were. Excited that their grand-mama was coming home. Can't say that we weren't all a bit that way. The house will be alive again now that its mistress is home."

Grace said, "It is good to be home, Liza."

I could see that Liza was a warm-hearted girl and probably not much older than myself. She donned the customary maid's white apron over a modest black dress. A little white cap sat atop her reddish hair that was pulled back neatly and twisted at the nap of her neck. There was not a timid bone in her body. She continued talking until all had their tea served, and then she dismissed herself. Jane, on the other hand, appeared shy. She brought in the gift bags Grace had asked for without saying so much as a peep.

James was the first to speak: "Mother, what do you plan to do? We thought perhaps you would like to move in with Catherine and me."

Victoria added eagerly, "Oh yes, Grand-mama, you could!"

Grace said to her granddaughter, "That would be fun, but Grand-mama loves her home." She then focused her attention back to James. "I do appreciate your offer, James, you know that, but I couldn't possibly leave my home."

James said, "We hate the thought of you being here alone, and when Miss Woodruff leaves—"

"Alone?" Grace quickly interrupted. "Why, James, I have Mr. And Mrs. Simms and Jane and Liza. I will hardly ever be alone."

Catherine added, "You know that you are welcome anytime."

Grace said, "Of course, dear."

Jonathan went on to say, "Mother, you will let us know if you need anything? We do know how you love your independence."

"If something needs to be done, I will not hesitate to let you know."

They seemed satisfied with what she said and did not question her desire to remain at home. Grace was far from being an invalid. I do believe she had more spunk than even I could muster.

Grace gave each of the children their gifts from Egypt. Their eyes lit up at the sight of these treasured items from such a faraway land. The girls were given a necklace and matching bracelet, and Martin a replica of the jeweled scarab similar to the one Mr. Rogers had, but of course, it was not made with genuine jewels.

When tea and visiting time with Grace's family came to an end, Jane showed me to the room that I would occupy during my stay.

The bed dominated the room, its four posts draped with heavy floral-designed fabric. Pillows of different shapes and sizes nearly hid the wooden ornate headboard. Feeling the effects of travel, it looked inviting. Perhaps later, a nap would be rejuvenating.

Jane asked, "Would you like for me to unpack your bags and put your things away, miss?"

"Thank you, Jane, but that's not necessary. Unpacking will give me something to do."

She left the room leaving the door open. I placed my luggage on the bed, opened them, and began to put my clothes into the empty armoire. It was then that I noticed the children standing at the door watching me.

I said, as I continued putting my things away, "You may come in."

Martin said, "We are not to bother you."

I said, "I see. Did you come to bother me?"

He said, "No."

"Then you may come in."

Before replying, he thought this bit of logic over. "I suppose that makes it all right."

"I don't see why not," I assured him.

He walked into the room, the girls following slowly behind him.

He was quick to ease his curious mind by asking, "Father says you work with your uncle and that he is an archeologist."

"That's right," I said, still folding my clothes to put away.

"Are you an archeologist?" he then inquired.

"Well—that is what I do."

"Girls are not supposed to be archeologists."

I was amused. "Oh—I can see that you are worldly-wise."

This saying, unknown to him, caused his brow to furrow. "I don't know much about the world. I'm learning though. Did you know that the earth is millions of years old?"

"It is not!" I told him. "Scientists that don't believe in God profess such things."

"Do you believe in God?"

"Yes, I do."

"If He is real, why can't we see Him?"

He was full of questions.

I said, "At one time people did see Him."

His blue eyes widened. "I didn't know that!"

"You can read it for yourself if you like. Do you have a Bible?"

"Not one of my own. But mother has one that she would lend to me."

I picked up my Bible, which lay next to my luggage. "Come here, I will show you."

They gathered around me as I opened my Bible to St. Matthew chapter one, verse twenty-three. I read it aloud: "'Behold, a virgin shall be with child, and shall bring forth a Son, and they shall call His name Emmanuel, which being interpreted is, God with us.'" I then clarified for them: "Emmanuel and Jesus are the same. He robed himself in flesh, thus becoming the son of God, and came to earth to be with man."

Victoria asked, "Why does He have two names?

"God has many different characters. He is a healer, a deliverer, a teacher, a prophet. Isaiah said His name shall be called Wonderful, Counselor, Mighty God, Prince of Peace, and Everlasting Father."

Adeline added, "Kings have long names."

She was very cute, standing in her lavender frock, her black hair pulled up into a ponytail with a huge white ribbon tied in a bow.

I agreed, "Yes, they do. The Bible also tells us that Jesus is the King of kings and Lord of lords."

Adeline's blue eyes grew larger. "Then He must have a really big name."

"His name is a name above all names."

"I'm glad I don't have to spell it," said Mary—or was it Margaret, I had yet to know which.

Martin informed me, "They are just learning how to spell their names."

"Oh, I see."

The same said, "My name is easier to spell."

I took a deductive guess: "Then you must be Mary?"

She bobbed her head happily. "Mama says my eyes are hazel and Margaret's are brown."

I looked closer at the two, and sure enough, Mary's eyes were hazel. "Thank you, Mary, now I shall be able to tell you two apart."

Happy to have aided me, she smiled brightly.

"You children were told not to bother Miss Woodruff," came Liza's authoritative voice at the threshold. She waved her hand at them as if shooing a fly. "Now off with ye!"

They hung their heads and slowly made their way out.

To cheer them, I said, "I tell you what, after I have had a short nap, would you children be so kind as to show me around your grand-mama's place?"

Victoria said, "You'll like the garden."

"I'm sure I shall."

So, after my nap, as planned, all five children eagerly showed me the grounds. The garden, we had decided, would be our last stop. There we could rest after our long stroll.

It was quite a little journey to the creek and back, and indeed the garden was a welcoming sight. We entered from the side yard, through a large wrought iron gate. As we passed a succession of tulips, daffodils, pearly peonies, foxglove and Siberian irises, we were ensconced in a most divine scent. We made our way toward a wooden bench and there we sat.

I glanced around and saw, through an opening in the hedge, another kind of garden: a wide, semicircular sweep of lawn lined with trees and wildflowers, and thoroughly layered with Boston ivy, pillar roses and clematis. Also visible was a most magnificent water fountain with some Greek goddess holding a vase from which water continually poured out. It looked impressively ancient.

I told the children, "How lovely this is!"

"I come here to read, when it is not raining or too cold," said Victoria.

Adeline added, "Grand-mama sometimes has tea here."

"I like the creek better," said Martin. "Flowers are for girls."

"Mr. Smithy is not a girl," Margaret told him curtly. "And he takes care of them."

"And quite a task it is," I told them. "It takes a caring hand and infinite knowledge in horticulture to create such a place as this."

"Horticulture?" Martin spoke out as if I had just made up the word. "Mr. Smithy told me he has never had any of that fancy schooling."

"You don't have to go to school in order to learn a trade. Mr. Smithy has probably worked the land all his life, and knows enough about cultivating it to grow anything he wishes."

Victoria said, "Grand-mama told us that Mr. Smithy is gifted, and that God made him that way so he could take care of his earth."

Mary's brow furrowed. "Poor Mr. Smithy, he will have to work very hard to take care of the earth. Miss White says the earth is very, very big and it would take a lifetime to travel around it."

I laughed, and then assured her, "Mr. Smithy will not have to do it alone. There are others to help him."

"That's good," she sighed. "I like Mr. Smithy. I don't want him to go away."

"I'm sure he is planning to stay right here."

Mary asked, "Are you going away?"

I told her, "You know I am only visiting. I hope to go back to Egypt within six months."

She said, "You could stay with Grand-mama. She does not have anyone now that Grand-papa is gone."

"Well, there are Mr. and Mrs. Simms, Liza and Jane, and Mr. Smithy. And then she has all of you to visit her. Your grand-mama will do just fine. You must understand my uncle is also alone. I would not want to leave him."

Adeline asked, "Was he sad when you left him?"

"Oh—very much."

Margaret wanted to know: "Why did you leave him then?"

"Because there were problems afoot and he felt that I was in danger."

Martin was next to ask, "What kind of danger?"

"There are bad men stealing ancient treasures from the tombs."

"Does that make it dangerous?" Victoria asked.

"It could. Especially if those men will stop at nothing to get what they want."

Margaret's mouth dropped open, and then she went on with her questions. "What man? Was he a robber? Did you know him?

I was amused with their interest. "Curiosity killed the cat—you know."

Mary was thoroughly disgusted. "Why did he do that!?"

I could not help but laugh.

Martin was quick to inform her, "Curiosity is not a person—you silly goose!"

"What is it then?"

"It means that you are so inquisitive about something that you will ask a hundred questions," I told her. "Even if it gets you into trouble."

By the look on her face I was certain she still did not understand what that had to do with the cat.

We heard Grace calling to us. Martin called back, "We are over here, Grand-mama."

She joined us, and I said, "It's lovely here, Grace."

She smiled proudly. "Mr. Smithy does a superb job."

Victoria became excited. "May we have tea in the garden, Grand-mama?"

"It is too late for that today, but perhaps tomorrow, weather permitting."

Enthusiastically, Victoria clapped her hands together. "Oh, goody! We shall have tea in the garden. It will be like a party. May we have a party, Grand-mama?"

"Certainly," said Grace. "We will dress up for tea and have us a little party."

"Dress up!" Martin repeated with a certain amount of repugnance. "Can't we just have tea in our play clothes?"

"But we want to dress up," said Victoria.

"Girls!" Martin replied, his voice insinuating that that was the reason we were overcome with frivolity—our gender was to blame.

Grace said very tactfully, "You don't have to come, Martin, if you have other things to do. But I'm sure Miss Woodruff would love for us to give her a most splendid English tea."

Being the little man that he was, he stuck his chin out and placed his hands on his hips. "Well—" he began rather importantly. "I haven't anything else scheduled." He looked at me as if I were the culprit that caused this bit of ado.

I smiled and corroborated his importance by saying, "A party is not complete without English gentlemen."

"Yes," he agreed. "I shall invite John to the party."

Grace informed me, "John lives with his aunt. She owns the property adjacent to mine."

With all that settled, we retired from the garden to prepare ourselves for supper.

The following day, the tea party brought a certain amount of commotion as the servants made the necessary preparations, bustling here and there. Even the children's parents were brought into the excitement of it all and joined us out in the garden.

Chairs were brought out in order for everyone to have a seat, and as if the queen herself planned to attend, we dressed in our best, with hats adorned with ribbons and flowers; garments of the finest fabric; and a table set for tea.

Martin looked sweet wearing knee britches and a matching jacket. Of course, I did not tell him so. I could only imagine his response to such a feminine word as *sweet*. He walked up to me, with whom I assumed was the boy that he had said he would invite to the party—I believe the name was John.

"This is my friend," Martin informed me. "John Blithe. John Blithe, this is my grand-mama's guest, Miss Woodruff."

John Blithe was a thin boy and a foot shorter than Martin. He, too, had donned knee britches, but with suspenders and bow tie, instead of a matching jacket.

I said to little John Blithe, "Hello, John. It is a pleasure to meet you."

John, perhaps not knowing English etiquette, which was not offensive to me, replied with eyes growing large, "Say! Are you the one from Egypt, then?"

I guess I was the next best thing to a mummy. I smiled as Martin elbowed him in the ribs and then made his reprimand: "That's not what you're supposed to say."

John frowned.

"It's quite all right, Martin," I said. "We must remember it is a guest's prerogative to do as they please."

Martin said, "But he should be told." And then he went on to explain, "I would want to be told what I should do, or not do, so people won't think me a dolt."

I said, "Well, then, perhaps later you can explain it all to your friend."

"Yes, I can do that."

Poor little John, I knew that Martin was not scolding him to be cruel, but to be of help. When I noticed the Welsh corgi by John's side, I decided to lighten the mood by inquiring, "Who is your little friend here, John?" I bent over to pet the dog.

He beamed. "Owyn."

At the mention of his name, Owyn looked up at John.

"I see he is loyal," I went on to say.

"He never leaves my side."

"A true friend, indeed. How lucky you are."

John asked, "Do they have dogs in Egypt?"

"Why, yes."

Martin went on to awe him by saying, "Grand-mama says the Egyptians have a dog that is a god."

John looked at Martin and then me. "Is it a real dog?"

"No, not like Owyn," I told him. "The Egyptians called him Anubis. He was a part of their mythology."

"What's a myth—?"

"A mythology," I said, helping him with the word.

He nodded his head enthusiastically.

"Egyptians told stories too, and now we call it Egyptian mythology."

"Like Cinderella?"

"Yes—something like that."

He continued to ask questions: "It is a fairy tale about a dog?"

"Anubis is an Egyptian story. They believed him to be a god of the dead. He was the guardian of the tombs and a judge of the dead."

"What kind of dog was he?"

"A jackal."

Martin said, "A jackal is a wild dog that is smaller than a wolf."

"That's right," I confirmed.

John wanted to know: "Have you seen a mummy?"

I smiled; he was so curiously interested. "Yes, I have seen a few."

"Are they really wrapped up in all that cloth?"

"Yes, they are."

"Martin," Grace said coming up behind him. "You and John go and get the croquet set."

"We can play croquet?" asked John.

Grace said, "All of us will play."

Martin wrinkled up his nose. "Even the girls?"

Grace tapped him on the head. "Even the girls. One day you won't mind so much."

After tea, we set out with our croquet mallets, and although we looked the part of distinguished gentlefolk, the very word "croquet" implies trickery and sneakiness.

As we all stood at the first metal wicket to begin the game, Jonathan asked, "You must tell us, Miss Woodruff, are you a passionate player?"

"Mr. Hubert, if winning the game is of importance to you, it will ease your mind to know that I am a novice. I have only played the game on one other occasion."

He looked pleased. "Oh—well, we will remember not to be too hard on you."

"Don't believe a word he says," his wife Vanessa warned me. "He is a ferocious player."

I gave a rise to my brow. "I will be on guard."

And so the game began.

Now there was one thing, that day, I learned about croquet. The word had derived from the French name for a shepherd's crook. The "croquet" means "little crook." I would say the sport has something "crooked" about it, and the expression "by hook or by crook" literally refers to the manipulation of one's croquet mallet.

We had worked our way, "smashing and splitting" each other, as they would say, to the seventh wicket. In turn, I was behind Jonathan. When my turn came up, there was only one thing to do, and that was to clobber my opponent's ball with my own mallet, thus doing what croquet is best known for—"the send."

After I had knocked Jonathan's ball askew, he looked at me rather pointedly. "I do believe you told us a falsehood. It seems you know the game very well."

"I believe I told you that I had only played on one other occasion. I did not say that I was not good at it."

Perhaps one should question the game's morality, for it seemed to bring out all the evil passions of humanity. I could see it in Jonathan's eyes. I knew that I was in for it. By the end of the game he had managed to clobber me twice. I placed forth, Grace third, Jonathan second, and James first. The children were still taking their turns.

As we stood watching the children, Grace said, "When they leave us things will quiet down considerably."

"Yes, I have given that some thought."

"I know you are accustomed to being busy."

"I will have too much time on my hands, Grace."

Jane brought out lemonade in tall, slender glasses. We took ours and Grace went on to say, "William has some papers that need to be organized. Would you like to help me do it?"

"Yes, of course!"

A thought came to me, and I asked, "Does the professor have notes on hieroglyphics? Could I learn from them?"

"Oh—indeed, yes! And I too, know a little."

"That would be marvelous! Would you help me with it?"

"I would like nothing better."

I was satisfied. My time away from Uncle Harry and Egypt would not be wasted. I could work here and learn, and then return to Egypt the better for it.

Chapter 14

With the children gone, Grace and I began to sort through Professor Hubert's paperwork. Her plan was to piece together her husband's writings into a book, to share what knowledge he had acquired through his own personal studies. She felt it would benefit those interested in Egyptology, and in the deciphering of Egyptian scripts—hieroglyphics, as well as hieratic and demotic ideograms.

Within a matter of weeks we had successfully categorized all of the professor's manuscripts. We had divided his work into three piles. One stack contained his own personal experiences, a journal of sorts, in which he told his life's happenings. Another stack of papers consisted of information that he had collected through the years from all of his archeological expeditions; and the remaining stack was his study on hieroglyphics.

I was drawn to the Egyptian etchings. What fun it would be, if in a tomb, to find papyrus or a stone with such etchings and understand their meaning; that is, if the meaning were not a curse of some sort. I was determined to learn, and through weeks of study I began to memorize signs and their interpretation. The professor believed that Egyptian writing consisted of three types of signs: ideograms, phonetic signs and mute determinatives. The ideograms represent visible objects. Thus the man with a raised stick drawn on the paper I held signifies "to beat." A bird with its wings outstretched "to fly," etcetera.

Abstract ideas, I found, were far more difficult to decipher. But again the Egyptians used images such as the curved scepter of the pharaohs to signify "to rule," the lily, the heraldic flower of Upper Egypt, "the south." The dotardlooking figure of a man with his walking stick represents "old age." Also another important step to the existence of hieroglyphics was what he called determinatives, which are mute signs added to the end of words to give a more accurate definition to words of the same orthography, but different phonetically.

And so my daily studies continued, and with that my knowledge of Egyptian hieroglyphics increased. I had nothing else to devote my time to, and after six months had transpired I could read most of what the professor had copied down onto paper easily enough.

The children came to visit us often, and whenever I would sit in the library to study, Martin would join me. I had grown rather fond of Martin, and I could not help but see his passion for learning what he could of the Egyptians. In that we shared the same interest and desire.

The first six months of my stay with Grace passed quickly. Uncle Harry and David wrote to me often, and I gleaned, from what information Uncle Harry was willing to convey to me, that they had not yet found the culprits behind the robberies and that many were weary of it all. Even Dr. Mehreiz was posting guards at the Egyptian Museum.

Dr. Clairborne had written to me once. It was a "friendly" letter. How was I doing? How was I spending my time? Was I enjoying my stay in England? Those were the things he asked. I was tempted to write an outlandish letter, one making up stories of danger and peril. Or of a handsome highlander that whisked me away to marry. I could write falsehood, to ruffle him. To what purpose, I was not sure—perhaps, because he was part of the reason I had to leave Egypt to begin with, "to keep me from danger," and other such nonsense. *Dangers could pop up anywhere*, I thought. But deep inside I knew that Uncle Harry and Max were only looking out for my best interest. So, my return letter was conventional, nothing out of the ordinary. I replied as any English lady would: I'm doing fine, thank you. I am spending my time in the garden and helping Grace with the professor's work. England is treating me kindly...I am safe and secure...etcetera.

I was learning the art of domestics. I could now cook quite well, thanks to Grace. Mr. Smithey, the gardener, was teaching me how to care for certain flowers. My time was spent doing both, but my heart was longing for Egypt, and when a year had gone by, and still no word from Uncle Harry saying that I could return, I became extremely homesick.

I think Grace sensed my despair. One morning, after I had returned from the garden, she asked if I would like tea.

We went out onto the patio and Jane brought out the server. Grace poured.

"I received a telegram," she said, as she handed me a hot scone from a silver tray. "From a close friend. A Mrs. Silvia Bastian. She owns a townhouse not far from the British Museum. She suggested that we pay her visit. I think we should go."

I welcomed the invitation. I was running out of things to occupy my time. I had memorized all of the hieroglyphs the professor had etched onto paper, and I had perused his manuscripts. The gardening and cooking were becoming second nature. The children would be returning to their schoolwork, thus their visits would not be as frequent. So my response came without hesitation: "That would be wonderful," I told her. "When do we leave?"

So, within two days, we were on our way.

Mrs. Bastian—or "Silvia," as she wished to be called, was a plump woman, with a kind face. Her blondish brown hair she wore in a neat coiffure atop her head. Grace had informed me that she was a widow of two years. Her husband died after suffering a heart attack. Her blues eyes lit up as she warmly welcomed us. She led us into the parlor and then rang for the maid to bring tea and refreshments.

"You've redecorated," Grace noticed.

"The entire house," she told us. "I tired of the old. In some ways I think redecorating was a way for me to get on with life after George passed away."

Grace said, "Well—it's lovely."

"After you have rested, I will show you the entire house. I can't take all the credit. I had a decorator come in and help. It's such an undertaking, you know."

"Indeed," said Grace. "A decorator?"

"Yes," Silvia confirmed. "A new business opened up a year ago. An interior decorator is what they call him."

"A him?" I questioned curiously, quite certain I had not heard her correctly.

"Imagine that!" Grace put in. "Not only a decorator, but a man. I can't imagine any man doing what has always been done so efficiently by women."

"He is very good," Silvia said.

Grace glanced around the room. "Well—from the looks of it I'd have to agree."

After our tea, she showed us to our separate rooms, where we were left to rest. Wallpaper, on which roses seemed to be floating, made the room that I was given a very pleasant one. *A man,* I thought, amused. *And he did all this.*

"My—my," I laughed out loud, "What would Dr. Clairborne think of that?"

I noted the cherry-wood furnishings: Queen Anne style. There was a writer's desk in a corner, and chairs with cabriole legs and backs were curved to fit the spine. A small table suited to serving tea was placed near a very large window.

Upon her word, after we had our rest, and before we dined, Silvia showed us the rest of the house. Never in all my life have I graced a home so elaborate, nor so huge—three stories and an attic. Every floor had its own theme. The bedrooms were all Queen Anne decor. The kitchen, dining room, and all the rooms on the first floor had the new modern look. The kitchen had all new GE appliances, which the cook kept sparkling clean. We were seated in the dining room, with a high ceiling and splendid windows. Faux panels of swags and medallions were painted on the walls. Lace tablecloths over a contemporary table, and to complete the modern touch, the dining chairs were covered with bold blue-and-white striped fabric.

"I am amazed," said Grace, after we concluded our tour. "I must meet this man of wonders."

"And you shall," said Silvia. "But be prepared to redecorate. You'll not leave his shop until he has convinced you to do so."

"I suppose the old house could use some fixing up."

Silvia liked that comment and said, "I want in on the fun."

"I would love for you to be involved," Grace said.

Silvia said to me, "Will you come with us, dear?"

"Of course! I would not want to miss meeting this 'man of wonders.'"

"One day you will want to decorate your own home. Is that not so, Grace?" She did not wait for Grace to reply; she continued, "Have you a sweetheart?"

I smiled and gingerly gave my head a negative shake. "No."

"What's this?" she looked at Grace. "This cannot be! She's too lovely."

Grace smiled. "Oh—it's not as bleak as it sounds, Silvia. She has just not made up her mind which gentleman she prefers."

Silvia let out a chuckle. "Now that's the way to do it! I know a few young men that you could add to your choices."

"I haven't a clue as to what Grace is talking about," I told Silvia. "Just because I know a few unmarried men, does not mean that I have them on some list labeled 'possible future husband.'"

Silvia threw back her head and laughed. "You are amusing," she said to me. "Grace, we must throw a party while you two are visiting. Now that I have redecorated, I need to open up the house and invite over close friends and acquaintances. It'll be fun!"

"I'm sure everyone would love to see what you have done with your home." Grace went on to suggest, "You should invite the decorator to the party."

"Why, yes!" she spoke out excitedly. "That is a most splendid idea. We must start making our plans immediately." And with that said she arose from her seat to get a pen and notepad, and then proceeded to make out her guest list.

"This party will probably give his business a boost," I said, as dinner was being served. "Not only will they marvel at what he has done, but they will also get to meet him firsthand."

By the time we finished our meal the party plans were complete. It was scheduled for the following month, which meant that Grace and I would be extending our stay. I was not much for sitting around, I needed to stay busy, and so I came to a quick decision to go to the British Museum the following day and volunteer my services. Surely, they could use help filing, categorizing, or even allow me to be a tour guide through the Egyptian exhibits. I told Grace of my plans.

"You are so much like your Uncle Harry," she said to me. "If you're not surrounded by old things, then you are not happy."

Silvia laughed. "I would think then, that we must make her very happy, Grace."

I said, "Please understand," I began, "it is not because I don't enjoy being with you ladies—"

"Say no more," Grace interrupted. "You go and volunteer your services. It will be a great experience for you. And the museum, I am sure, could use your help."

"Yes, you do that," Silvia said.

I smiled and thanked them both for understanding.

The British Museum's collection of art and antiquities houses the finest collections in existence. It is one of Britain's architectural landmarks. The lower floors, which consist of thirteen rooms; the main floors, thirty-five rooms; and the upper floors, thirty-seven rooms. The Egyptian exhibit was on the upper floor, and that was where I went first. I wanted to see the Rosetta Stone before inquiring to whom I must speak with in order to volunteer my services. I found the slab of black basalt encased in glass. I read the inscription: It was found by French troops in 1799 near the town of Rosetta in Lower Egypt. The stone was inscribed in 196 BC, with a decree praising the Egyptian king Ptolemy V. Because the inscription appears in three scripts—hieroglyphic, demotic, and Greek—scholars were able to decipher the hieroglyphic and demotic versions by comparing them with the Greek version. So there I stood, studying the piece of antiquity, bearing the inscription that was the key to the deciphering of Egyptian hieroglyphics, when a tap on my shoulder, from behind, broke my concentration. I turned and said, "Yes?"

"Are you the young woman that has come to work?"

How did she know? Did Grace already inform them of my coming? Maybe it's the navy suit I'm wearing—very business like.

I said, "Yes, I am."

"We have been waiting. Since you are not with the group on tour. Well, I thought, perhaps, you must be the young woman that has come about the job. Please follow me."

I was still confused, but I followed her back to the main floor to an office where she told me to be seated. She shut the door, leaving me alone. I glanced around the room. Bookshelves lined one wall, pictures another. A large window behind the heavy wooden desk allowed the morning sunlight into the room. The door opened, a gentleman walked in, I stood. He crossed the room to where I was standing, astute looking in his gray, pin-striped, double-breasted suit.

"So good to have you," he said as he shook my hand in a business-like manner. "I'm Mr. Finley. Please have a seat and tell me about yourself."

I did and when I explained about working with Uncle Harry in Egypt, he looked at me rather strangely and said, "I don't recall your resume having that information."

"My resume! But I did not submit a resume, Mr. Finley."

He pulled out of his desk drawer a file, opened it up, and began to peruse it. "Are you not Miss Gentry?"

"Oh dear!" I exclaimed, my hand going to my throat. "I believe there has been a misunderstanding. I am not Miss Gentry! I am Miss Elizabeth Woodruff. I came here today to volunteer my services."

He eyed me over his wire-rimmed spectacles. "And your uncle is Harry Woodruff?"

"Yes—that's right."

He closed the folder. "I've heard about Harry Woodruff; and I do believe I've read something of you too, Miss Woodruff." He smiled, and then went on to say, "Something about being bitten by the curse."

I smiled back. "The story was somewhat exaggerated."

"Stories do tend to get that way."

He sighed heavily. "Well—Miss Woodruff, I need a secretary, and the woman that I was going to hire has not met our scheduled interview time. And I am one for punctuality. How would you like the job?"

I was flabbergasted! What was I to say? I had to be honest with him, so I explained, "That would be wonderful. But I think you should know that my intentions are to return to Egypt as soon as my uncle tells me that I may do so."

He leaned back in his chair and began to tap the end of his pencil on the desktop. "Do you know when you will be returning to Egypt?"

"No. You see, there is a bit of unrest, and my uncle thought it best that I stay with a friend until it all blows over."

"That is all understandable. If you accept the position, I will hire you on temporarily. Of course, it will be with the understanding that when your uncle sends for you, you will be relieved of your position. The pay is good."

This was going better than I had imagined. I had come to the museum to volunteer my services, but instead I would receive pay! "A very generous offer, Mr. Finley. How could I refuse?"

"Jolly good!"

"When do I start?"

"Would today be too soon for you?"

I looked down at my navy suit; I was dressed for work, and since I had no plans for the day, other than to browse through the museum—*why not.* "I have no other engagements today. I can start immediately."

"Good! Good!" He stood; I stood. "Your desk is out front," he went on to explain, "directly in front of my office."

I followed Mr. Finley to the desk he spoke of, and my eyes immediately went to the accumulated stack of papers which sat atop it. Evidently, he had been without a secretary for some time and that thought was confirmed when he said, "As you can see, I have been without help for a good month. I don't expect all of this to get done today, Miss Woodruff. It took a month for these papers to pile up, and I expect it will take two to get through it. Take your time. You'll need to sort through each piece and read over it before filing it away. Much of it is documentation for artifacts that the museum has acquired. Any of these documents that needs a response, just set it aside and we will look it over together. There are file cabinets in the adjoining room that you'll need to peruse." He pointed in which direction. "If you have any questions, please feel free to ask me, or Mrs. Holloway, the woman you met earlier, and we will assist you as best as possible." With all that said I was left to the task of sorting through the papers.

I sat down on the cushioned chair, now eager to get better acquainted with my desk. A black phone sat to my right, and next to it a notepad and pen. A heavy black typewriter sat directly in front of me, one that would have been rather intimidating, had I not the previous experience in how to use a similar contraption. The desk contained three drawers on the right and one in the middle. I opened them one at a time to find rubber bands, paper clips, notepads, ink pads, all the things I would need to do what a secretary is required to do.

Mrs. Holloway showed me to the break room, where coffee was kept hot at all times. There was a Frigidaire in which we could keep our lunch cool, and an oven to warm it. Tables and chairs were also provided. My thirty-minute lunchtime was designated at 12:30. We had two breaks: one in the morning, and one in the afternoon. She then went on to explain that all incoming phone calls would go to my desk. It would be up to me to either take down messages or forward the call to Mr. Finley. My new responsibility was to make certain that Mr. Finley was not unnecessarily disturbed; which not only meant telephone calls, but walk-in visitors as well.

My first two weeks passed quickly. I did not get a lot accomplished, but spent most of my time learning the filing system, answering telephone calls, and sorting through the stack of documents that needed to either be filed away or perused by Mr. Finley. I was looking at one such document when a woman, several years older than myself, walked up to my desk.

I put aside what I was doing. "Can I help you?"

She smiled. "Yes—please. I'm here to see Mr. Finley."

It was eleven o'clock and Mr. Finley did not have any appointments scheduled for the remainder of the morning. It was now up to me to thwart what might be considered an unnecessary interruption; and that unnecessary interruption was standing in front of me looking rather nervous. I was not at all certain I could handle this.

I told myself to take it a step at a time—ease into it. I started by asking, "Do you have an appointment scheduled with Mr. Finley?"

She surprised me by saying, "Yes."

Perhaps I had been mistaken. I quickly pulled out Mr. Finley's appointment book, checked the date and time, his next appointment was not scheduled until later in the afternoon, and that was with a gentleman from the university by the name of Professor Straten, and she was not Professor Straten.

"I'm sorry, but according to Mr. Finley's appointment book he is not scheduled to see anyone at this time."

She was an attractive lady, dressed in a smart black skirt and white blouse. Her blonde hair was pulled back and twisted at the nape of her neck—business style. Rather large blue eyes looked at me, pleadingly, as she explained, "My appointment was scheduled for two weeks ago."

My genuine smile turned plastic, for I knew that this woman had to be Miss Gentry—the very one whose job I had been given. I was soon to be looked upon as the one who took her job! The thief. The conniver. The cold-hearted woman that steals from the less fortunate. *Gads! What was I to do?*

I girded up my thoughts and calmly asked, "Your name, please?"

She responded innocently, "Miss Gentry."

This was no dream. She stood in front of me in the flesh. I would have to deal with this. "Miss Gentry, if you will please have a seat, I will inform Mr. Finley that you are here."

"Are you his *new* secretary?"

I was growing warm around the collar. "Yes, but only temporarily."

She pulled out of her purse a hankie and began to dab at her eyes. "Oh, dear—I'm too late. You see, my elderly mother had an accident, and I was not able to make the scheduled interview. We haven't the money for a telephone. I so needed this job."

The tears were flowing now, and I was certain Mr. Finley would not appreciate them. I, on the other hand, felt the need to resolve her plight. "I'm sure something can be arranged, Miss Gentry. As I said a moment ago, I am only working temporarily. Please have a seat and I will explain to Mr. Finley your situation."

"That's wonderful! I don't know how I'll ever repay you for your kindness."

"I will do what I can, but Mr. Finley is the one that does the hiring and you will still have to speak with him."

"Yes—of course."

I rapped on Mr. Finley's door and then went in. He did not intimidate me in any way, but there were several things about Mr. Finley that I had learned. One—he praised punctuality and expected just that from his workers. Two—he did not like pop-in visitors, not by anyone, including the museum's board of directors. Miss Gentry had violated both. I was certain these faults would not be in her favor.

"Yes, Miss Woodruff, what is it?" he asked, not bothering to look up to see, if in fact, it was his watchdog secretary; the guardian of his office door; the one that allows no one to pass through without his permission.

"Miss Gentry has arrived."

He eyed me over a pair of reading glasses that sat perched on his nose. "You may tell her that the position has been filled."

"But Mr. Finley," I bravely proceeded. "I am only here temporarily and—"

"I will run an advertisement for a new secretary when that time comes."

"I am hoping to return to Egypt very soon," I quickly added, "There was an accident and Miss Gentry was not able to make her scheduled interview."

He set down the document he held and leaned back in the leather-cushioned chair, eyeing me intently. "You are suggesting that I should interview Miss Gentry?"

"Well—if she meets the job qualifications, it would save you from doing it later."

"And what do you suggest that I do with you if I hire Miss Gentry?"

I had not thought of that. I was about to convince Mr. Finley to fire me. "Yes—I see."

He smiled almost wickedly. "Well—Miss Woodruff?"

I nervously cleared my throat. "I could show Miss Gentry the filing system, and what is being done with all the paperwork. Of course, my original intentions were to volunteer my services."

He waited a moment, perhaps to think over what was best to do, and then he said, "You may show Miss Gentry in."

I did, and when Miss Gentry took a seat, Mr. Finley also asked that I be seated.

He asked the customary questions that one would expect from an employer, and Miss Gentry replied, as one would expect from a prospective employee. I thought all was going well, until Mr. Finley said, "I can't hire you for the position, Miss Gentry, as I have hired Miss Woodruff for that job. However, I'm sure we could use your help catching up with the work that has so quickly accumulated during the absence of my previous secretary. Also, Miss Woodruff has informed me that she will, in the near future, be leaving us to return to Egypt to help her uncle. When that time comes her job will, once again, be available. If you are still interested in the position, then we will talk about it at that time. For now I will hire you on as part-time help."

I thought Mr. Finley handled the situation rather diplomatically. I had just read the previous night about the wise Solomon, who masterfully suggested that a child be physically divided between two women in order to find out who the real mother was. Mr. Finley, of course, was no Solomon, but at that moment I held him in the highest regards, for not only did I still have my paying job, but also Miss Gentry was extremely pleased with the outcome.

In the weeks that followed, Miss Gentry proved to be very efficient. I think Mr. Finley was very pleased with our progress, and with our organizational skills. Miss Gentry worked an average of twenty hours a week, and when she was on the job, I turned the secretarial tasks over to her. I did the less desirable, such as filing, running errands, assisting the visitors.

On one particular morning as I was going about the task of filing, a gentleman approached Miss Gentry's desk. I could not see them, but I could hear their conversation quite clearly.

"I have an appointment with Mr. Finley," I heard the gentleman say.

"You are—?" Miss Gentry was obviously checking the appointment book; after a moment I heard her say, "Mr. Rogers."

"That's right," he replied. "And you must be the new secretary."

"Yes, I am."

The voice was familiar. *Mr. Rogers? Helen Corinth's Mr. Rogers?* I wondered.

I covertly peered out as Miss Gentry opened Mr. Finley's door to announce Mr. Rogers.

He was Helen Corinth's Mr. Rogers!

If he knew that Miss Gentry was the "new secretary," then he had known the previous one. This was not his first time seeing Mr. Finley. What business did he have with Mr. Finley?

I remembered the scarab. Perhaps he and Mr. Finley were friends and he wanted his opinion on its worth. Or maybe Mr. Rogers was interested in selling it to the museum?

One week later, displayed under a glass case was the very same jeweled scarab. Mr. Rogers did sell it to the museum. I was glad, for truly that is where it belonged.

I walked slowly, looking down at the glass case, which was the length of one wall. The antiquities were displayed in divers ways. There was one particular piece that caught my eye. It was a necklace with the cartouche of some king or…?

I leaned forward to get a closer look. The cartouche was that of Princess Ihi. I remembered the piece; it was one of the jewels in the alabaster box that had been stolen from the princess's tomb. Although Max had managed to recover the jewelry box, most of the jewels had not yet been found. And this particular piece managed to make its way from the black market to the museum…but how?

I stood straight, contemplating just what I could do to discover its origins. Every piece of antiquity in the museum involved some sort of paperwork. I could start with that and see where it would lead me. It was possible the necklace found its way into the museum as innocently as Mr. Rogers's scarab. If that were the case, there would be no trail to follow. Nonetheless, I was anxious to get started. If I could uncover anything that would reveal those behind the robberies, it would be to my advantage…I could go home.

Chapter 15

Every piece of antiquity acquired by the museum was assigned a catalogue card with specific facts and historical significance. The information I was looking for would be found on the upper right hand corner of the card. It would tell how the piece was procured by the museum. To most, this information was of little value, but to me it could be the difference between staying in London and going home to Egypt.

Mr. Finley was out for the day, and I was aching to get started on my investigation.

Miss Gentry peered around the filing room door. "Are you still at it?" she asked. "It's quitting time and I'm ready to go home."

"I have some research to do before I leave," I said, trying not to sound suspicious or anxious. "You go ahead."

"Research?" she said, questioning my sanity.

I put the last folder into place and then slid the file cabinet drawer shut. "I'm planning to go through all of the catalogue cards on the Egyptian collection."

She gave a look of distaste. "Is this something I need to help you with?"

I laughed. "No. This is something I'm doing on my spare time—off the clock."

"How—exciting," she said, but didn't mean it. I could tell by the sound of her voice, she thought I was daft.

She knew all about my life in Egypt—the tomb of Smenkhara; Uncle Harry; Philip; David, and even Dr. Clairborne. "Well, I would rather be with my uncle in Egypt right now."

"You must really be homesick, kid."

"Yes, I am," I said truthfully.

"Maybe it won't be much longer."

"That is what I'm hoping."

"Well, if you're sure you don't need my help, then I'll leave you to do your research. I'll see you tomorrow."

We said goodbye, and then she headed out the door.

My heart began to beat excitedly. What information would I uncover? And would it be enough to help solve the tomb crimes?

I whispered a prayer. "Please help me, Lord. I just want to go home."

My first thought was to find the cards on Mr. Rogers's scarab and Princess Ihi's necklace. I knew these two items were black-marketed objects, and I was curious to know what information was given concerning their procurement. I did not expect to find incriminating evidence. However, if similar information was used on such objects, a trail could be linked to the antiquities rightfully obtained, or those acquired from the black market. Perhaps, even a connection to certain individuals.

In my right hand I held the card on Mr. Rogers's scarab, and in my left hand the card on Princess Ihi's necklace. I began to compare the two. The department to which both belonged was written first: Egyptian collection; below that, the date the objects were acquired—and below that from where the piece came. This caught my attention, for both indicated that they came from personal collections.

I took out the complete drawer and placed it on the table. I sat down with pen and paper, and began to flip through the cards. Any of the Egyptian antiquities listed from "personal collections," I wrote down. Within thirty minutes I had completed the tasks, and had ten objects from which the museum had acquired certain Egyptian pieces through personal collections.

Now what? I thought. *What should I do next?*

How could these objects be traced to certain individuals? How? My mind was blank. Nothing—absolutely nothing came to mind of what to look for next, or where to look.

"Well, I guess I'm no Sherlock Holmes," I said to myself. *Grace and Silvia are probably wondering what is keeping me. I'll go home and tell all to Grace. Possibly she will have a suggestion on what I could do next.*

She did. "I don't think you should be doing this," she said to me. "Your uncle sent you here to keep you safe from all of that."

"What harm could possibly come by thumbing through catalogue cards?"

"It's not the catalogue cards, but the information you're seeking out. If, indeed, the culprit is near and he gets wind of what you're doing, it could put you in danger, and we don't know what lengths these men will go to. A worker was already murdered—remember? That's why you were sent here in the first place."

"I won't do anything foolish," I promised. "But if I could learn who brought in these pieces, I could wire that information to Uncle Harry."

"That does seem harmless enough. But you must promise me that you will do no more than that. This is dangerous business."

"Of course," I assured her.

"Well, let me have a look at what you have."

I showed her the list and explained my encounter with Mr. Rogers on ship. "He said that he had purchased the scarab at the hotel in Cairo, from an old vendor. I think he felt guilty having it under such conditions. That's probably why he decided to sell it to the museum. How Princess Ihi's necklace found its way into the museum is another story. I think if I could link these objects to someone we just might find our culprit. At least one of them."

She asked, "Does Mr. Finley see to every individual that brings in an artifact from personal collections?"

I shrugged my shoulders. "I really don't know if he does or not. He did see Mr. Rogers. I suppose I could ask him."

Quickly she said, "No, you mustn't do that!"

"Why, Mr. Finley is harmless, Grace. He is a good man."

"That may be true, but what if he begins to question all this and delves into the matter? It could not only put his life in danger, but his family's as well."

"Yes, I see. You're right. I would hate myself if anything happened to Mr. Finley."

"Indeed."

The hour was getting late and I was ready to go to bed—the day's events had finally taken their toll on me, and I was exhausted. "Perhaps tomorrow I will be able to think about all this more clearly," I told Grace as I stood. "I shall say good night."

Before I walked away, Grace took hold of my hand. "I know you long to go home, dear, and I want that for you too. But it might be best if you leave this alone and let the authorities hunt down these culprits. I don't want to see you hurt."

I thought for a moment, carefully weighing out what she said. Of course, Grace was right. I had no business meddling any further into the matter. I gave my head a nod. "You're right. I will not delve into it any further. Uncle Harry would not be pleased."

Grace gave a sigh of relief. "I can't tell you how much that relieves my mind."

"I never intended to worry you, Grace. I'm sorry."

She smiled. "I know," she said, giving my hand a gentle squeeze.

We said good night, and I headed up the stairs to the room that Silvia had prepared for me to use for the duration of my stay. The room had its comforts, but before I slipped into bed, I spent time in prayer. Prayer was better than any type of sleeping remedial, for it always gave me great peace. I quoted aloud, as I lay my head on the pillow and shut my eyes: "I will both lay me down in peace, and sleep; for thou, Lord, only makest me dwell in safety."

The next morning when I arrived to work, Miss Gentry—who asked that I "please call her Annie," was waiting for me. Her blue eyes were wide and her face a little peaked. She was the first to speak, and it was not the customary "good morning."

"I thought you would never get here," she said, as I approached her desk.

I checked the time on my pendant watch. The time was directly on the hour. I was not a minute late. "What are you talking about?"

She explained. "I arrived fifteen minutes to the hour, hoping with all hope that you would already be here. You usually are."

"I overslept this morning," I said, frowning at her behavior. "What's going on, Annie?"

"You're not going to believe this!" she said, in a rush of words. "I've taken a dead man's job."

"What!?"

She drew out of her purse a folded newspaper clipping. "The prior secretary, whose position has been filled by me—" she then pointed a finger at herself "—was found dead."

"Let me see that."

I took the clipping that was now three months old, and read it. The article went like this:

Mr. Melvin Henderson, 45, was found dead at his home,
4429 Arlington St, where he resided for fifteen years.
He was secretary of the British Museum
to Mr. William Finley.
After much investigation into the matter of his death, authorities have ruled it

accidental.

Survivors include two sons, Frank and Charles of this city, one daughter Linda Stouder of Derbyshire.

Funeral arrangements are incomplete.

I held the article for a moment, thinking over what this could mean. "Ruled accidental?" I said to Annie.

"Gives you the goose bumps."

It did. "Yes, I suppose you could say that," came my comment.

"My aunt gave me that clipping just yesterday. She saves the papers for the bottom of her canary's cage. Last week, she was cutting out a new bottom and found *that* article."

I could see that "that article," was the cause of Annie's fears, and I was not at all comfortable with this bit of news, not after what I had discovered yesterday. I didn't want her to sense my unease, so I said, "It's not like his ghost is going to come back and haunt you for taking his job, Annie."

"Maybe he was murdered," she whispered.

I grabbed her by the arm and nearly dragged her into the filing room. "Listen! You have to stop talking like that! The paper said it was an accident."

"Yes," she snapped back. "But it also said after much investigation."

I looked at her evenly. "I think the best thing for us to do is forget about this."

Her blue eyes narrowed at me. "I think there is something going on that you're not telling me."

The less I explained, the less danger she would be in. "I've already told you about the tomb robberies. Do you remember Mr. Rogers, who came in last week to see Mr. Finley? I know him. He had a scarab that was black-marketed. He sold it to the museum."

Her eyes grew wide. "Do you think Mr. Rogers—?"

"No. He bought the piece in Egypt, from an old peddler of sorts."

Her imagination began to work. "Do you think this Mr. Henderson knew something and was murdered because of it?"

"The article said it was ruled accidental. I think it is best if we leave it at that."

"What if they think that I know something? This is really starting to scare me."

"You don't look so good, Annie. Why not take the day off and come in tomorrow. After you've rested, you'll see all of this differently."

"Do you think so? I didn't get much sleep last night—worrying about all this."

"Go home," I demanded.

"I think I'll do that."

As she turned to leave, I gently took hold of her arm. "And Annie—everything is going to be just fine. If there is something to this Mr. Henderson's death, it will eventually come to surface. Don't let it scare you—okay?"

"I just wish I had half your courage."

"I'm really rather cowardly. I just do a lot of praying."

She smiled. "All the stories you've told me about the tombs, the curses, and staying out in the desert. You're far from being cowardly. I've only dreamed about such adventures."

"You'll have to come and visit us in Egypt, Annie."

"Wouldn't that be something," she said more to herself than to me.

She picked up her purse from off the desk and waved a goodbye.

"See you tomorrow, Annie."

As she headed out the door, I made myself comfortable at her desk. I opened my purse and carefully slipped the newspaper article inside it, and then I took out Mr. Finley's appointment book. I made it a habit, before the workday began, that I would check the day's appointments. I thought it important to familiarize myself with who would be coming in to see Mr. Finley. He had no morning appointments, but was scheduled to have lunch with Mr. Corinth at noon. His afternoon was free until three o'clock, and then a Mr. Niles from India was to see him.

With that done, I shut the book. A thought came to me as my fingers toyed with the black leather cover: *Why not match the dates on my list with the names logged in Mr. Finley's appointment book? Perhaps names could be linked to the purchases of those objects from personal collectors.*

Mr. Finley was not due in for another hour, and the museum would not open up to visitors until ten. I had time to do a little more research. Suddenly, I was stabbed with guilt. I did tell Grace I would not meddle into the matter any further. But I had already gone this far; I couldn't just stop now! I would do it quickly, and then turn the information over to Uncle Harry. That was my plan.

I took the list out of my purse and set it next to the appointment book. By now my heart was beating excitedly.

The first object on my list was a winged scarab pendant. I compared the date the piece was acquired by the museum to the dates and names in Mr. Finley's book. There were names written in the book on the exact date the scarab was purchased, but I felt they were not at all connected, as one was with Mr. Corinth, and the other appointment with the dean of the university. I flipped back through the pages and found Mr. Howard Carter's name logged in to see Mr. Finley exactly one week prior to the date on the catalogue card. Mr. Rogers's dates were similar. He came in to see Mr. Finley; the museum bought the piece, which was catalogued exactly one week preceding the purchase date.

I believed Mr. Carter's name could easily be linked to the pendant on my list. After all, he was the one who discovered the tomb of King Tutankhamun. This pendant was an Egyptian piece found in the king's tomb. It had to be from Mr. Carter's personal collection.

By the time I came to the fourth piece on my list, it was clear to me that this was the way it was done: The collector saw Mr. Finley, the piece was purchased, or donated to the museum, and exactly one week later, that piece was catalogued and placed under glass for public viewing. Thus far, nothing seemed unusual.

I went to the next piece written on my list; it was a pharaonic gold coin, Thirtieth Dynasty, with hieroglyphs on the surface. I quickly flipped back several pages in Mr. Finley's book, and there I noticed between the pages, a square piece of paper. I picked it up and could not help but gasp—for that list was very similar to the list I was now perusing; the one I had penned yesterday from the catalogue drawer. I compared my list with the one I found, and they were both almost exactly alike. Evidently, whoever had written this one, also went through the catalogue drawer as I had. And to my further deduction it would had to have been Mr. Henderson!

"The deceased, Mr. Henderson," I said to myself. "What did you get yourself into, Mr. Henderson?"

"What did you say?" came Mr. Finley's voice from behind.

I slammed the appointment book shut. "Mr. Finley—Oh, I was just checking your scheduled appointments for the day."

He gave a nod of his head. "I see. Where is Miss Gentry?"

My face grew warm. *I must be turning ten shades of red,* I thought. It was like wearing a sign with the word *guilty* written across it. "Miss Gentry—yes…um—she is feeling ill. So she will not be in today."

"Hope that it's nothing serious."

"No, I don't think so."

"Miss Gentry seems to be working out well. I would say that it's jolly good that you convinced me to interview her. Have you heard from your uncle?"

"He writes regularly, but things are still unsettled there, and he has yet to tell me that I may come home."

"Well, fortunate for us, I'd say. Who will I be seeing today, Miss Woodruff?"

"You are scheduled to have lunch with Mr. Corinth at noon. And then you will be seeing a Mr. Niles at three o'clock this afternoon."

"Very well. When Mr. Corinth arrives just send him into my office."

"Yes, Mr. Finley."

He went into his office, picked up a small stack of papers and then informed me, "I need these letters typed and mailed, today—please."

I took them. "I'll have them typed and ready for you to sign after you return from lunch."

"Splendid!"

It took me the remainder of the morning to type up all of Mr. Finley's correspondence. Mr. Corinth arrived on the hour for Mr. Finley.

"Why—I do believe it is Miss Woodruff!" Mr. Corinth said, not disguising the surprise in his voice.

I politely stood. "Mr. Corinth, how nice to see you again."

"Indeed, it is a pleasure to see you again, Miss Woodruff," he said, looking around and frowning rather strangely. "I never would have expected to run into you here. Were you not visiting with Mrs. Hubert?"

"Oh—yes," I told him. "Presently, Grace and I—Mrs. Hubert and I, are visiting in London, with a Mrs. Bastain. I had some time on my hands and decided to use it helping out here at the museum. As you can see, I am filling in for Miss Gentry, Mr. Finley's new secretary; she is ill today."

"Well, I guess it's good that you are here. Mr. Henderson has been missed. He was the previous secretary. He died rather suddenly—an accident, they say."

"Yes, that is what I was told. How did it happen?"

"He fell from his balcony."

"His balcony?" I gasped.

"He leaned forward and it gave way."

"That's tragic!"

"Yes, it was very tragic." He said nothing for a brief moment; perhaps surmising over the late Mr. Henderson, and then his thoughts came back to the present. "Well, I mustn't keep Mr. Finley. We both know what a stickler he is about punctuality."

"Indeed," I replied, laughing.

Mr. Corinth smiled cordially. "It was nice to talk with you, Miss Woodruff."

"And you, Mr. Corinth. Mr. Finley said to tell you to go straight in."

As Mr. Corinth turned to walk into Mr. Finley's office, he bent over and picked up a slip of paper. Holding it up, he read it. "I believe this is yours. It was on the floor next to your desk."

He handed it over to me—I took it. It was the list of items I had penned from the drawer, listing the museum's personal collections. "Yes, it is—thank you."

The list would mean nothing to Mr. Corinth, and I was not worried that he had read it. But my thoughts went back to Mr. Henderson. I was quickly coming to two conclusions: Either Mr. Henderson's death was an accident, or he knew something and was murdered for it. And that murder was made to look like an accident. *Had the railing to Mr. Henderson's balcony been tampered with?* Perhaps that is what had been placed under investigation by the authorities?

I felt I knew Mr. Henderson's fate. What other bit of information did Mr. Henderson come across that caused his demise? And how close was I to knowing the truth about the black market, and the leader behind it? Was this leader someone at the museum? An official? The only official I knew was Mr. Corinth—and he was a family man. Mr. Finley would not hurt anyone. But who were the others? If only I knew more about them, about their lives and their activities, then perhaps this mystery could come to an end.

Several days later, and to my trepidation, I felt I was being watched.

Chapter 16

Several weeks had passed since Annie and I learned of the news concerning Mr. Henderson's death. We talked no more about it, and I did not tell Annie about the list I found in Mr. Finley's appointment book; nor did I tell her that on several occasions I sensed I was being watched. Besides, it was just a feeling. I did not actually catch someone in the act. Maybe my nerves were just a little jittery. One thing I felt almost certain of, Annie was not in any danger, and I did not want to alarm her in any way. If she showed signs of being fearful or nervous, it would only make her appear as if she were onto something. The best thing to do was to keep it all to myself—which I did.

If only I could tell Max or Uncle Harry, they would know what to do, I thought, longing once again for home, to talk with Uncle Harry—to see Max.

I was sitting on the porch swing at Silvia's, enjoying a mid-morning cup of tea, and my thoughts were lingering on Max. I inhaled the sweet scent of hibiscus, and then shut my eyes. I had felt safe in Max's arms—that is, when I finally discovered the true Maxwell Clairborne. How silly it had been of me to think him criminal, and how glad my heart was to learn otherwise. What were my feelings toward Max? I missed him, and yet he could anger me so. To him I was nothing but trouble. That was a fact he had made clear when he suggested to Uncle Harry that he send me safely away.

I smiled, thinking how furious Max would be if he knew what I had been up to lately. Yes, he would chastise me once again for "meddling" where I had no business meddling. But I was not really meddling. Things—just happened. I would have had to turn a blind eye not to have seen the scarab, and not to have noticed Princess Ihi's necklace. It was not my fault that it was there before my eyes, and I just happened to know the necklace had been stolen along with the alabaster box. I was not seeking out trouble. Max, of course, would not see it that way.

Did it matter?

Maybe.

Why? I asked myself. *Why would it matter if Max were upset with me?*

Mr. Babcock, the mail carrier, interrupted my thoughts. He strode up the walk and onto the porch, his mail satchel hanging to one side. "I can see you are enjoying this lovely morning, miss," he said to me.

"Indeed, I am, Mr. Babcock. And how are you doing today?"

"Fine, indeed. If I can keep Mrs. Blitz's dog from chewing off my leg, that is."

Mrs. Blitz's establishment was two houses up from Silvia's, and her pit bull, whose name was Captain Sinbad, was notorious for chasing the milkman and mailman out of her yard. "You certainly face many dangers to deliver the mail," I said to him.

"Ah—most of the time no harm comes by it. But there have been times," he went on to tell me, "when my life was on the line." He gave a laugh. "I have one of them letters for you this morning," he proudly announced.

"From Egypt?"

"That's right."

I was excited, and quickly took the letter he handed to me. "Miss Silvia says you have been to Egypt, and that you plan to go back. Says it's your home."

"Yes, I live there with my uncle, Harry Woodruff—he's an archeologist."

"What adventure," he said, imagining such a place. "While you travel up the Nile, warding off the crocodiles, I'll be traveling up the avenue here in hopes that I can ward off Mrs. Blitz's dog."

I laughed. "You should insist that she keep him penned."

"Nah, the dog looks forward to it. Chasing me, that is."

"Oh, I see. Then it is sort of a sport between the two of you?"

"You could call it that," he said. "Well, miss, you have a nice day."

"Thank you, Mr. Babcock. And you do the same."

He left me to read my letter. It was from David.

My dearest Beth, was how his letters always began, his next sentence would follow with: *I hope this letter finds you well?* He then went on to express how he missed me, and that Egypt was indeed a dead place without my presence there to liven things up a bit. Knowing that I could not tolerate sitting still, he asked what I was doing with my time. He wrote that Dr. Mehreiz had informed him that several men had been apprehended as members of the black market. However, they were only men used as puppets; the real culprits were still at large. He went on to tell me of trivial things, and then in closing, he briefly wrote: *Your Uncle Harry is not well*, and then: *I thought you should know.*

Just like that! No explanation. No reason why.

I let my hand that was holding the letter drop to my lap. What exactly did David mean by "not well"? Did Uncle have a lasting illness, or was it something that would pass in a few days' time? Why was David not specific about this!? He knew me well enough to know that I would want to be told the details: What was wrong? How was *he* acting? Has *he* seen a doctor? Has *he* been confined to bed rest?

Then I thought, *Uncle Harry is working too hard—to the point of making himself ill.* I was not there to help him, and not only was he doing his job, but mine also.

"Oh, Uncle Harry," I whispered to myself. "You should let me come home."

It was getting late, and I promised Silvia and Grace that I would meet them for lunch. I needed to dress for the occasion, so I took the letter and went up to my room. I changed into an elegant navy suit. The straight skirt fell to the tops of my ankles, and the jacket was double breasted. I pulled my hair back, pinning it at the nape of my neck, and then, what made the suit complete, was the tea hat with soft, chenille-like veiling.

I allowed myself plenty of time for a leisurely walk to the quaint cafe. It was situated on the corner of Wisteria Avenue and Main Street. I decided to take an avenue that I thought would be more scenic. I so enjoyed looking at the homes.

I was about one block from the cafe, when I arrived at the corner of Hampton Boulevard and Arlington Street. Now Arlington Street was the street on which Mr. Henderson had resided. I chose to go down Arlington, hoping to get a glimpse of his home. I could not remember the house number, but I noticed that most of the homes on Arlington had mailboxes with the residents' names painted artistically on the side. After passing four or five mailboxes, I came to Mr. Henderson's. It was in front of a clean, white house with dark-green shutters. It was well kept and did not appear in need of any repair. I quickly noticed a woman tending the flowerbeds. She straightened and looked my way, for I had stopped in front of the house.

She said, "Hello. Have you come to look at the house?"

"Hello," I said, in return. The house was up for sale.

She came to where I stood and extended her hand. "I'm Linda Stouder."

"Elizabeth Woodruff," I said, as we shook hands. "You are Mr. Henderson's daughter?"

She looked at me curiously. "Yes, that's right. Did you know my father?"

"Not exactly," I said. "I was helping Mr. Finley until his new secretary arrived. I just heard about your father. I am very sorry for your loss."

She looked away. I could see the tears pooling in her blue-gray eyes.

She was an attractive woman. I'd guess to say mid-thirties. She was not what you would consider heavy, but she was on the verge of being what many called "pleasingly plump." Her auburn hair was pulled back and held in place by a large barrette. The flower-printed frock she wore was loose fitted—easy to move around in.

"Are you here to see the house?" she questioned me again, and then, with a hint of annoyance, she added, "Or have you come to see the scene of the crime?"

Obviously, Mr. Henderson's death had drawn unwanted visitors. "Well—I'm not really sure that it is either of those reasons," I told her. "But I am surprised that you would openly refer to your father's death as a crime?"

The subject was hurtful. Again she looked away.

"I'm sorry," I apologized. "I know it must be difficult to talk about. I thought you might be able to tell me about your father."

She met my gaze with narrowed eyes. "Why would you need to know about my father?"

I did not want to add to her grief, and yet I was interested to know the family's perspective on what they thought could have been the cause of their father's death. "Well," I began cautiously. "I read the news article. It mentioned that there was an investigation. And I am aware of certain…things. Things that have made me curious about his death."

"What sort of things?"

"I really would not want to say something that is only speculation on my part," I explained. "I have no proof—"

"I would like to show you something," she interrupted. "Please, follow me."

She led me up the staircase to the second floor, and then into a bedroom, which I assumed had been Mr. Henderson's room. She confirmed this by saying, "This was my father's room."

It was a masculine room, of dark wood and leather—not the decor of a woman. "Your mother?"

"She died five years ago. An incurable disease is what the doctors called it."

"My parents are both deceased. I live with an uncle."

"I'm sorry," she said, softly.

"I love my uncle. He is very much a father to me."

She gave me a compassionate smile. "That's good, that you have someone."

"I am very thankful that he and my aunt took me in. She is dead now, but Uncle and I get along splendidly."

She opened French doors that led out onto a balcony. "Come look," she said.

She pointed to the concrete ledge where both sides of the balcony floor had crumbled. The railing was no longer there. Probably more for the sake of safety, rather than the memory of what had happened.

I knelt down to have a better look.

"The authorities said it had weathered away," she told me, but then quickly added, "I don't believe it. You can check the entire house, not anywhere will you find signs of deterioration. My father was a stickler about the upkeep of this house."

"Did you explain that to the detective?"

"Oh, yes. But he had nothing else to go on—no other leads. And he pointed out that perhaps my father was not aware that it needed repair. If you'll look," she said, pointing to the center of the concrete ledge, "there are no signs of weathering or deterioration any other places along this ledge. I would think if the concrete was starting to deteriorate, that it would also show signs of doing so in other places as well."

"Yes, I would think so," I agreed. "Do you know of any reasons why someone would want to murder your father?"

"The detective asked me the same question…and no, I can't think of any reasons why someone would want to murder my father. He was a good man. I cannot even begin to imagine why someone would do such a thing."

I could think of a few reasons, I thought dismally. *He knew something or someone linked to the black market.*

"Now I must know," she said. "Why do you ask?"

What was I to say?

Adamantly, she continued, "You must tell me. And if you know anything, you must go to the authorities."

"What I know is only speculation. You must promise me, that what I share with you will not be shared with anyone else. Not until I can get what information I know—including the mysterious death of your father, to the proper authorities."

"Are you with some sort of secret agency, or something like that?"

I laughed, for I could almost envision Max's reaction to what she said. "No, of course not. But you could say I am aware of a number of mysterious happenings."

Briefly I explained to her all that had happened with the tomb robberies, and the artifacts stolen from Princess Ihi's tomb. I told her about the black market. I told her what I had discovered at the museum, and that I felt her father may have been on to something...something incriminating.

I finished by saying, "I know men that have been working feverishly to find and capture the culprits. They are the ones that I need to get this information to. Not Scotland Yard, and not the constables. This needs to be handled carefully. We wouldn't want to place other lives in danger, nor would we want the culprits to get away because we failed to handle this properly. I do hope you agree with me."

"Yes! Of course!"

I noticed the time, and knew that I would be late meeting with Grace and Silvia. "I must be going. I'm having lunch with friends, and I don't want to keep them waiting."

I followed her out of the house, and before we departed, she rested a hand upon my arm. "Thank you. This has given me some amount of comfort. You must promise to stay in touch with me—often. I must know what is going on."

"I will," I promised. "Goodbye, Linda."

I left her and hurried down the street. It would take me another five minutes to get to the corner of Wisteria and Main Street.

The traffic and pedestrians were unusually busy. A wedding celebration at a white church with a pointed steeple seemed to be the cause. I saw the bride and groom making their way out of the church. Friends and family threw rice at them, and their laughter could be heard above the wedding guests' cries of jubilation.

I thought of Philip, and felt that life had somehow cheated us. He and I, perhaps, would have married. "I wish you were here, Philip," I whispered in the breeze.

As I stood there, contemplating what might have been, I did not notice the growing crowd of people that had gathered near me to watch the wedding procession, and what happened next struck me with horror.

I was standing near the curb, watching the wedding celebration, and as I had mentioned, my thoughts were elsewhere. It happened in a matter of seconds. I was pushed forcefully from behind. There was nothing I could do to regain my balance. I was falling forward into the street and in front of several carriages being pulled by powerful horses. It was inevitable; the huge carriage wheels would run me over.

I was going to die!

As I fell, I Immediately spoke out the name, "Jesus!"

I did not have time for repentance, nor did I have the time to reacquaint myself with the Almighty…I didn't need to; I conversed with the Lord daily.

After the incident, I was surprised to find myself alive, and in one piece. My hands and knees were badly scuffed, and my skirt torn.

There was commotion about me. One gentleman extended a hand to help me up. "Are you okay, miss?" he asked. "Do you think you can stand? Have you broken anything?"

I assumed he meant bones. "No…I don't think so."

When I stood pain shot up my leg.

A lady said, "It was a man. He was in a terrible hurry."

"Yes, I saw him too," said another lady. "I don't suppose he realized what he'd done—running off like that."

"No, I suppose not," I said to the two women, and then I informed the gentleman that helped me to stand, "It's my ankle, I've twisted it."

He suggested, "May I hail you a cab?"

"Yes, thank you."

The cab was hailed and the gentleman assisted me into it. He noticed then that I was missing a shoe and went back for it.

"Look here," he said. "The heel is broken off. I do believe it is what saved you from a very fatal accident. It got caught in the drainage grill near the curb, and kept you from falling further out into the street. You're a very fortunate young lady."

I was still a bit dazed, but agreed that indeed I was very fortunate. I thanked the gentleman for his kindness, and then gave the driver instructions to take me to Silvia's. I was too shaken to have lunch at the cafe.

As the cab driver directed the horse and carriage around a corner, it was then that another shocking discovery took place, for standing near the edge of the street was Mr. Rogers! He stood still and watched as the carriage went by. A certain amount of unease crept up my spine, and my imagination immediately began to think of a number of possibilities: *Was Mr. Rogers a part of the tomb robberies?* His name had appeared in Mr. Finley's appointment book on several occasions. "Oh, God," I whispered. "Was the hand that pushed me out into the busy boulevard, Mr. Rogers's hand?"

The words spoken by the gentleman that had assisted me came to mind: "You were saved from a very fatal accident."

Was it an accident? I asked myself. *Or was it meant to be murder?*

This thought caused me to go limp. I laid my head against the carriage seat and shut my eyes. *It just couldn't be possible,* I thought dismally. *Was someone aware of what I was about, and were they now trying to murder me, as they had managed to murder Mr. Henderson? And was Mr. Rogers involved?*

What was I to do—to think?

When the carriage came to a stop, Grace and Silvia met me. They had just arrived home from their luncheon. Grace was very upset when she saw my condition.

"What has happened!?" Grace gasped.

As they helped me into the house I explained the entire incident.

They insisted on calling for the doctor. When he arrived, he looked me over. He said I had no broken bones, but a badly twisted ankle, and a very bruised arm. I was to have bed rest for the remainder of the week. He gave Grace a painkiller to give me each evening to help me sleep; she was to mix it in a cup of warm milk or tea.

So, I spent my days in bed. The morning hours I spent talking with Grace and Silvia, and the afternoons reading and napping.

One afternoon, Grace had opened up the bedroom windows. A lovely breeze blew into the room. It was an enchanting afternoon. I could hear the birds, and the scent of flowers from the garden below drifted into the room. I had just finished rereading David's letter. I was thinking about Uncle Harry's illness when I drifted off to sleep.

It was the dream that helped me come to a decision. I dreamt that I was standing on Mr. Henderson's balcony. I felt a refreshing breeze on my face, and in my dream I could hear the birds. I was wearing a white robe that tied at the waist with a cloth belt of the same fabric. I got up from where I was sitting and walked to the balcony rail. The railing stood out to me. It was black railing that spanned the entire balcony. It looked strong, sturdy, and unmovable. There was a garden below, a beautiful garden that I wanted to see. As I leaned over the balcony to look below, it gave way. I was falling—falling to my death. It was then that I awoke, my heart beating rapidly.

After calming down from the effects of the dream, I noticed that David's letter was clutched tightly in my hand. The dream had shaken me. Was it a warning that someone was trying to kill me?

I relaxed my hand, and smoothed out the letter; folded it and placed it back inside the envelope. Uncle Harry was ill and I was no longer safe in England.

I should go home! Uncle Harry needed me and I would be safe with Max near. I would tell both Uncle Harry and Max all that I knew, and what had happened to Mr. Henderson—and what had happened to me. It was imperative that they know. I would not send this information via telegram. I would do it personally.

I threw aside the covers and with great care I stood. My head began to spin. I sat back down on the edge of the bed, waiting for the dizziness to subside; when it did, I stood.

I dressed, and then took out my luggage. It was then that Grace came into the room.

"What are you doing?" she asked—no, she demanded to know.

"I'm going home."

She gaped at me and then repeated, "Home?"

I did not beat around the bush, but came right out with it. "Someone is trying to kill me."

"What!?"

I told her all that I thought, and what I had dreamt, and then I gave her David's letter to read.

After Grace read the letter, she said, "If you think someone is trying to kill you, you should certainly go to the police."

"I can't, Grace. They really would not know what to do. I must tell—" I could not give her Max's name, not because she could not be trusted, but because I promised Max I would tell no one that he was the agent Moses. "I must tell Uncle Harry; he can get the information to Moses. Moses will know what to do."

"Do you think Mr. Rogers is behind this? Perhaps you should warn Mr. Corinth."

"I don't know what to think," I told her honestly. "I just know Uncle Harry's ill and needs me, and I no longer feel safe here."

She was silent as I continued to pack my clothes. "I don't want anyone to know I'm leaving. I may be followed, so it's best that I do this secretively. We'll send my luggage to the shipping yard the day before I depart and then when it's time to go, I'll go out as if I'm going shopping."

"Oh, dear," came Grace's worried whisper. "Harry put me in charge of you and I have failed miserably."

"You have done no such thing. You cannot be held accountable for other people's behavior."

"You will be traveling without a chaperone. You know how Harry feels about that."

I smiled. "I am almost twenty-three, Grace. I think I can manage on my own for a few weeks. Think about it as a way of helping the cause of women's rights."

"If anything happens to you, I'll never forgive myself for letting you go alone."

I told her, "If anything happens to me here, you'd never forgive yourself for not letting me go."

She gave a heavy sigh. "I really can't stop you. And if you are in danger…well, I do suppose it is best that you go home. I know Harry will watch over you like a hawk—Max too. I do hope Harry is not seriously ill."

"As I am hoping the same."

We decided that my trip should wait until I was able to walk on my ankle. So, two weeks later, I was dressed and ready for my so-called outing.

Silvia gave me a warm farewell embrace, and Grace kissed me on the cheek.

"Be very cautious, dear," Grace advised.

"I will," I assured her.

I left them standing on the porch and hopped up into the cab, which was drawn by two black horses. I told the driver that I wanted to shop first. I bought a pair of new white gloves to go with the white-and-blue-striped suit that I would wear upon my arrival to Cairo. An hour later, I was embarking.

I was thrilled. Finally, I was going home.

Chapter 17

I arrived safely at Cairo's port, and, as usual, the dockside was bustling with activity. I was anxious to see Uncle Harry and to know how he was doing. Not wanting to be encumbered with my trunk, I gave instructions for it to be delivered to Uncle's home.

As I was making my way down the dockside to hail a buggy, standing not far off, and a head taller than most, was Dr. Maxwell Clairborne. I could not make out his features, but I could easily recognize that familiar stance. He could not have known that I was arriving today—no one knew. He was, or so it appeared, giving instructions to a dockside worker concerning a large wooden crate.

As yet, not wanting to confront him, I did an about-face and quickened my pace.

Had he seen me? Again, I was wearing that infernal white hat, the very hat that, according to Max, made me stick out like a beacon.

I yanked the hat off my head and mumbled how daft I was for wearing it.

I kept on going and did not chance a glance back. I hadn't gone far when Max came up beside me, matching my strides.

"I don't believe this!" he said.

So much for a warm welcome, I thought, with some amount of humor. I continued walking at a hurried pace. "You don't believe what?" I asked indifferently.

"Best put that hat back on or you'll ruin that lovely complexion of yours.... I know Harry wasn't expecting you."

He gave me the needed ammunition. I stopped and faced him. "Why did you not write and tell me that Uncle Harry was terribly ill?" I asked, refusing to be intimidated by him.

"Who told you he was terribly ill?"

Trying to muster up some confidence, I straightened my shoulders. "It doesn't matter whom," I told him evenly.

"No, it doesn't. But I would hardly call mild exhaustion a fatal illness."

"I didn't say fatal, I said terribly ill."

"If you mean to use it as an excuse—it would not be one that is justifiable."

"By whose opinion?" I countered. "Yours? And why should I need an excuse to come home, if I so desire?"

"You know why," he said, a bit acerbic. "It is still not safe here."

"Oh—and you think I might be safe elsewhere? Think again, Dr. Clairborne."

I began to walk away and he followed beside me. "And what is that supposed to mean?" he questioned.

"That you think I might be safe elsewhere?"

"No. Why would I need to think otherwise?"

He took hold of my sore arm, bringing me to a halt. I winced; he noticed. With a gentle hand he pulled up the sleeve of the white-and-blue-pinstriped jacket I was wearing. My arm and wrist were still showing signs of a badly discolored bruise.

"What happened?" he asked—no, he demanded to know.

"I fell."

"The truth."

"My shoe got caught in a grid—"

"This has something to do with that remark you made."

"I don't know what you mean."

His keen eyes challenged me. "Yes, you do."

My head was beginning to pound and I was not feeling at all well.

He asked, "Where is Grace?"

I said nothing.

"Don't tell me you came alone?" he said, with increasing irritation.

I was tired and growing hot in the sun. "Max, please. I'm not feeling at all well...I would like to go home."

He led me to a bench that was shaded by a frond overhang. "Sit here and I'll go for a buggy."

Willingly, I gave myself over to his care. Although I disliked his barrage of questions, it felt good to have him near.

He bent down, his hand resting on the back of the bench, and he was eyeing me with concern. "I'm sorry if I seemed a little rough."

I smiled up at him. "I expected it."

"Oh—I see. I'm back to being the ogre."

"Something like that, yes."

"Have you seen a doctor?"

"What?"

"The arm…and wherever else?"

"Oh—yes, of course."

"You are going to tell me all about this when you've rested and are feeling better. And I want the whole story, Beth, not just pieces of it."

He had not changed any; he could always discern more about a situation than one wanted to reveal. I looked away from his penetrating gaze. "I had intended to tell you—everything."

"I have a feeling I'm not going to like it."

"You won't," I said, looking back up at him.

He eyed me with a look of severity. He was probably thinking that whatever had happened could have been avoided by my not meddling.

He stood straight and looked off into the distance. "I'll go for that buggy."

I watched him walk away, wishing that he were not always so severe.

When the buggy and driver arrived, Max helped me up into it. He paid the driver and gave him the needed instructions as to where I was to go, and then he turned to me. "We will talk later."

"Thank you for your help."

The driver snapped the reins across the donkey's back. The buggy lurched forward, and Max was left standing in the street.

He was as I remembered him. I wondered if he thought that I had changed any.

When I arrived home the house was quiet. It was possible that Uncle Harry would be at the site working. If that were the case, I could easily hire transportation out in a day or two.

I heard movement coming from the kitchen, so I made my way there. As I drew nearer I could hear Mrs. Bilgas humming a tune, and the sound of dishes being placed in cupboards. I walked in; she jumped, her hand immediately went to her heart.

"I'm sorry," I told her. "I didn't mean to frighten you."

"The wonders of pharaoh!" she declared, her white teeth beaming against dark skin. "Look at what has appeared."

"Trust me," I laughed. "I'm no mirage."

"Indeed, no."

She gave me a hug and then placed me at arm's length. "You have not changed." Her keen eyes looked me over. "Well, maybe you have acquired a look of—maturity. It is there in your eyes…the mirror to the soul."

"A lot has happened," I told her.

"Ah—yes. I can see that it has made you wiser."

I smiled. "That may be debatable by some."

"I was not told you were coming home. I would have freshened your bedroom and prepared a festivity."

"And you would have gone to too much trouble." I picked a grape off a cluster that sat on the kitchen counter in a bowl. "Uncle Harry doesn't know yet that I have come home. Where is Uncle Harry?"

"He is resting. He will be very surprised to see you."

It was not like Uncle Harry to nap in the middle of the day. "David wrote and said that he is ill."

"It is not good that he works so hard," she told me.

"Is that the trouble: he is just working too hard?"

"That is what the doctor thinks."

"Well, I'm home now. Not only will I be able to take over some of his tasks, but I will make sure that he doesn't overwork himself again."

"That is good. Now, you must be hungry. You sit and I will make you a cup of tea and something to eat."

"Just tea, please. I will wait until supper time to eat."

As I drank my tea and ate the slice of cake that Mrs. Bilgas said I must have, we talked about her family.

I was just finishing the last morsel when Uncle Harry barged in. It was apparent that my presence gave him a bit of a shock.

"Beth—it is you!" he said, after a moment.

I got up from my chair and gave him a hug. "Uncle Harry," I said, kissing him on the cheek.

"When I heard your voice, I thought I must be dreaming or delirious with fever."

"No, I'm really here and it feels great to be home."

"You don't know how many times I've wanted to send for you," he told me. "I had to remind myself that your safety was more important than this old man's loneliness." He gently took me by the shoulders. "Look at you. You haven't changed any."

"But of course she has changed," Mrs. Bilgas told Uncle Harry as she replenished my cup of tea and set down a cup of coffee for Uncle. "You can see it in her eyes."

Uncle looked closely and then gave me a wink. "Ah—yes, I see what you mean, Mrs. Bilgas. Our little girl has grown into a fine young lady."

I clued Uncle Harry in. "Mrs. Bilgas thinks I have become wiser with time. What do you think, Uncle Harry?"

"We should all grow wiser with time. One's life should never regress."

Mrs. Bilgas removed her apron. "I will leave you two. You will have much to talk about. Supper is in the oven warming, and there is enough for two."

"Thank you, Mrs. Bilgas," Uncle said.

After Mrs. Bilgas left us, I refilled my cup with hot tea, and sat back down opposite Uncle. He'd lost a little weight—not so much that it should cause one to worry, but enough to notice. "David wrote and said you've been ill."

"Nothing serious," was the answer he gave. He looked at me from across the table; his eyes held a certain amount of speculation. "Is that why you've come home, because you think I'm ill?"

I could not lie. "It is one of the reasons."

"It is still not safe for you here."

"Well, that brings me to the other reason. I was no longer safe in England, either."

His calm expression grew intensely dark. "What happened?"

I told him everything.

Now, Uncle Harry is a very patient man. He is longsuffering and gentle, but as with any man, when his family is threatened, such evil is not tolerated. "I'll not let anyone harm you," he said with vehemence.

I knew then what extent he would go to in order to keep me safe and alive. I could see it in his eyes, and hear it in his voice. I asked, "Are those behind all of this not soon to be caught? It has been well over a year."

"I think that it is very soon in coming. Just a matter of time," Uncle said. "And with the information that you have—Well, perhaps it will be of some help. I'll notify Dr. Clairborne, he'll want to speak with you."

"Dr. Clairborne said he would be out later."

Uncle Harry looked puzzled.

"He was at the dockside when I arrived. We already had words," I explained.

"Dr. Clairborne and I both felt it best that you and Grace be distanced from all this. But, he'll understand, once you've explained."

"Dr. Clairborne, understand? Hmm—I'm not so sure about that. Most likely, he will think that I've meddled where I should not have."

"He will be enraged that you were threatened in such a way. If I ever get my hands on the man—"

I did not like to see him so upset. I laid my hand over his. "I'm okay, Uncle Harry, and when all of this is over the authorities will justly punish those involved."

He grasped my hand. "Thank God that you are all right!"

After he let go of my hand, I leaned back into my chair and studied him for a moment. "Uncle Harry, what did the doctor have to say about your health?"

"Nothing that you need to worry about."

"Be honest with me. And whether or not I need to worry about it is irrelevant. I want to know what the doctor said and what the problem is."

"Was," he corrected me.

"Now, either you tell me, or I will go to the doctor and find out for myself."

"You've become very bossy."

I laughed. "And you've become very obstinate. Now, are you going to tell me what the doctor said, or shall I pay him a visit?"

"The doctor said I had a mild case of upper respiratory infection—symptoms very similar to what miners, who spend hours underground, come down with. A little rest and more sunshine will eliminate the problem."

"Dr. Clairborne said something about mild exhaustion?"

"Mild exhaustion is not a health problem."

"It is if you are not taking care of yourself. And Mrs. Bilgas said the doctor thought you were working too hard."

"When has a little hard work ever killed a man?"

"I'm sure that it has."

"Bah!"

"I won't let you overwork yourself. I'm going back out to the site with you."

"That is probably best. I don't intend to let you out of my sight. I will see that you are kept safe. Even if I have to hire you a bodyguard, then that's what I'll do."

I laughed. "A bodyguard? Really, I don't think that's necessary. However, it wouldn't hurt to hire several guards on-site."

"I have already done that."

"Oh yes, I had forgotten."

"I would feel better if someone vigilantly watched out for you."

"I think you and I can manage that."

"Not while I'm working. My mind is absorbed and too occupied to be watching out for you. The more I think about it, the more I like the idea. A bodyguard is what you need."

"But Uncle Harry—" I began to protest.

He stopped me by raising a hand. "Beth," he said sternly, "I have made up my mind."

I knew not to argue with him once his mind was made up. "All right. I'll agree to anything, if you will just let me go back out to the site with you. I have already missed so much."

"You have missed some, but mostly the tedious things. There is still much to do."

"I've longed to be there, Uncle Harry. Every day I have wondered what beautiful things you were finding and restoring."

"We are just starting on the burial chamber. You haven't missed seeing and working with the finer things."

I smiled. "I'm excited—all over again."

He laughed. "You have it in your blood, my girl. You're a true archeologist."

"I've been taught by one of the best. What are books when compared to the experience gained by working with the best? I'm sure to be the envy of every student studying Egyptology and archeology. When will we be going out to the site?"

"In a few days."

"I'll be ready. But what of you—are you sure that you're up to it?"

He smiled. "You'll be happy to know that I've obeyed doctor's orders and took a week of rest. Otherwise, I would be out at the site this very moment."

Uncle looked rested, but I was determined to keep a close eye on him. The excitement of the find would make it easy to forget about overworking. I would be his reminder.

"Have you seen David?" I asked.

"He is with Colonel Whittley."

"Colonel Whittley!"

"He is helping him finish up with Princess Ihi's tomb."

"That's good. I'm glad to hear that. David will be a great help to Colonel Whittley."

I wondered if the colonel hated the princess as much as I did.

Later that evening, and after I had rested, Max stopped by. Uncle Harry let him in; I was in the kitchen cleaning up after our meal, the one that Mrs.

Bilgas had prepared for us. I was just removing my apron when Max walked into the kitchen.

"Hello, Beth."

I laid the apron on the counter. "Hello," was all I said, and then we stood looking at one another. He looked good. I had forgotten how gray his eyes could look in dim lighting. His hair, though as dark as ebony, was a nice color against skin that had been tanned by the desert sun. He was wearing dark gray trousers, and a white, crisp linen shirt. He looked comfortable, relaxed.

Expecting him, I chose to wear a silk chiffon skirt, with tiny glass beads worked into the design, and a cool, white cotton-silk blouse. My hair was pulled back and held in place by a barrette, and soft curls were left to hang freely. However, I could not have appeared as relaxed as he—the butterflies in my stomach wouldn't allow it. I knew the reason for his visit: I would have to explain all that had happened, and somehow I felt that he would find I had acted foolishly. I guess I cared what he thought.

It was actually a comfortable temperature outside, so he suggested that we go out onto the patio to sit. I was wondering where Uncle Harry had wandered. I wasn't sure I wanted to explain the whole story to Max, without Uncle being present to support me. It was silly of me, but I was actually feeling nervous about telling Max all that had happened. As if what had occurred was my entire fault—or something.

"Harry said he'd join us later," Max then informed me, as if he could read my thoughts. "He said he has some paperwork that needs his immediate attention."

That's just dandy! I thought.

Max didn't waste any time. "What happened, Beth? I'm in no hurry, so please, start at the beginning."

I thought for a moment and was going to start the story from the time that I was hired to work for Mr. Finley at the British Museum, but then I remembered Mr. Rogers and the scarab.

So, I told Max everything, from the time that I had met Mr. Rogers on ship, up to the time of being pushed out into the street.

I could tell by the set of his jaw he was disturbed, and maybe even a little annoyed.

"I wasn't trying to find trouble, if that is what you are thinking," I wanted him to know.

"You shouldn't have pursued it, Beth. You almost got yourself killed."

I could feel my dander rise. "I would hardly call it pursuing."

"You should have just left it alone!"

"Left it alone?" I snapped back. "How can you say that? I didn't do anything—daring. I simply checked the files, and made a list."

"You did enough to make someone suspicious, and then you were obviously being followed. When you went to Henderson's house, to snoop—"

"To snoop!" I snapped back. "I didn't go there to snoop. How was I to know that his daughter would invite me into the house?"

"And you just couldn't resist," he pointed out.

I had had enough. I stood and glared at him. "I really don't think I have anything else to say to you!"

Max sighed in frustration. I turned and stormed away, bumping into Uncle Harry as he was stepping out onto the patio. I went to my room and cried angry tears. My room faced the patio, and I could hear Uncle Harry and Max talking in low tones. I knelt by the open window to hear what I could of their conversation.

Uncle Harry was saying, "Your assumption about Henderson was right."

"You realize what this means?"

"Yes, I think I do. This narrows your search down to about four men."

"Three, actually. You can count Finley out. He's clean."

I wiped the tears away. *So, my information was useful.* This thought was gratifying. I had not acted so foolishly after all.

"I think I've upset her," I heard Max say.

Uncle agreed, and then said, "I thought sending her away from all this was the right thing to do."

"It was! We had no idea she'd end up at the museum."

"Maybe it was meant to be," Uncle said.

"What!?" came Max's voice.

"Well, we've prayed that this would come to an end," I heard Uncle explain. "You have to admit, all that has happened narrows it down."

"It was too dangerous, Harry. Eventually we would have narrowed it down without the need for Beth to put her own life at risk. What really worries me is the fact that they know she's on to something. They probably think she is in with the underground operation. This isn't over yet, and knowing their track record like I do.... Harry they'll come looking for her."

Hearing Max actually say it caused my blood to run cold. "Someone would actually hunt me down?" I whispered fearfully.

Once more, I was causing them trouble. Max would probably never speak to me again.

"I'm going to hire a personal bodyguard for Beth," Uncle Harry told Max. "Have any recommendations?"

I could not make out Max's answer. I decided I had heard enough and was beginning to feel I had treated Max badly. I freshened my face and went into the kitchen. Mrs. Bilgas's cake sat on the counter in a glass-covered cake dish. I sliced both a piece of cake and filled two mugs with fresh, hot coffee. All of this I neatly arranged on a silver tray and carried out onto the patio.

"A peace offering," I said, hoping they understood that I was not trying to be the cause of their troubles. I first gave Uncle his plate and coffee mug.

"How nice, Beth," I heard Uncle say as I turned to give Max his portion.

I could feel Max watching me, and it made me nervous. What was he thinking: what a nuisance I was? *It would serve him right if I spilled the hot coffee onto his lap,* I thought with a certain amount of humor, as I *carefully* set the mug in front of him to keep from doing just that. It was as if he willed me to gaze into his eyes. I did, and saw, not the disapproval I was expecting, but concern.

"Thank you, Beth," he said.

"You're welcome."

"I apologize for upsetting you."

"No need to apologize," I was now willing to admit.

"You're not going to join us and have a piece of cake?" Uncle asked.

"I'll join you, but I had a piece earlier."

"Did you enjoy your stay with Grace?" Uncle asked me, as I took a seat opposite Max.

"I did, very much. Her home is lovely, and her family came to visit with us often. You'll be happy to know, Uncle, thanks to Professor Hubert's manuscripts, I have become quite good at reading hieroglyphics."

"That's splendid! And will be very helpful."

"I'll miss Grace and her family. Especially Martin—he and I did so much together."

Uncle gave me a strange look. Max stopped eating his cake and stared rather curiously. It took me a moment to realize why: Neither of them knew who Martin was, and both were obviously thinking that the nine-year-old boy was an English gentleman whom I had come to be on familiar terms with. I found this rather amusing and decided to have some fun with it.

"He's very sweet," I went on to say. "I so enjoyed his company. We loved studying the hieroglyphs together."

"Martin?" Uncle inquired.

"Martin Hubert," I told him. "Professor Hubert's grandson."

Max was still watching me closely, and Uncle Harry wanted to hear more. "He visited there often?" Uncle asked.

"Yes," I told him. "We became very close friends."

"I see."

"I intend to stay in touch with him," I said, wanting to laugh at their expressions, for I knew what they were both thinking: I had fallen in love. "If it would be okay with you, Uncle Harry, I would like to invite him here."

"You want him to come here?" Uncle asked, probably wondering just how serious was my relationship with Martin.

"Yes, if that's all right with you."

Uncle looked thoughtful, while Max, looked—jealous?

Surely, that was not the case. Max and I were not romantically involved. So, just why was he looking at me like that? Again, he was probably thinking how unorthodox I had become: traveling alone. Inviting what he presumed was a man to my home.

"Of course, you may invite anyone you like," Uncle finally said. "As long as proper arrangements are made. Cairo's hotel is accommodating enough—even for an Englishman."

It was time to end the fun. "Since Martin is only nine, Grace will probably come with him."

"Well, why didn't you say so?" Uncle remarked.

"She prefers to shock us," Max added, with a certain amount of sarcasm.

"Do my actions tend to shock you, Dr. Clairborne?" I asked, ready to do battle for the cause of women's rights.

"Your actions tend to make me a little—nervous."

"You do set us on edge at times," Uncle agreed.

I laughed. "I think you both have a tendency to overreact."

"Keeping you out of danger has been one of the toughest jobs I've ever had to deal with," Max told me. "You would think you could be just a little accommodating, Beth, and try to stay out of trouble."

Even if he was teasing, my feelings were bruised. I was nothing more than a job to him.

I did not care to converse with them any longer. I placed the empty cups and dessert plates onto the silver tray, excused myself, and carried them back into the kitchen. At about the time I finished washing and putting away the dishes, Max stopped by the kitchen to say goodbye.

"If you would like to go out one evening, I would be glad to take you," he offered.

Serving as protector?

"That's okay. It's not necessary for you to go through the trouble. Uncle and I will be traveling out to the site in a few days, so we won't be around. I hope that will make your job easier."

He looked puzzled for a moment, but soon caught my meaning. "Why do you take everything I say the wrong way?" he asked, perturbed.

"I know you have a very difficult situation here, with the robberies and all. I really didn't intend to make your job more troublesome. I'm sure the last thing you need right now is a silly woman on your hands to have to look after."

"Beth," he said, with a certain amount of patience. "For one, you're not some silly woman on my hands, nor are you just another facet to my job. I thought you would understand that by now. It's because I care."

"I know," I said. "You are that type of man. You care what happens to others."

"Not just others, but I am concerned a great deal about what happens to those I consider to be my friends. I didn't want to see you mixed up in all this. These men are dangerous."

"Yes, I have discovered that."

"Don't go out alone."

Again, I could not help but feel he was doing his job. "I won't," I said. "Uncle Harry will see to that."

"Good."

I saw him to the door. He said good night and then pointed to the door lock. "Make sure you secure it."

"Of course."

Max waited at the doorstep until he heard the lock click, and then he walked away.

I did not want to be a burden to anyone, especially Max. He needed to devote his full attention to apprehending those involved with the tomb robberies and the murder of Mr. Henderson. I decided then that it would be best not to see Max for a good while. It would be the only way that I could help him. I would help eliminate part of his job…me!

Chapter 18

The excitement was growing. Uncle and I would leave in the morning to begin work once again on the tomb of Smenkhkara. Meticulously, I went over the itemized list of things to take, each time adding to it. Also, laid out and ready for tomorrow, were my safari clothes: a khaki split skirt, white cotton blouse, and the boots. Everything was in order.

I closed my luggage and then took a good look at my room. I would miss the comforts, but the thrill of working at the site always took the place of not having them. By the end of the day total exhaustion always made sleep come easy anyway.

I could hear Uncle Harry in the study moving and shuffling papers around. His cough was getting worse and it caused me to worry. I decided a cup of hot tea would perhaps ease his discomfort; I entered the study with it. He was bent over a stack of papers, sorting out what to take with him.

"You really should go see the doctor before we leave," I told him, handing him the cup.

"No need to. He would just tell me to continue taking the medicine he prescribed, and to make sure that I'm not down in the tomb for more than six hours a day."

"You will do that, then?" I asked for my own solace.

He gave a nod of his head. "I will do it."

I bit down on my bottom lip and studied him for a moment. "Maybe we should postpone going out, Uncle Harry."

He looked up at me through the tops of his reading glasses. "Nonsense," he said. "I'm fine. Besides, staying here is not going to make this cough go away.

It sort of comes and goes. I think the weather has a lot to do with it."

I gave a heavy sigh.

"We don't have time for worry, Beth. Mrs. Bilgas will be here this afternoon to help you go over the food items we need to take. Do you have your things ready?"

He was trying to divert my thoughts from his health to the safari. "I'm ready," I couldn't help but say excitedly.

"Good, good," he said, as he shoved papers inside a folder that he planned to take with him. He stood straight. "Well, I think that just about does it. Everything's ready but finishing the two interviews set up for this afternoon."

"A freelance archeologist?" I asked, knowing he would need help.

"No, your bodyguard."

He had not forgotten.

"How do you know they can be trusted?" I asked.

"Dr. Clairborne recommended them."

"Oh, I see. I suppose that makes them trustworthy."

He laughed. "Yes, I would think so. They are employed by him when the need arises."

I wondered if the two men Uncle would be interviewing were the same men that had been used as my escorts the night of my rendezvous with Moses?

Probably.

When Mrs. Bilgas arrived I followed her into the kitchen. She was waving a slip of paper. "I have it all written down," she told me. "Your uncle needs to be fattened up, and it wouldn't hurt you a bit too."

"I like being thin," I told her. "It makes it easier to squeeze into difficult places inside the tombs. Places where others can't go."

"And that makes you happy?" she asked.

"It's great!"

She shook her head sadly. "It's not a place for a lady."

"Who said anything about my being a lady?" I laughed.

"What to do! What to do!" she said, waving her hand in the air as if giving up on the idea of my ever becoming one. "I see how that doctor friend looks at you."

"Whaaat!?" I said, wondering what she saw that my eyes had not.

"Ah—see, you don't even notice."

"I notice that he gets very annoyed with me."

"Why do you think he worries about you and looks out for your safety?"

"He's doing his job. He worries about the others too."

"But he does extra things to make sure you are well taken care of."

"And how do you know this?"

She gave me a wizened smile. "Because I heard him talking with your uncle."

The conversation was becoming very interesting. Just what did Mrs. Bilgas know that I did not?

"And—?" I prodded.

"Dr. Clairborne had a man," she whispered secretively, "that even followed you to London."

I was shocked. "An agent? You have got to be mistaken!"

"No, it is true."

"Why would he do such a thing and not tell me?" I asked angrily. "And Uncle Harry was in on this too? They should have told me!"

"They did not want you to be frightened."

"Well, just where was my protector when I was pushed out into the street—I would like to know?"

"Hmmm, that is a very good question. Maybe Dr. Clairborne dismissed him."

I laughed, and then became somber. "I'll be glad when all of this is over," I said. "I'm tired of it, Mrs. Bilgas."

"Yes, it is not good."

Another bout of coughing came from Uncle's study. "I really wish he would go see the doctor before we leave," I told her. "It's worse today. I'm really worried about him."

"He should stay home."

"I asked him if he thought we should, but you know Uncle Harry, not much could slow him down."

"It's that tomb," Mrs. Bilgas said as she began to pack our food into the large trunk.

"Why would you think that?"

"It is the way things are. The dead always punish those who intrude."

"Why, Mrs. Bilgas, are you referring to the curse?"

"You both should leave the dead alone, is what I say."

"You know Uncle Harry doesn't believe in ancient Egyptian curses."

Her dark eyes widened as she looked at me. "Do you?"

It had been a long time since the curse even crossed my mind. So much was happening with the tomb crimes to even give it place for thought, but I remembered Philip and all the events surrounding the excavation of Princess

Ihi. How could I ever forget the curse? I looked over at Mrs. Bilgas. "Yes, I do."

"Then you must warn your uncle."

"It won't do any good. He considers it all nonsense."

"You realize half of the workers left the site. He will have a difficult time finding new men."

I was perplexed. "Why? Uncle didn't say anything to me about it. Are you sure?"

"That is what my husband heard. When the workers found a cursed tablet, and your uncle collapsed inside the tomb. Well, they said it was the curse, and half of them walked away."

"Uncle collapsed?" I gasped.

"He did not tell you?"

"No, and he probably doesn't intend to. I will go and talk with the doctor today."

"He is not in town."

"Where is he?"

"In one of the villages. He goes there once a month for several days to take care of their sick."

"Well, I guess Uncle won't be seeing him before we leave then," I said, the disappointment growing. So many things were putting a damper on the excitement of going back out to the site: Uncle's illness; a murderer possibly hunting me down, and now the curse was once again raising its ugly head. The thrill was quickly diminishing.

"You will need to be careful," Mrs. Bilgas felt the need to say.

"Sometimes, I wish the tombs had never been discovered. Philip would still be here; the robberies would not have taken place, and poor Mr. Henderson would still be alive."

"What is it that your Bible says: To love money is an evil root?"

I smiled. "Yes, that is exactly what it means. 'The love of money is the root of all evil: which while some have coveted after, they have erred from the faith, and pierced themselves through with many sorrows,'" I quoted. "A wealthy man can be greedy of gain and do evil things to acquire more; whereas a man with little will steal and kill to have it. It doesn't really matter where a man fits in socially; money has its power over both poor and rich. It's where the heart is that matters."

We finished packing the food items, and then I helped with dinner preparations. After she finished her daily tasks, she left us.

Later, Uncle called me into the study. My newly acquired guards stood as

I entered the room. Uncle had completed the interviews and had decided to hire both men for the job. Their height and build alone were enough to ward off anyone that would dare be a threat to me.

Uncle Harry made introductions and then explained what they must do. I was to be guarded day and night. While one was resting, the other would keep vigil. They were to get a good night's rest, pack what they would need for the safari, and be ready to travel out to the site by eight in the morning.

They promptly agreed to their charge, shaking Uncle's hand to seal their contract, and then they bid us good evening.

After the evening meal, and with our trunks ready by the door, Uncle decided to retire early. "Tomorrow," he told me, "will be a taxing day."

He looked very fatigued.

I agreed and also went to bed an hour before my usual bedtime, but sleep did not come; the curse plagued my thoughts.

Uncle was a stickler for documenting every piece of antiquity. One small bead found on the floor in a tomb would not go unnoticed by Uncle. He would record what and where he found it, the condition of the piece, and the date of its find. If I wanted to know more about the cursed tablet found in Smenkhkara's tomb, I would find that information logged somewhere in Uncle's notes—I was sure of it.

I threw back the covers, slipped on my house shoes and robe, and then quietly made my way to Uncle's study. I found four leather-bound journals dated from the time I left Cairo until my return home, each containing one hundred pages of notes and drawings. My search could take awhile, so I decided to fix a cup of hot tea.

When I returned from the kitchen with the cup of hot tea, I sat behind Uncle's desk with the first journal and began to carefully go over each item documented. The information I sought was not in the first journal, however, about the middle of the second, I found the information I was looking for—the tablet.

Uncle noted: "Number 136, Lintel bearing a curse against tomb robbers. Valley of the Kings; Eighteenth dynasty; limestone. The reproduction of the text in hieroglyphs." He had not bothered to translate, but the hieroglyphs on the tablet were sketched on the bottom half of the paper, and thanks to Professor Hubert's manuscripts, I knew that I could decipher them.

Taking a pencil from Uncle's desk drawer, I began my work. The enigmatic combinations of plants and body parts, geometric figures and birds, soon took on meaning. Words were formed, and then the sentence. Once completed, I laid the pencil down and read it as a whole: "I will drive back the robbers of this tomb. I am the flame of the desert, and I will consume all that enter with the fire of vengeance."

Fear hit me hard. The words were menacing—evil. Uncle may not believe in curses, but I did, and I was terrified. I wondered then, what would become of us? Uncle was already fighting some sort of illness—was it possible that the curse was at work against him? He believed God to be greater than any curse, and I knew that to be true, but why did I fear it so? I had such little faith, and doubt seemed to be my constant companion.

I folded the paper I had used to translate the hieroglyphs and went back to my room. Sleep would not come easy, so I did not bother to get back into my bed. Instead, I paced in the only small space available between the end of my bed and armoire. I had to sort this out. I didn't suppose there was a way to reverse a curse. I had not heard of a way.

I began to pray. I told God all about my fears and doubts, and asked him to help my unbelief. I spent twenty minutes in prayer and fifteen reading in the book of Psalms. Peace came and finally I was able to sleep.

It was about three in the morning when I awoke. I sensed that something was wrong—a feeling, call it intuition. I got out of bed, slipped on my house shoes and threw on my robe. I had to make sure Uncle was all right.

I tapped lightly on Uncle's bedroom door, but there was no answer. "Uncle Harry," I whispered as I slowly opened the door. Immediately, I could tell something was wrong. The room was dark, but I could hear the raspy sound of his breathing. I felt panic rising within me.

"Uncle Harry," I said again, as I lit the candle on his bed stand.

He still did not answer me. I leaned over and laid the back of my hand across his forehead. He was burning up with fever. I took hold of his hand. "Uncle Harry," I sobbed. "What can I do?"

He was not responding.

There was a basin of cool water against one wall; I took a washcloth and dipped it into the water, and then placed it gently across his burning brow. He mumbled something. "Uncle Harry, I'm here," I told him. But what good was I? I did not know what to do. I needed the doctor, and he was away. How helpless I felt. There was nothing that I could do for him, nothing at all.

I sat on the edge of Uncle's bed, trying to pull myself together. I had to do something. Mrs. Bilgas, perhaps, could help. She was a very resourceful individual. She had raised a houseful of kids and would know what to do about fevers.

I would go for help. I went to my room and quickly changed into a dark skirt and white blouse, and a good pair of walking shoes. I did not want to draw attention to myself, as I would be out alone, so I put on a dark cloak with a hood.

Before walking out the door, I went back into Uncle's room. He was burning with fever and shivering uncontrollably. "I will be right back with help, Uncle Harry," I said worriedly.

Not giving myself time to panic, I quickly left his room and ran out of the house. My intentions were to go for Mrs. Bilgas, but then I remembered that Max was in town. *He had cured me when I had become ill from that insect bite. And he is a type of doctor,* I thought reassuringly. *He would know more about medicines than Mrs. Bilgas, and probably have what Uncle would need on hand.*

So, my plans quickly changed, and I headed for Max's place. Although I had promised myself not to be a bother to him again, I had no choice and I needed him desperately. I needed his ability to cure. I needed his strength right now, for I was so terribly weak. I needed his faith to fill in where doubt was telling me God could not help. Uncle was ill, but I was spiritually sick. The realization, that in this crisis, my faith and trust in God was suffering.

When I stepped up to Max's door and finally knocked, I stood waiting, anxiety shaking me to the very bone. The minutes seemed like hours. "Please hurry, Max."

He opened the door, the look of surprise when he saw me was apparent. "Good God, Beth!" he said, as he grabbed my arm and quickly pulled me inside, shutting the door behind me. "What are you doing?"

My breathing was uneven, and I was so upset I didn't even know if I could say a word without falling apart.

"Beth?" he whispered, gently prodding me to answer.

"It's Uncle Harry," I was finally able to say. "Oh, Max, he's dying."

Chapter 19

"I'm so sorry to awaken you at this hour, but the doctor is not in town." I began to sob. "Max, I need your help. Uncle Harry can't die on me. He's all the family I have."

I could say no more, but stood there crying, the tears staining my cheeks. Crying was not something I did often, but when I did the tears were impossible to stop.

"Beth," Max whispered and then pulled me into his embrace. "There is no need to apologize. I'm glad you came to me for help."

His hand held my head firmly against his chest where my tears were quickly wetting the front of his robe. His embrace was comforting, and I did not want him to let me go. I clung to him as if my life depended on it.

Suddenly, he put me at arm's length. "I'll only be a minute. Harry is going to be fine. Don't fall apart on me—I may need your help."

He left me, and again I felt alone, weak, frightened.

Within a matter of minutes he returned, dressed and carrying his black leather medical bag. "Let's go."

He took me by the hand and out the door we went, not wasting a moment's time. He did not know Uncle's true condition, only that I had said he was dying, therefore, time was vital—a precious commodity that many people waste without considering it can never be redeemed.

When we arrived, Uncle Harry's condition had not improved. I stood back as Max did his examination. I paced and prayed, waiting for the outcome; waiting to hear if Uncle's final hours upon this earth were coming to an end. I could not imagine life without him. I did not want to imagine life without him. However, if it did happen? If he did pass from this life...

"Beth." It was the second time Max had calmly said my name, but only the first that I consciously heard it. He brought me out of my thoughts as he stood in front of me. "Upper respiratory infection. I gave him something to bring the fever down and to help fight the infection. He's going to be okay, Beth, but it's going to be a long night. Why don't you go back to bed? I'll sit up with Harry."

I shook my head slowly. "I won't be able to sleep, Max. I can't leave Uncle's side until his fever goes down and I know he is resting easy."

Max checked his vital signs every fifteen minutes. Uncle continued to improve, along with my trepidation. I glanced over at Max, who sat on the opposite side of Uncle Harry. I was truly thankful for his presence and for his abilities. He had saved Uncle's life.

At that moment I realized that Max had become an important part of my life. *No,* I thought with clarity, considering the hour, *he has become a part of my heart and I could easily fall in love with him.* This thought must have been chiseled on my features. Max caught me looking at him, and before I could conceal such notions, his brow rose inquisitively.

"I'll go for coffee," I said, leaving the room quickly.

When the coffee began to brew, Max stepped into the kitchen. "I want to know how you are holding up?"

"After a few cups of coffee, I'll be fine," I lied. My hands were shaking so bad Max took the sugar bowl from me before I managed to drop it.

"I think you need to sit down and let me fix your cup."

I balled my hands into fists to stop the shaking. Max covered them with his, watching me closely.

"I'm afraid," I confessed.

"Harry will be all right."

"It's not that."

He bent down, eye level with me. "Afraid of what, Beth? When is Harry hiring those bodyguards?"

"He already has." How could I explain my fears about the cursed tablet? Max's views about ancient curses were not so dissimilar from Uncle's: he would think it all foolishness.

I removed my hands from his, and then nervously smoothed them across my face and through my hair. "I discovered that Uncle found a cursed tablet. Max—this is all a part of some curse, I can feel it. I may get through this today, but what about tomorrow—or the next day?"

He straightened, giving it some thought. "Beth, your uncle's life is not subject to some three-thousand-year-old curse. You know how he believes. His faith in God is stronger than some curse originated by a now-dead priest."

"I deciphered the hieroglyphs. It was horrible, Max. Uncle Harry had made note of it in one of his journals. Where do you suppose that tablet is now?"

"You're not listening to me," he said almost sternly. "That tablet has nothing to do with Harry's state of health."

I said nothing, for truly I believed that it did.

Max poured our coffee into two mugs, and then he led me to a chair. He took the seat next to mine. "If anything," he began, "it would be something tangible."

I wasn't sure what he meant. "You mean like something he touched?"

"Something like that—yes."

"It was," I agreed. "That cursed tablet."

"What part of the tomb has Harry been working in?" he asked, ignoring my insistence that Uncle's illness had something to do with the cursed tablet.

I thought for a moment before answering. "I think the burial chamber."

"He has not found an adjoining chamber that, perhaps, not many but himself have entered?"

I shrugged my shoulders and then slowly shook my head. "Not that I know of." I narrowed my eyes at him. "Where are you going with this, Max?"

"I want to go take a look at where Harry's been spending most of his time these past six months."

"Best ask Uncle Harry. Will he come out of this stupor soon?"

"Now that the fever is down. When the sun rises, I think he'll come around."

He said nothing more, but took a drink of his coffee. I could tell his mind was working—sorting it out. He would search for a logical explanation, a reason for Uncle's condition. But I had little faith: I wanted to find a way to reverse a curse.

At about 7:00 a.m., Uncle Harry came to. Max had just completed checking his vitals. I had, at some time, drifted off to sleep; my arms and head were still resting on Uncle's bed when Max's movements awakened me. The sun rays were beginning to stream through the window. I had to blink to adjust to the brighter light. "Is he okay?" I asked Max, my voice still sleepy.

"Ask him for yourself," Max said, giving me an encouraging smile.

"Uncle Harry?"

Uncle slowly turned his head to look at me. "You don't look so good."

I laughed. "You had me worried," I told him, wanting to cry for joy.

"What happened?" he then could only whisper.

Max was the one who answered. "You have a bad case of upper respiratory infection, and had a fever that would put down a strong horse."

Uncle studied Max for a moment. "I won't ask how you managed to find this out in the middle of the night."

"Probably best," Max agreed, knowing Uncle wouldn't like the thought of me walking the streets at night unescorted. "Harry, you'll need to take it easy for a while."

Uncle moaned. "I don't have time for this."

"Uncle Harry," I said sternly, "you'll do whatever Max tells you to do!"

Max smiled down at Uncle. "You're outnumbered, two to one."

"I wouldn't have the strength to do otherwise," Uncle told us.

I worriedly bit down on my bottom lip. Would Uncle Harry be able to fight off this infection? Would he ever be well enough to finish his work at the tomb? The tomb didn't matter, he could easily hire someone else to complete the job, and it was his recovery that was of utmost importance.

"How about something to eat?" I asked, wanting to help him regain his strength.

Uncle took hold of my hand. "Not right now."

"We do need to get some fluids down you," Max told him. "You don't run a fever that high and not have some dehydration." He turned to me. "We'll start with water—room temperature, then in a few hours, clear broth."

I nodded my head to his instructions and then went for the water. I took the water to Uncle, propped up his head, and held the cup to his lips. He drank it slowly.

When my two bodyguards arrived, Max explained the situation and sent them home. He told them he would be staying for the remainder of the day and would keep a close eye on me, but asked that one of them return later that afternoon.

After they left and we gave Uncle a good amount of clear broth, I shoved a pillow into Max's hands. "Uncle has a very comfortable sofa in his study. Go rest."

He took the pillow and smiled. "There are times when you can be very aggressive."

"Only when I have to be. You don't like it?"

"I think you need sleep worse than I do; you're a bear."

I smiled. "I'm going to take a quick shower and then curl up on the recliner beside Uncle Harry's bed. I'll sleep, and if there's any change I'll come wake you."

Later, I awoke to the smell of food. My hair was down, and in thicker areas, still damp from its washing; the ends were starting to curl up in an uncontrollable way. *How long had I slept? And the smell of food!*

I noticed Max leaning on the doorjamb, a cup of coffee in one hand, casually watching me. I was suddenly conscientious of how I must look: tousled.

He smiled. "Hungry?"

"Famished. What time is it?"

"Almost two."

"Oh my—I didn't mean to sleep so late. You should have awakened me."

I stood up and began to smooth out the wrinkles in my khaki skirt. "I must look a mess."

"On the contrary," he remarked, still looking me over.

I felt a blush coming on. "Did you fix it?"

He was not thinking about the food; that was obvious with his answer. "Fix what?"

"Lunch."

He stood straight. "Yes, and it's ready."

I followed him into the kitchen to see what he had prepared. "Can you cook?"

"I can make do."

On the stove were sausage and scrambled eggs with biscuits and hash browns. "This looks great! I'm impressed."

"Well, I'll remember what to do if I ever want to impress you."

We ate at the table. "This is really good, Max, but I should be the one fixing your meal. I can't thank you enough for what you've done. You saved Uncle Harry's life."

"He's still going to have a rough couple of days." He rubbed a hand across his chin. "I'll head home, shower and shave, pick up the medicine Harry will need for tonight, and be back before dark."

"You'll stay again tonight?" I asked with hope.

"I think I better."

"I wouldn't know what to do if Uncle Harry had another spell like last night. I would just have to come after you again."

"Yes, I know."

I could tell by the tone of his voice that that was another reason why he thought it best to stay the night: so I would not wander out alone. How would I ever repay him? "Don't worry about fixing yourself something to eat, I'll have supper ready for you when you return."

"Thank you."

"Go ahead and go home, Max. I think I can manage Uncle's care for a couple of hours," I told him.

"I'll wait," he told me.

"For what?"

"One of your guards."

"Max—!"

He held up a hand to stop my protest. "Don't go in that direction, Beth. You've already discovered how dangerous these men can be. Humor me, if you must, but I'm not leaving until one of them arrives."

"Very well," I whispered obediently, as I began to clear away the dishes.

Five hours later, Buckingham Palace's famous changing of the guards took place: Max and my present bodyguard, whose code name was Joshua, made their switch. Max had changed into khaki trousers, and an off-white chambray shirt. He looked relaxed, comfortable.

"How's Harry doing?" was the first thing he asked upon his return.

"Thirty minutes ago he was sleeping like a baby."

I followed Max into Uncle's room. He checked his vital signs and then stood over him. "Well, Harry, everything looks good, you are running a slight fever and it will most likely increase as night falls. If it's all right with you, I want to give you the same treatment."

"That seemed to work," Uncle Harry told him.

"Harry, what part of the tomb have you been working?" Max then asked.

"The burial chamber."

"Have you discovered any new adjoining chambers that not many but yourself have had a chance to enter?"

"Yes, Abdul and I discovered an adjoining cubical a month ago."

I was surprised. "Why did you not tell me about it?"

Uncle looked my way. "My plans were to show it to you today."

Max asked, "Can you tell me about it? Anything unusual?"

Uncle thought for a moment. "It is were the king's vital organs were placed inside four cylindrical cavities made of calcite-alabaster. Some papyrus, but I think it was a chamber specifically made for the protection of the king's vital organs. That is why I believe the tablet was placed inside that chamber instead of the burial chamber."

"You mean the cursed tablet?" I asked.

Uncle skirted my question by adding, "The organs are in four canopic jars with the heads of the Sons of Horus, who is responsible for the magical protection of the king's internal organs."

"Is the cursed tablet still there?" I wanted to know.

"No. The workers learned of it, and so I had it removed."

"I would like your permission to have a look inside that chamber, Harry," said Max.

"You still have the key. You don't need my permission to go in."

"I prefer that you know," Max told him.

"Abdul knows that I have given you access to the tomb. He will not ask questions."

Max nodded.

"What are you thinking, Max?" Uncle then went on to ask. "You've questioned me concerning my whereabouts in the tomb, and now you want to have a look for yourself? I did a candle test; the air seemed fine."

"There are other ways, Harry."

"Other ways for what?" I asked Max.

"Written words alone can't ward off intruders," Max explained. "I want to gather dust samples and see what I can find."

"So, you think I have come in contact with a booby trap of sorts, and that is why I am ill."

"That is what I'm thinking," Max admitted. "A fungus, perhaps…maybe poison."

"Poison!" I blurted out.

"Poison is as old as the history of mankind," Max explained. "The first pharaoh, Menes, grew poisonous plants around 3000 B.C. and actually had their effects recorded. It has been discovered that the Egyptians used opium, hemlock, henbane, arsenic, and monkshood. Aconite is produced from monkshood; just five milligrams are deadly. Socrates died by drinking hemlock. Cleopatra mixed poisons expertly. It would not surprise me to find in any Egyptian tomb, traces of poison or bacteria that have survived for thousands of years. It is very conceivable that narcotic fungi could protect the Egyptian tombs. Just breathing such fungi would certainly touch anyone on entering a tomb and be a massive deterrent to any grave robber."

"Do what you like," Uncle Harry told him. "And please let me know what you discover."

"This is frightening," I said, beginning to understand exactly what Max had meant by the curse being something tangible. His theory was logical and made sense, completely unlike my theory that was based on hokum and evil incantations.

Again, the tombs were not looking so grandiose.

Chapter 20

Three days later, and with Uncle Harry up and about, Max left us to go and gather dust samples from the tomb of Smenkhkara. I was relieved that Uncle's health was daily improving; he was beginning to be his usual self. And thanks to Max, the curse was no longer a dark secret from the realm of the spirit world, but rather something of this earth after all. I trusted Max to discover the real cause behind Uncle Harry's illness, and no matter what his findings, Max would know what to do about it.

I was still curious about the cursed tablet that had been discovered in Smenkhkara's tomb. I wanted to see it for myself, so when Mrs. Bilgas arrived, I walked to the museum with my bodyguard shadowing me.

It had been some time since I had seen Dr. Mehreiz. He noticed me first. "Why Elizabeth!" he said in greeting. "It is so good to see you. How's Harry doing?"

"He has been very ill."

"The last time I saw Harry, he'd lost a little weight. I wondered then if he was working himself too hard."

"Yes, that, and he is battling a severe case of upper respiratory infection accompanied with extremely high fevers. Dr. Clairborne has been treating him for the infection. He is doing much better now."

"Splendid," he said. "What brings you here?"

"Well, I'm hoping you can tell me what my Uncle Harry did with that cursed tablet he found in Smenkhkara's tomb. I'd like to see it for myself."

He looked at me a bit strangely. "You want to see it?"

"Do you know what he did with it?"

"Yes, he brought it here. Harry had it removed because the workers were afraid to be on-site with it. He lost almost half of his manpower because of that tablet."

"Yes, I know."

"You're not afraid of it."

"The curse?" I asked.

He gave a nod of his head.

"At one time," I admitted. "But Dr. Clairborne has given me a better understanding of what makes the curse effective."

"Hmm, I see. Well, follow me. I'll show it to you."

He looked behind me and noticed Joshua. "He follows," I said. "Uncle Harry wants me guarded until the tomb robbers are caught."

"Very well, then." He motioned with his hand for us to follow him.

We entered a back room where antiquities were dispersed in an unorganized way. The room, I knew, was where items were placed until given a permanent location inside the museum's public viewing areas. The tablet lay on top of a table against the back wall, covered by a large white cloth.

"This is it," Dr. Mehreiz told us, as he lifted the cloth from the limestone tablet.

Dust particles from off the tablet began to float in the air; I could not help but be alarmed. "Stand back until the dust settles," I quickly warned. "Dr. Clairborne believes that the dust could be a type of poison." I then focused my attention on Dr. Mehreiz. "Have you touched this tablet at all?"

"No, Harry's the one that set it up back here. I've only seen it one other time, and that was right before Harry covered it with this cloth."

"That's good," I said with relief. "Don't let anyone else come near it until Dr. Clairborne has finished with his test."

I looked down at the limestone tablet, already understanding the meaning of hieroglyphic inscription. The tablet no longer seemed to me an evil thing, but now had the historical significance it deserved. "It's fascinating," I told them. "And it is in excellent condition."

"Not many would see it as a rare find. Most hope to avoid finding such a piece," Joshua spoke out.

"Yes, I know," I said, laughing. "Until Dr. Clairborne explained to me about the poisons the Egyptians used, I truly believed cursed tablets held certain powers. But it makes better sense, don't you think, that poisons were used to help activate whatever curse was placed upon some tomb. At least, that is Dr. Clairborne's theory."

When we were through looking at it, Dr. Mehreiz carefully laid the white cloth over the tablet. I insisted that he go and wash his hands immediately. He did so, and then Joshua and I left him.

I had done it! I had come face to face with my greatest fear: a cursed tablet. It did not frighten me. It did not hold some unknown power over me, threatening me with impending doom. There were still unexplained questions in my mind: Lord Carnavon's mysterious death, for one, and I could still not dismiss the fact that Princess Ihi was in Captain Smith's quarters aboard the *Titanic*, and that his behavior had been recorded as being somewhat irrational. I would have to talk with Max about all of it. He would have an explanation.

As we were coming out of the museum, we ran into Mr. Corinth. He was coming into the museum as we were going out. He stopped; I stopped.

"Mr. Corinth!" I spoke first. "How good to see you."

"Miss Woodruff, I believe," he said with a smile. "How are you doing?"

He took my hand in greeting, and then released it. "This is Joshua," I said introducing my guard, for it seemed the appropriate thing to do.

"A pleasure," Mr. Corinth said, as he shook Joshua's hand in greeting.

Joshua did not smile, but did shake his hand, and then said, "Sir, it is good to meet you."

I could tell Joshua was taking note of Mr. Corinth, doing his job as my protector. "Mr. Corinth is the director of the British Museum," I told Joshua, hoping to ease his mind by telling him just who Mr. Corinth was.

Joshua only gave a nod, seeming unimpressed.

"You have returned to Egypt to stay, or are you visiting with your uncle?" Mr. Corinth asked.

"I plan to stay. And you, are you here visiting, or taking care of business?"

He smiled. "Both."

"How is Miss Gentry?" He did not immediately respond, so I clarified the question by adding, "Mr. Finley's new secretary."

"Oh—yes. She seems to be working out just fine. Mr. Henderson's death was a shock to us all."

"Yes, I was sorry to hear what had happened to Mr. Henderson. His daughter believes he was murdered, Mr. Corinth."

He appeared thoughtful, maybe concerned. "I can't imagine why anyone would want to murder Mr. Henderson…can you?"

"His daughter said the same. She could not think of a reason. I personally did not know him, but it does appear that foul play should not be ruled out. I believe that once the mastermind behind the tomb robberies is apprehended—Well, it would not surprise me if Mr. Henderson's death were not linked to whoever is behind all these tomb robberies."

"You are probably right," he agreed. "Perhaps, the authorities can be persuaded to look further into it."

There was a brief pause in conversation, and then he said, "We are sorry that you are no longer a part of our staff, Miss Woodruff. Mr. Finley said you were in a bit of a hurry to leave."

"There were certain reasons why I had to return home immediately."

"Well, I hope those reasons were not serious ones."

"Uncle Harry has been very ill. I thought I should be here with him."

"That's understandable. I had heard that Harry was a bit under the weather. I trust he is doing better?"

"Yes—he is much better, thank you."

"How is the excavation coming along?"

"Uncle's illness has slowed down the progress."

"I'm sorry to hear that."

"He'll be back at it in no time."

"Well, I must be going. I have a meeting to attend. Do tell Harry I said hello. Good day, Miss Woodruff."

"Good day, Mr. Corinth."

For the remainder of the day, my conversation with Mr. Corinth stayed with me. He, too, did not rule out the possibility that Mr. Henderson could have been murdered, and that it could be linked to the culprits behind the tomb robberies. Perhaps, Mr. Corinth would think about that possibility and have the authorities look further into the cause of Mr. Henderson's death.

The next day Uncle Harry went to the museum to do a little work. I stayed home to unpack a few things, as it was not likely that we would be traveling out to the site for several more weeks—Max's orders. So, I began to unpack what I knew we would need. The house was quiet, so I jumped when the doorbell rang.

A boy, not much older than twelve, tall and lanky, dark eyes, hair, and skin, stood on the doorstep, smiling. "You are Miss Woodruff," he asked. "This letter for you."

I took the letter he handed over to me, thanked him, and then gave him a coin for his services. I shut the door and went back into Uncle's study to read my letter.

It was from Max. He was at the tomb and had found something significant. I was to come out immediately.

I packed a few things into an overnight bag, wrote Uncle Harry a letter telling him where I was going, and that Abraham, my alternate bodyguard, would be with me. He was not to worry, Max would see me safely home. I placed Max's letter to me, and my letter to Uncle Harry on the table by the front door. He would not miss them.

I picked up my hat, which hung on a hook by the door, then explained to Abraham where we were headed.

One thing that Uncle Harry did not specify to my vigilant guards, and that was to stop me from doing anything Uncle would consider foolish. So, Abraham did not dispute, but followed obediently.

Abraham led me to the river. We took one of the boats and went to the site.

The valley looked dreadful under the glare of the late afternoon sun. And although it was windless, sand managed to find its way into my hair and clothing.

The place was deserted, and I was beginning to have qualms about coming without Uncle. I did not see any signs of Max, and began to worry that I had missed him.

I had Abraham light one of the torches, and then, with me leading the way into Smenkhkara's tomb, we descended slowly, staying close.

I called out to Max several times but he did not answer.

"I fear something is wrong, Abraham."

"We should go back," he warned.

"But what if Max is hurt and needs our help. Come, we are almost to the end."

I heard the horrible thud as we reached the end of the passageway. I turned to find my guard on the floor, lifeless, and a man standing over him, holding a torch. I froze.

"Well, I see you got my message," he hissed wickedly.

I did not know who this man was, but I did know that he was dangerous. He was a large and well-muscled man, one that would use his strength to bully. He was holding a gun, and it was pointed directly at me.

"What do you want?" though afraid, I managed to ask.

He gave a menacing laugh. "What do I want?" he said, shaking the gun at me. "I think I should be asking that question: It's…what do you want?"

I must remain calm, I thought. "I don't know what you mean."

"You've been asking too many questions. Have you not heard the saying: Curiosity killed the cat?"

"This is absurd!"

"You will tell us who your leader is?" he then advised.

"My leader?"

"Don't play innocent, Miss Woodruff. It won't work with me. Clever of them, to use a woman."

He thinks I'm working for the underground operation! "I'm not an agent—if that is what you are thinking."

He threw back his head and laughed. "Your uncle, then?"

"You leave Uncle Harry out of this!" I snapped back.

"Maybe. If you tell us those involved with the underground operation. I might be able to spare him. As for you, I'm sorry to say, you know too much. A pity."

I was afraid. "What do you intend to do with me?"

"Oh—I don't intend to touch you," he then explained. "However—" his smile widened, "you have heard of the curse of the pharaohs. We will let the curse take care of you for us."

It was then that I realized he had used the words "us" and "we" several times. He was not working alone. He was working for someone else, doing the dirty work, as they say. What could I do to save myself from his diabolical plans? He had a gun and I had nothing. If only Abraham would awaken, or was he dead?

"You see," he went on to explain, "when they find you, there will not be any marks on your body, not a hair of your head will have been touched. That will most certainly confuse even the best of them. Not even Scotland Yard will be able to solve this one." He then pulled out a candle. "It's laced with arsenic. A simple method, but the vapors are deadly and untraceable; they are supposed to have killed Pope Clement VII in 1534 and Emperor Leopold I of Austria in 1705. I will place it out of your reach, and—"

He stepped forward and yanked the key to the tomb's padlock from my belt loop.

"I will lock you and your friend in the tomb," he said, pointing to Abraham on the floor. "You will both die. They will blame the curse."

"No they won't! I have too many friends that are intelligent enough to know better. And you, sir, will be found out eventually. You will not get away with this, and neither will your leader."

"Well, we shall see. Now, if you wish to spare your uncle's life, then you will tell me who the leader is of this underground operation."

I thought a moment. What could I do? Maybe there was a way out of this? "All right, I will tell you. But first, you must tell me who is the mastermind behind the tomb robberies."

He shrugged his shoulders. "What good will it do you to know? You'll be dead."

"Then it won't matter if you tell me."

"Why do you want to know? You should be pleading for your life instead."

"Would it make a difference if I did?"

"No."

"You don't have to do this. My uncle would be willing to give you any valuable antiquity in exchange for my life. I'm sure it would be worth more than what you are being paid now."

"You do know how to bargain. But I am already being well compensated. You see—my leader has access to any piece of antiquity you could ever imagine. And I can pick out any one of them."

Silently I prayed, for I knew that I was doomed. There was no bargaining with this man. He was going to kill me, and unless Abraham awakened and was able to overpower him, we would not live to see another day. And yet, through it all, I wanted to know who was behind the robberies.

"Your leader is a clever man," I then said. "Tell me, who is he?"

It was then, out of a dark corner, stepped—Mr. Rogers?

Chapter 21

"Unless you want to be shot in the back," Mr. Rogers warned the man. "I suggest you drop the gun."

The man turned, still holding the gun. He was about to shoot Mr. Rogers, when the snap of a whip knocked it out of his hand, hurling it to the tomb floor.

"We prefer you alive," came Max's voice from the shadows.

Max stepped forward, the tail of his whip still encircling the man's wrist. "Are you okay?" he asked me, as he worked to bind the man's hands with rope.

Everything happened so quickly; I just stood there dumbfounded.

"Beth?" Max asked again, concerned, looking my way.

Rogers came forward. "I'll finish up with him," he told Max, taking the rope from his hand.

Max came to me, and took me in his arms. "It's over," he said gently. "Are you okay?"

I began to shake. I suppose the aftereffects of it all began to take its toll on me. "Yes," I was finally able to say.

His embrace tightened as he gave a sigh of relief. "I prayed I would make it in time."

"How did you know?"

"I was with Harry when he read your letter. I knew that it was not me who asked you to come here."

He let go of me and knelt beside Abraham, who lay seemingly lifeless on the tomb floor.

"Is he alive?" I asked.

"Yes, but he'll wish he wasn't when he comes to. He'll have a nasty headache when he awakens."

When Abraham came out of his unconsciousness, he moaned. Max gave him a few minutes and then helped him to his feet.

"If I can get you out of this tomb," Max told him. "I'll be able to have a better look at that bloody bump on your head."

"Here, I'll help," I offered, coming around to Abraham's other side.

"Fine guard I make," Abraham said, trying to walk steady.

"It's not your fault," I told him. "We were stealthily waylaid."

"But that's what guards are for: to thwart such happenings."

"Let's not worry about that now," I told him. "We must get you out of here so Max can make sure that you're all right."

"Rogers, everything under control?" Max asked over his shoulder.

"We've got our man," Mr. Rogers assured him.

"Let's get out of here," Max ordered, and we began a slow ascent. The remaining daylight outside the tomb was a welcome sight.

Until the authorities from the Antiquities Service Department arrived, Mr. Rogers kept a vigilant eye on the prisoner, while Max and I saw to Abraham's wound. He had quite a knot on his head. I helped Max wash the blood out of his hair with water before he stitched up the wound.

"This is all my fault," I told Abraham. "I am so sorry I got you into this."

"The next time," Max then spoke out, as he began to stitch up the laceration. "You just tie her to a chair. She'll be less trouble that way."

"You are quite humorous, Dr. Clairborne."

His smile widened. "I'll give you something for that headache," he told Abraham, as he put his things back into his black leather medical bag. "And then when we get the tents erected the best thing for you to do is lie down."

"We're staying?" I asked.

"It'll be nightfall soon. No sense traveling in the dark if we don't have to."

Uncle Harry arrived with an entourage: Dr. Mehreiz and the Antiquity Service Department authorities, which, I learned later, took charge over our prisoner. About ten of Uncle's men were also with the group; they began to erect the tents that Uncle brought with him, loaded on the backs of camels.

Uncle Harry hugged me tightly. "I would have come with Max earlier, but I was worried I'd only slow him down. I knew Max would get to you in time—thank God."

"Oh, Uncle Harry!" I cried out. "This was all so horrid."

After everything was in order, I sat next to the campfire; Uncle Harry and Dr. Mehreiz were on the opposite side. Max came and sat next to me.

"How's the prisoner?" Uncle asked Max.

"I would just as soon see him hang," Max voiced. "His intentions were to kill Beth."

I remembered the candle. "Max, he had a candle dipped in arsenic. He was going to use it to kill Abraham and me. If someone else gets a hold of it—"

"We've already got it," he assured me.

"That's good."

"He'll testify, then?" Uncle inquired.

"To save his own neck. Yes. He doesn't deserve leniency. His intent was to murder. I don't care if he is our prime witness and tells the court he's working for Corinth."

"Corinth!?" I blurted out. "Nathaniel Corinth? You think Mr. Corinth is the mastermind behind the tomb crimes?"

"Yes, he is the mastermind behind all the robberies," Uncle informed me.

Mr. Corinth! It was not possible! He was a family man. An intelligent human being that should know better. "This can't be! Why? Why would he be a part of such goings-on? He seemed such a nice man." And then I realized that if Mr. Corinth was the mastermind, then it was his orders that could have brought about my demise.

I felt sick.

I stood quickly, my emotions in turmoil. "I don't feel so well. I'm going to go get something to drink." And although it was dark, I turned and began my way to the tent where a cooler and folding tables were set up for our meals. A jug of tea was kept in the cooler. I grabbed the jug and poured a sufficient amount of tea into a mug.

My head was beginning to hurt, and my stomach had an odd feeling. Strange, how the body reacts to unpleasant news.

"Are you okay?" Max asked, coming up behind me.

I turned to face him. "A little disturbed. What makes men do such things, Max?"

"Power. Greed. Sometimes even reasons that they think make it justifiable. Corinth, for instance, feels that it is more important to preserve, or take what others don't value."

I remembered then my conversation with Mr. Corinth aboard ship. "Yes, he did seem concerned about preservation, and mentioned that many would sell their most priceless treasures to any foreigner for a few dollars. But to murder..."

"I think we can rule Mr. Corinth's crimes as obsessive behavior, one that got out of control."

"What do you know about Mr. Henderson's death? Was he murdered by someone working for Corinth?"

"Are you sure you want to hear this?"

"Yes, Max. I need to know."

"Although Mr. Corinth would not murder himself, he hired men that gave it no thought. Perhaps, one situation led to another, and Corinth got in way over his head."

I began to remember bits and pieces of my encounters with Mr. Corinth. "I made a list of items I had penned from the drawer, listing the museum's personal collections. Mr. Henderson had done the same, and was murdered for it. Mr. Corinth also saw my list and it wasn't long after that, that I was pushed out into the street. I was right in thinking then that someone wanted me dead."

"Yes, James saw the man that pushed you out into the street. And we knew that this same man had met up with Corinth on several occasions; that's when we narrowed the crimes down to Corinth."

"James—who's James?"

"Mr. Rogers."

"Mr. Rogers. Tell me, is he the agent that Mrs. Bilgas said you sent to England to follow me?"

Even though it was dark, I could tell he was smiling. "I confess."

"Confess!" I repeated. "Caught is more like it. And I can't imagine why you would do such a thing."

"Because I care."

"But to have me followed."

"I worried constantly that you would get into some sort of trouble and I wouldn't be there to help. Rogers was able to keep an eye on you, where I could not."

I could sense the rising chemistry between us. "You worried constantly?" I whispered.

"Every day," came his reply.

"You thought about me?"

He gave a short laugh. "Yes. And you say that as if you don't believe me."

"Well, I—"

It was then he gently took hold of my hand and pulled me into his arms. "Beth, how long is it going to take for you to figure this out?"

My hand was resting upon his chest. His heart, beating as rapidly as mine, and being close to him was certainly making my head spin. "Figure out what?" I asked, gazing up at him.

"I'm in love with you," he confessed softly, and before I could say anything, he lowered his head.

His lips were warm and soft as they settled on mine, causing me to go limp in his arms. It felt right, as if he and I were meant to be together.

When the kiss ended, his embrace relaxed. "Max," I said softly. "I thought the only feelings I ever managed to arouse in you were those of frustration, annoyance, anger."

He laughed. "I think those feelings also come with loving you."

I wasn't sure I liked his answer. "Really. Perhaps, then, I would be more trouble than what I'm worth."

He smiled. "Oh no! You are worth a great deal to me. Why do you think I've made certain you were closely watched and looked after? And what are your feelings, Beth? Could you learn to care as deeply for me, as I do for you?"

"With all my heart," I whispered sincerely.

"Do you think Harry will mind about us?"

I laughed. "You've saved my life and his. I don't think he'll mind too much. And he does like you."

"That's sure to be in my favor," he said in jest.

"Truly. What about us could he possibly not like? You are a good man."

Again, he pulled me close. "Good enough to marry one day?"

"I think that's a definite possibility."

He kissed me again, and then said, "After all of this is behind us, we'll discuss that possibility."

I gently pulled away from him. "Max, what will happen now?"

"You mean with Nathaniel Corinth."

"Yes."

"Rogers and I will leave before sunup along with several officials from the Antiquities Department. Corinth will be placed under arrest, tried for his crimes and then sentenced."

"I feel for his family."

"I'm sure it will be a great shock to them. A man is a fool to not weigh out the consequences of his actions, especially when his family will be affected by what he does."

"How long will you be gone?"

"Several weeks; maybe a month."

"That long?"

He smiled. "You'll miss me then?"

"You know I will."

"One thing is certain: I'll be back as soon as possible."

"I'll count on that."

The day's events suddenly left me feeling drained. I let my head fall to his chest, to rest there for a moment.

"You're exhausted," he said, holding me steady. "I think it's time to say good night. I'll walk you to your tent."

Holding tightly to my hand, Max walked me to my tent. There we said goodbye. "Please be careful, Max. Mr. Corinth is obviously a dangerous man."

His thumb brushed against my cheek. "I'll be careful," he promised. "There's someone I intend to come back to."

He kissed me good night and then left me. I hated the thought of letting him go, knowing that I would not see him for weeks to come. I was already missing him terribly.

The following weeks Uncle Harry and I worked out at the site. His health seemed to be improving, and I watched him closely, insisting that he do as the doctor had ordered and only work six-hour days. So, from early morning until noon we worked in the burial chamber, the remainder of the workday was spent above ground. I, of course, did all of the cataloguing. Occasionally, I stood by to watch Uncle Harry and Mr. Riley with the preservation process. Mr. Madison, the photographer, was also present on-site doing his job. In a matter of weeks, according to Uncle Harry, the excavation of Smenkhkara's tomb would be complete.

We were into the middle of the third week when Max arrived. I was up before dawn and had already made a pot of coffee. I poured myself a cup and faced the horizon to watch the sunrise. I was taken by surprise when Max came up behind me and enveloped me in a bear hug.

"Good morning," he whispered into my ear.

"Max!" I turned, splashing coffee everywhere.

He took the cup out of my hand and placed it on the table next to us. "Now," he said with a smile. "Let's do this right."

My arms went around his neck, and his around my waist. He kissed me properly and then released me. "You're beautiful in the morning," he said.

"That's because I've already had a chance to comb my hair. Earlier, you would have come face to face with Medusa."

"The snake goddess?"

"No, Max, the snake Gorgon."

His hand touched the curls against my back. "Somehow, I don't believe that."

"When did you arrive?"

"A little after midnight."

"You should have awakened me."

"I wanted to."

"And why didn't you?"

"That bodyguard of yours wouldn't let me. He said you'd gone to bed with a headache and weren't to be disturbed."

"My bodyguard!?"

"Yes, you remember, Abraham."

"But I no longer need a bodyguard."

"He feels that you do."

"What's going on?" I asked suspiciously.

Max raised his hands in the air. "I'm not the one that put him up to it, if that's what you're thinking. I assume he feels badly that you were accosted by one of Mr. Corinth's men, and that he failed to be the one to help you."

"You think he's feeling guilty?"

"That's probably all that it is. Humor him for a little while—it'll pass. Besides, now that I'm here," he said, taking hold of my arm, and drawing me close. "I'll take over for him."

"Doing your job once again?"

"I love my job."

"Do you?"

"With all my heart."

I smiled, his words making my heart swell.

"What are you doing up so early?" he then asked, as he released me to pour himself a cup of coffee.

"I wanted to watch the sunrise."

He handed me my cup and together we faced the horizon. He stood behind me with one arm around my waist, the other holding his cup of coffee. I let the back of my head rest against his chest. "Did everything go well?" I asked, referring to Mr. Corinth's arrest.

"It did."

"I'm glad it's over with, Max." I sighed contentedly and then said, "So much has happened in the last two years. Good and bad."

"The bitter with the sweet."

"Is that the way life will always be: the bitter with the sweet? I was so certain the curse of the pharaohs was a dark evil that would eventually kill us all. But then, you explained it all so clearly."

"Some of it can be explained."

"I believed that the tragedy of the *Titanic* was due to the curse found under Princess Ihi's pillow. When Uncle Harry became ill and I had discovered he'd found that cursed tablet. The words were menacing. It was terrifying to read: 'I am the flame of the desert, and I will consume all that enter with the fire of vengeance.' I was certain Uncle had become another victim of some ancient Egyptian curse. Do you think I'm foolish?"

"No. And you're not the only one that thought the *Titanic* sank because of the curse. It's the kind of story people love to tell around a campfire. I've heard it more than once: The mummy whose curse killed archeologists and Egyptologists indiscriminately before taking the ill-fated passengers of the *R.M.S. Titanic* to their watery graves! It was written up in the *Herald*, Beth. I do know that because of her great value, the princess was placed in the command bridge. It is a fact that her coffin was heavily encased in gold. We know that gold and uranium are often found in the same mines. I believe that the ancient Egyptian priests understood the laws of atomic decay, and that they were familiar with the effects of uranium. The question still arises: was Captain Smith affected by radiation? Small amounts of radiation can cause serious damage to health, and make people act irrationally. The effects of uranium can destroy the body's cell structure. It is possible that many amulets as well as artifacts contained deadly radioactive elements, designed to carry out the death formulas."

"Then you believe that Captain Smith did act irrationally because of being in close confinement with Princess Ihi?"

"I believe Captain Smith was having an adrenaline rush with his new ship. He was testing her capabilities; her speed; pushing her within what he probably considered reasonable boundaries."

"Yes, I see what you mean. Like a man and his automobile, or his horse."

"Yes."

"You have an explanation for everything."

He laughed. "No, Beth, not always. So, don't expect it."

The sun was slowly rising over the horizon. It was beautiful, and I was content. The sky and the desert sand were awash with purple, reds, orange and gold. "It's so lovely," I whispered reverently.

"There is your flame of the desert, Beth," he said of the sunrise. "And it is our God who created it."

I smiled. My feelings for him blossomed. "I love you, Max."

He turned me toward him, cupping my face in his capable hands. He kissed me. "I've been waiting a long time to hear you say those words."

As the sun rose to its fullest, I knew that the future was for us to make; to be written in stone, for the world to read, like that of an ancient Egyptian tablet. We smiled at each other; and the love I saw in his eyes held promise. I knew then that I wanted to live my life with Max. I wanted our love to be a love not built on the shifting sands of passion, but on the firm rock of deep and abiding love. With God as our spiritual Rock it could be nothing less. Life was good and seemed brighter because of the darkness that had prevailed for a time. Yet, I could now look ahead without fear. I had Max by my side.

CPSIA information can be obtained at www.ICGtesting.com
Printed in the USA
BVOW072242050613

322586BV00001BA/72/P